THE MOUSSE WONDERFUL TIME OF YEAR

OXFORD TEAROOM MYSTERIES

BOOK TEN

H.Y. HANNA

CONTENTS

H.Y. HANNA

CHAPTER ONE

They say it's the most wonderful time of year, for family reunions and festive cheer, good food and drink, joy and laughter... and murder.

The middle of the afternoon is usually a time when Oxford railway station is fairly empty, except for the occasional pensioner, or mother and child, out on a day trip. When I arrived, however, the concourse was heaving with people milling about, clutching bags of gaily wrapped gifts or dragging wheeled cases behind them as they negotiated the ticket queues and checked the train timetables. Their faces were flushed, their eyes bright and expectant, and they seemed almost oblivious to the brightly coloured tinsel and gaudy decorations hanging around them, as they hurried onto the platforms to wait for their trains.

Music drifted out from the station shop, rising above the hubbub of the crowd—Bing Crosby's rich baritone crooning: "*Silver bells... Silver bells...*"— and I felt a familiar tingle up my spine. They might have been over-commercialised and predictably cheesy, but I couldn't help the rush of warmth and nostalgia that came over me whenever I heard those classic songs. I hummed along softly under my breath as I pushed my way through the crowd, emerging at last onto the platform.

There, I paused for a moment—partly because moving from the warmth of the station into the frosty air of the open platform made me catch my breath. It had been an unusually cold December, and the local newspapers and radio stations were chattering with excitement at the rare prospect of a "white Christmas" in Oxford. While this part of England did get cold enough to have snow most winters, it tended to happen during the dark months of January or February. This year, though, it seemed that Bing Crosby's dreams might be answered in Oxfordshire.

I also paused because another wave of sentimentality struck me. *There might not be clouds of steam billowing from the train engines, no uniformed conductor, whistle to his lips, standing by the carriages, and no men in fedoras embracing elegant women in passionate farewell, but there's still something eternally romantic about train platforms*, I thought. Then I laughed to myself. I was sure most of the harassed-looking passengers wrestling with coats and bags around me were not thinking of bygone eras and wistful goodbyes.

Still... I smiled suddenly as the crowds parted and I saw him: a tall man with brooding good looks, his dark hair ruffled by the chill wind sweeping the platform, and his eyes—a startling shade of Celtic blue—narrowed against the elements. I started towards him, thinking to myself that I, at least, was living up to the cliché. I had come to the station for a romantic farewell. But not forever. Just for Christmas.

"Gemma!"

I laughed as he swept me up in an embrace as passionate and dramatic as anything in a vintage Hollywood movie. Devlin O'Connor—detective inspector with the Oxfordshire CID, my long-lost college sweetheart and now reunited boyfriend—grinned as he released me and said:

"I thought you weren't going to make it."

"Sorry. The Christmas tree at the tearoom toppled over just as I was leaving. Thankfully none of the customers were standing nearby, but it still made an awful mess and I had to stop to help Cassie put it up again. She was still rehanging the ornaments when I left."

"Wasn't it secured at the base?"

I rolled my eyes. "Yes, but obviously not strongly enough for the weight of a certain furry body climbing to the top to play with the ornaments!

When everyone warned me about cats and Christmas trees, I thought they were all exaggerating. Now I'm paying for not taking them seriously. Since it went up, the tree has been knocked over five times, half the ornaments are broken or have gone missing, the lights are completely tangled, and there are pine needles everywhere..." I shook my head. "How can one cat cause so much trouble?"

"Very easily when her name is Muesli," said Devlin, chuckling.

I eyed him covertly. It was so nice to see Devlin laugh again, with that familiar twinkle in his blue eyes, since his habitual expression the past few weeks had been a preoccupied frown. He'd been working so hard in the run-up to Christmas—the CID had been swamped with even more cases than usual—and I had been busy myself, with the holiday season bringing a rush of catering orders and customers to the Little Stables Tearoom. The result was that we had hardly seen each other, and I'd been looking forward to finally having some time off and doing some things together over the Christmas break.

But when I heard that Devlin's mother had invited him to spend Christmas with her, I'd swallowed my disappointment and urged him to go. They had only just begun to rebuild their fragile relationship and this seemed like a great step forwards. Keeley O'Connor might have been wild and irresponsible, with an attitude more suited to a careless teenager than a woman in her late forties, but she was also warm and genuine, with an irrepressible charm. I'd found myself inadvertently liking her when we met during her recent visit to Oxford and I knew that, for all his outward ambivalence, Devlin needed his mother. This would be the first time in many years that he'd gone home for Christmas, and it was a chance for him to bond with Keeley again. Still, now that I was faced with the prospect of a lonely Christmas without him, I found myself wishing that I hadn't been so unselfish.

"I wish you weren't going away," I blurted out.

"Me too, Gemma," said Devlin with a sigh. "I know I shouldn't say this, but a part of me would much rather stay here with you."

"Even if it means spending Christmas with *my* mother?" I asked with a laugh.

"It can't be any worse than what's in store for me." A look of uncertainty clouded his handsome features. "Maybe spending Christmas with Mum wasn't such a great idea..."

"No, no, you have to go, Devlin," I said quickly. "I think it's a fantastic chance for you and your mother to spend some quality time together, to really get to know each other again."

Devlin pulled a face. "More likely a chance for me to make sure she doesn't get too stoned, or arrested on Christmas Day for drink driving." He hesitated, then added, "I don't suppose you'd like to come and spend Christmas in the north of England?"

I shook my head regretfully. "You know I can't, Devlin. My mother would have a fit. Christmas is a big deal in our household. She always insists on following all the traditions—the mince pies, the plum pudding, holly and ivy everywhere, the Queen's speech on Christmas Day... There were several times when I couldn't make it home for Christmas during the years I was working in Australia and I still don't think she's forgiven me. Besides, we've got special guests coming to visit this year—cousins from America—so I definitely have to be around to help entertain them."

A sudden rush of wind down the platform alerted us to the arrival of the next train, and Devlin put his arm protectively around me as the carriages rolled towards us.

"That's my train. I have to go," he said with a grimace. Then he turned me around to face him and said, with mock sternness: "Now behave yourself, Miss Rose. No stumbling over any dead bodies while I'm away."

"What do you mean? I haven't come across a body in nearly two months!" I said, grinning. "Besides, it's not as if I go around looking for them, you know," I added indignantly.

"I know, Gemma, but you're just as bad as your cat in some ways. Trouble follows you everywhere. You seem to get yourself mixed up in a murder investigation every time my back is turned."

"Aww, come on—aren't you being a bit paranoid? I thought Christmas was a time of goodwill to all men. Everyone will be busy celebrating with their families and things should be quieter overall."

"Don't you believe it. Crime actually goes up this time of the year. Home burglaries and robberies, domestic abuse, sexual assault, drink driving... even just pickpockets and thieves targeting those out doing their Christmas shopping," said Devlin, nodding at a woman walking past us, her arms laden with presents.

"Well, you don't have to worry about me. I'm not planning to be out and about in town much. I'll be busy in the tearoom until we close and then I'll just be at my parents' place, helping around the house and entertaining the relatives. I think the most exciting thing I'll be doing will be lighting the brandy on the Christmas pudding!"

Devlin looked unconvinced. "And try to keep those nosy old friends of yours out of mischief too."

I smiled. "You mean the Old Biddies? Oh, don't worry—I'm sure they'll be far too busy to have time for snooping this holiday season. Haven't you heard? After their success on the talent show back in October, they've decided they like being in showbiz."

"They're not continuing that 'granny band' idea, are they?" said Devlin, raising his eyebrows.

"No... at least, not in exactly the same format.

They've decided to form a band of granny carol singers instead," I said with a laugh. "'The Twelve Greys of Christmas': that's what they're calling themselves. They're going around singing carols and collecting money from the public to donate to local charities."

"I wouldn't put it past them to be able to meddle and snoop, all while singing Christmas hymns at the same time," said Devlin darkly. "Just do me a favour and keep them away from any suspicious deaths. With so many senior officers away, Oxfordshire CID is operating with a skeleton staff this Christmas and the last thing they need is another murder investigation, especially one with four bossy old hens running the show."

"Yes, Inspector O'Connor," I said cheekily.

Devlin's face softened and he lowered his head to give me a goodbye kiss.

"I'll miss you," I said, my voice wobbling slightly.

He touched my cheek gently with the back of one finger, his eyes tender. "I'll miss you too, Gemma. But I'll be back before you know it and then we'll do something nice together in the new year, hmm?"

He pulled me into a long, lingering kiss. I was breathless when at last we broke apart.

"Be good," said Devlin with a grin, giving me a little tap on the nose. Then he lifted his holdall and boarded the carriage.

I stood and watched as the train left the station, disappearing slowly into the distance. Another icy blast of wind swept across the platform and I shivered, feeling suddenly bereft. Then I gave myself a mental shake and turned briskly to leave. I glanced at the large station clock as I walked back across the concourse: I'd promised my mother I'd meet her for tea in town, but there was still plenty of time. *I might even have a quick look around the shops first*, I thought. I'd already done most of my Christmas shopping—all except for a gift for my best friend, Cassie. Somehow, I still hadn't found the perfect present for her and, with Christmas just four days away, time was running out.

Immersed in my thoughts, I didn't notice the man heading for the station exit at the same time, until we collided with each other in the doorway. I stumbled backwards, tripped on his case, and would have fallen if he hadn't caught me.

"Oops!" I said, struggling to regain my balance. "Th-thanks."

"Not at all. It was my pleasure," he said, his eyes sliding over me appreciatively.

He was a good-looking man, somewhere in his mid-to-late forties, with an air of suave arrogance and a taste for the finer things in life, if his expensive clothes and monogrammed leather case were anything to go by. He smiled, his teeth brilliantly white, and I realised that his arm was still around me even though I no longer needed his support.

"Thank you," I said again, awkwardly, as I

stepped sideways to disentangle myself. "Sorry... I didn't see you heading for the door at the same time."

His arm tightened imperceptibly around me for a moment before he released me. I stiffened. Was it my imagination or had his hand brushed the side of my breast as he let me go?

He gave me another dazzling smile and said: "When a man has the chance to catch a beautiful woman in his arms, there's nothing to apologise for. I've always thought train stations to be very romantic and it's nice to have the fantasy come to life." His eyes flicked over me, noting my lack of luggage, and he said, "I take it that you haven't just arrived in Oxford?"

"No, I live here. I've just been to see my boyfriend off," I said, stressing the word *boyfriend*.

He smiled again, unperturbed. "What kind of boyfriend leaves a gorgeous woman like you alone for Christmas?"

"He... he had to spend Christmas with his mother." The defensive words were out before I realised, and then I felt annoyed with myself. Why was I justifying myself to a stranger?

"Anyway, thanks again." I gave him a curt nod and turned to go.

"Wait!" He put a hand on my arm. "I'm sorry. I seem to have offended you in some way. I didn't mean to. Please forgive me!"

"No, I..." Now faced with his contrite expression

and excessive apologies, I felt suddenly embarrassed, as if I were the one who had been rude. I mumbled, "I've just... um... I need to go. I'm meeting someone for tea."

"Ah! Afternoon tea—that most delightful of English traditions! I must say, I've quite missed it."

I eyed him assessingly. His accent was British, but overlaid with a slight drawl, like someone who had spent a great deal of time in the United States.

"Don't you live in England then?" I asked, curious in spite of myself.

"No. This is the first time I've been back in years." He quirked an eyebrow at me. "As the song says, I'll be home for Christmas..."

"Oh. Well... I hope you have a good stay," I said rather inanely. Then with a quick nod of farewell—and a sense of relief—I hurried out of the station.

CHAPTER TWO

When I arrived back in the centre of Oxford, I found the streets even busier than the railway station. The famous university city was a top destination for tourists and local visitors alike, and the centre of town always hummed with activity, but now, with Christmas just around the corner, it was completely mobbed.

The Michaelmas term was over—Oxford University terms were unusually short at just nine weeks—and most of the students would have already "gone down", leaving their rooms in college and returning to their homes, but there still seemed to be a huge number of people filling the streets. They gawped at the festive shop windows and Christmas market stalls, juggled carrier bags filled with purchases, and tottered into pubs and cafes, seeking mulled wine and hot chocolate to warm their cold hands and feet.

I paused for a moment beside Carfax Tower, the twelfth-century landmark that had the distinction of being the tallest structure in town, for no other building in central Oxford may be built taller. This crossroads also marked the unofficial "heart" of the city, the junction for Oxford's four main streets, and I'd stood here many a time when I was a student. Now I gazed down the streets stretching into the distance, at the iconic "dreaming spires" that made up Oxford's famous skyline, and felt a sense of nostalgia again.

It was strange to think that this time a little over a year ago, I had only just returned to England. The eight years working overseas seemed more like a dream now, and it was almost hard to remember the horror and disapproval that had greeted my decision to abandon a high-flying corporate career and return home to open a traditional English tearoom. *But now, a year on, the gamble has paid off*, I thought with a smile. My little tearoom was thriving, I loved my work, Devlin and I were back together, and yes, I'd even learned to cope with living so close to my mother.

Well, most of the time anyway, I thought as my phone rang and I answered it to find my mother's well-modulated tones on the other end of the line.

"Hello, darling. Would you like your flannel underwear in white or red? The red ones come with a reindeer pattern and the white ones come with snowmen."

"I don't want flannel underwear at all, Mother," I said in alarm.

"Or they do them in a nice blue as well, with a pattern of penguins," my mother continued, as if I hadn't spoken. "Dorothy Clarke got some for her daughter, Suzanne—you remember Suzanne, darling? She works in the University Alumni office. Dorothy says they're marvellous. The flannel underwear, I mean, not the Alumni office. So soft and warm, and they don't chafe your privates."

"*Mother.* I said I don't want any flannel underwear," I said, feeling my blood pressure start to rise.

"Dorothy says they even prevent urinary tract infections. Fancy that! Suzanne suffered terribly with UTIs, you know, even though she was always drinking gallons of cranberry juice, but she had this dreadful burning sensation every time she—"

"*Eeuuww!* Mother!" I protested. "I'm sure Suzanne wouldn't appreciate us discussing her genital health. And I *really* don't want any flannel underwear. I'll never wear it, and then it'll be a complete waste of money—"

"Oh, nonsense, darling. Of course you'll wear it. I know! I can get you a pair in each colour, then you can mix and match. Although I suppose you really ought to separate the white ones for the white wash and..."

Her voice faded as I held the phone away from my ear for a moment and took a deep, steadying breath. *Grrrrr.* Why did my mother always have the ability to make me feel like I was thirteen again, sulky and impotent with frustrated rage?

"...anyway, I was also ringing you to tell you that I might be slightly late for tea," my mother was saying when I put the phone back to my ear. "I was supposed to meet Annabel in Home Furnishings to have a look at some chenille throws, but she's been delayed in Gift Wrap & Delivery, and she says—"

"What? Who's Annabel?"

"Don't say 'what', darling; say 'pardon'. Didn't I tell you that Annabel was joining us for tea? Annabel Floyd. Well, she was a Morecombe before she was married; you know, Sir Hugh Morecombe? She's his daughter. The Morecombes are one of the oldest families in the area. They have an estate— Thurlby Hall—just outside Meadowford-on-Smythe—"

"Oh... yes, I think I've passed it a few times when I was cycling to and from work. Or at least, the road leading to the estate."

"Yes, it's a vast property. The house is set well back, in the middle of parklands. Lovely old manor house, with the most magnificent entrance hall. Well, Annabel and I are both on the committee of the Sinterklaas Foundation. She's in charge of organising this year's Christmas event for the children; it's going to be a tea party at Thurlby Hall and—*oh!* There's Annabel now. I hope she can see me waving... Why don't you go on ahead and get us a table first? I hear that afternoon tea at The Randolph has become very popular and it must be even busier now with all the Christmas crowds—Oh dear! Annabel hasn't seen me waving and she's going the wrong way!"

"Can't you just call out to her?"

"Call out to her?"

"Yes, shout her name. Get her attention."

"Are you suggesting that I yell like a fishwife?" My mother sounded shocked. "A lady never raises her voice in public. I must dash, darling—I need to catch her before she gets in the lift. Toodle-oo!"

The line went dead. I stared at the phone a minute, then sighed and started up Cornmarket Street towards The Randolph Hotel. I hadn't gone far, though, when something in a shop window caught my eye: a luxury artist's set featuring tubes of oil paints in a huge selection of colours, a wooden mixing palette with thumb hole, metal palette knives, kneaded putty rubber, oil rags, and a range of hog-bristle brushes in different sizes, all contained in a beautiful varnished beechwood box with clasps and handles. I stared at it in delight. It would make the *perfect* Christmas present for Cassie!

Eagerly, I went into the shop, but when I was told the price, I gulped slightly. It was no wonder artists were always "struggling" if their supplies were so expensive! Still, business at the tearoom had been booming lately and I could afford to splash out a bit—especially on my best friend who had been such an amazing support the last year. I handed over my credit card and left the shop a few minutes later with the artist's set beautifully wrapped and placed in a Christmas gift bag.

Swinging the bag happily, I continued towards the hotel, smiling to myself as I imagined how Cassie's face would look when she opened her gift. I arrived at the front of The Randolph to find a small crowd gathered outside the entrance. It seemed like several new guests had all arrived at once; they were milling about in slight confusion as the porters attempted to sort out the luggage for check-in, and I paused by the group, waiting politely for them to go into the hotel first.

Then I felt something tug violently at my hand.

I gasped and whirled around, just as the gift bag was wrenched out of my grasp. A boy, his face hidden by a hood, pushed past me and began to run away with Cassie's present.

"Hey!" I cried, shocked and angry. "Stop! That's mine!"

I started to run after him but a man who had just come out of the hotel entrance was faster. He also had much longer legs and, in a couple of strides, he had grabbed the thief by the back of his hoodie. The boy dropped the gift bag and wriggled free, disappearing around the corner. I rushed up to the man just as he stooped to retrieve the gift bag.

"Thank you," I panted, taking the bag from him. "That was so—" I broke off as he turned around and I saw who it was. "*You!*"

The handsome man from the train station grinned at me. "So... we meet again. Fate certainly seems to be throwing us together, eh?"

"Er... yes," I said awkwardly, torn between dismay at running into him again and gratitude for his retrieval of the stolen present. "Thanks so much for rescuing this." I indicated the gift bag. "It would have cost a fortune to replace."

He gave a suggestive smile. "Well... you could thank me properly by having a drink with me."

I resisted the urge to roll my eyes. The man just didn't give up! "I'm sorry, I'm actually meeting someone for tea—"

"So you said, but have they arrived yet?"

"N-no..."

"Well then, you can have a drink with me in the meantime," he said smoothly, putting a proprietary hand under my elbow and steering me back towards the hotel entrance. He added quickly, as I started to protest, "Surely it's not too much to ask, after I've come to your aid... twice?"

I bit my lip. There was no way to refuse without sounding rude and ungracious. I declined a drink in the Morse Bar, however, which seemed more intimate, and instead suggested that we go into the Lancaster Room for tea. That way, my mother's arrival would hopefully cut our tête-à-tête short.

As luck would have it, a family was leaving just as we entered and we were shown to their vacated table by the window.

"I'm Ned, by the way," said the man as we settled into deep armchairs facing each other across the table. He quirked an eyebrow at me. "I hope you're not going to make me sit here drinking tea with a nameless lady?"

"Gemma," I said reluctantly.

Something about his overly confident, flirtatious manner made me unwilling to give any more information about myself than was necessary. It was as if the more he pushed, the more I wanted to resist. When a waitress came to take our order, I was quick to forestall him ordering the standard full afternoon tea, which would give him an excuse to linger.

"Just a pot of tea, please," I said firmly.

"Darjeeling? English Breakfast? We have a full menu of varieties to choose from," said the waitress.

I glanced at Ned. He looked amused, as if he knew what I was doing, and said blandly, "Whatever the lady prefers."

I asked for Earl Grey, my favourite, and then settled back in my armchair, looking around the room admiringly. There was probably no place as grand as The Randolph Hotel to have afternoon tea in Oxford. One of the city's iconic landmarks, the nineteenth-century institution, with its neo-Gothic architecture and lavishly elegant interiors, oozed Olde Worlde glamour and sophistication. Countless presidents and prime ministers have enjoyed its beautiful suites, and the famous Lancaster Room has been serving fine teas, homemade scones, delectable pastries, and finger sandwiches since it opened its doors in 1866.

I watched with keen interest as a waitress served a full afternoon tea to a nearby table, delivering a three-tiered cake stand bulging with delicious treats with great ceremony. Dainty cakes and glossy fruit tarts were nestled alongside colourful macaroons and rich trifles on the top, followed by freshly baked scones in the middle, and crustless finger sandwiches on the bottom. My companion raised an eyebrow and said:

"You seem to be eyeing that cake stand very intently. Are you regretting just ordering a pot of tea? We can ask for the menu again—"

"Oh no," I said quickly, flushing. "I... it was more of a professional interest, really."

"Professional interest?"

I hesitated, then gave a rueful smile. "I own a tearoom, so it's sort of an occupational hazard. I can't help observing and making notes whenever I'm out somewhere having afternoon tea. I suppose I'm always comparing and trying to improve or get inspiration—"

"Ah, you own a place like this?" He gestured around the room.

I laughed as I looked at the snowy white tablecloths and gleaming silver cutlery, the oil paintings on the walls, the baby grand piano in the corner. "No, no, not like this at all! Nothing this posh. It's a much more homely place—a small, old-fashioned, country English tearoom, in a building that used to be a Tudor inn."

"Sounds delightful! Where is it?"

"In Meadowford-on-Smythe. That's a village just outside Oxford—"

"Yes, I know Meadowford. Lovely high street. So... you own a tearoom there, eh? Well, well..." He smiled, looking like the cat who had got the proverbial cream.

His expression made me uncomfortable and I wished that I hadn't let him know about my tearoom. Now there was no way to stop him coming to find me! Looking over his shoulder, I was relieved to see a stout middle-aged woman in a waitress's uniform heading towards us, carrying a tea service on a tray. *Good.* Perhaps once he had drunk his tea, he would leave. Groping for some conversation to fill the silence, I said politely:

"So... are you visiting family for Christmas?"

He leaned back in his chair as the waitress came around the table to pour his tea. The knowing smile was still hovering at the corners of his mouth. "Yes, I suppose you could say that. I'm actually—"

He twitched and cursed as the waitress fumbled suddenly with the teapot and hot liquid sloshed out of the cup, splashing his hands.

"Hey! Watch what you're doing, you ham-fisted cow!" he snarled at the woman.

"I'm... I'm so sorry, sir!" she cried, flushing and bending to mop the table frantically. "I'm terribly sorry..."

I looked at the man next to me with a frown. My father always said that you could tell the character of a man by the way he treated the staff, and it seemed that my companion was showing his true colours. Having run a tearoom for over a year now, I knew that accidents happened, no matter how careful you tried to be, and his reaction seemed unnecessarily aggressive. I tried to catch the eye of the waitress to give her a sympathetic smile but she kept her face averted, hunched over with embarrassment, as she cleaned up the spill and hurried away.

"Really, you'd think the service would be better in a place like this," grumbled Ned. Then he turned back to me, his face smoothed into a pleasant expression once again, and said: "Anyway... where was I? Oh yes, the family Christmas. Well, it'll probably be a dead bore, to tell you the truth. You could help to liven things up, though, by agreeing to have dinner with me?"

I stared at him incredulously. Aside from the fact that he had to be at least fifteen years older than me, hadn't I made it obvious that I wasn't interested in him romantically? I'd never met anyone so thick-skinned or so persistent.

"I'm sorry... I... er... I'm very busy," I said stiffly. I wished I could simply tell him that I wouldn't have dinner with him, even if I had all the time in the world. But somehow, the strictures of politeness that I'd been brought up with kept me tongue-tied.

"Aww, come on! Your boyfriend isn't around, so why not? How about tonight? We could—" He was interrupted by his phone ringing. He answered it and I saw his face change.

"I told you not to call me on this number," he hissed. He glanced at me, then turned slightly away, saying in an undertone, "No, I don't have it yet. These things take time and I can't—what? London? Don't be ridiculous, I just arrived in Oxford... No! No, don't do that... All right. I'll come down. Where? Fine. I'll see you later."

He hung up and met my eyes with a bland smile. "Well, it looks like I will have to postpone the pleasure of taking you out for dinner. In fact, I'm going to have to leave now..." He glanced at the expensive Tag Heuer watch on his wrist, then rose from his chair. "But perhaps when I get back from London—"

I took a deep breath. Being polite was getting me nowhere. It was time to be blunt. I said coolly, "No. I don't think so. I'm sorry."

He raised his eyebrows, then he grinned, not remotely bothered by my rebuff. "Ah... the boyfriend is a lucky man. Well, perhaps I'll pop into your tearoom, then, if I'm still here in the new year. Surely you can't refuse me a scone and a cup of tea?"

I watched him leave and hoped fervently that he would be returning to the States by the time the new year rolled around.

CHAPTER THREE

The sound of my mother's voice brought me out of my reverie and I looked up to see her entering the tea room, followed by a slender, elegant woman who I guessed to be Annabel Floyd. They were both weighed down with several shopping bags. The *maitre d'* gestured in my direction and my mother hurried across the room, descending on me in a cloud of Givenchy perfume.

"Darling! Have you been waiting long? The lifts were taking an age so we decided to take the stairs instead, but when we got to the top, we discovered that they had moved the display to the basement! How dreadfully annoying! So we had to make our way down again. And then they didn't have the ramekins in the colour I wanted... but oh, there was a marvellous promotion for Le Creuset casserole pots just next to the display, so it was fortunate, really, that we had to go down to the basement as otherwise we might never have seen them. Thirty percent off—imagine! I purchased a twenty-four-centimetre pot in Marseille blue, and Annabel got the one in cerise, and then I found some mini ramekins..."

I glanced sympathetically at Annabel as my mother rambled on, wondering if the other woman was worn out from a morning of following my mother around the department store. She certainly looked pale and weary, and seemed slightly unsteady on her feet, stumbling as she reached the table. I sprang up and caught her arm, steadying her.

"Th-thank you," she said, flushing. "I'm sorry... so clumsy of me."

She was leaning against me and, for a moment, I caught a whiff of a strange fragrance. It was sweet and slightly sickly, almost like... *alcohol*. I glanced at the woman in surprise. Was she drunk? Then she moved away from me, sinking gratefully into a chair, and I wondered if I had imagined it. Still, as I resumed my seat, I couldn't help noticing that Annabel's hands trembled slightly as she picked up the tea menu.

I eyed her curiously: she was younger than I expected—I had imagined she would be my mother's contemporary, but she looked somewhere in her late forties. And although she was dressed in the same subdued, elegant style as the usual members of my mother's cashmere-and-twinset brigade, she seemed very different. It wasn't just the fact that she was ten to fifteen years their junior—there was a nervous air about her and a strained, uncertain look in her eyes, which was nothing like the usual self-assurance and complacent superiority (born from years of henpecked husbands and long-suffering children!) seen in my mother's friends.

Then I chided myself for my overactive imagination. Annabel was probably just tired from all the Christmas preparations and festivities, and as for the alcoholic breath... well, perhaps she had simply had a boozy lunch earlier. She wouldn't be the first person to do that, especially over the holiday season, and as long as she wasn't drinking and driving, it was hardly my place to judge. I turned my attention to my mother, who had finally finished rambling about her purchases and now seemed to be discussing the tea party that she and Annabel were organising.

"...so I told Annabel not to worry. I was sure you'd be able to help her—"

"Sorry, help with what, Mother?"

"With the nibbles for the tea party, darling! The caterers have left Annabel in a terrible lurch and now we have no food for the children and other guests."

"It's a dreadful inconvenience," Annabel agreed.

She had a soft, breathless voice that sounded perpetually apologetic. "I've been ringing around trying to find someone else but it's such short notice—only the day after tomorrow, you see. I suppose I could try to serve something else but we've already sent out the invitations, so everyone will be expecting a traditional afternoon tea, with cakes and scones and finger sandwiches and all the trimmings." She sighed. "I'd hate to disappoint them. Besides, I really want this event to be a success. It's the first time we're holding something like this and I'm hoping that it might become an annual feature."

"Er... it's a Christmas tea party, is that right?" I asked, trying not to show that I hadn't really been paying attention to my mother previously.

Annabel nodded. "Yes. I don't know if you're familiar with the Sinterklaas Foundation but it's a charity that helps children from underprivileged families. Many of their parents often can't afford the usual luxuries that we take for granted at Christmas. Even something as simple as a Christmas gift for every child can be a strain on a family with limited income. Last year we raised funds to buy presents for every child and went around distributing them for Christmas Day. But this year, I thought—why not go the whole hog and invite them for a proper Christmas party? Of course, with children involved, I decided a tea party would be more suitable than a dinner party, and we could have all the Christmas treats, like mince pies and plum pudding, crackers and games, and provide stockings with gifts for every child... It will be a chance for them to experience the kind of Christmas that many of us take for granted."

"That sounds wonderful," I said, touched by her generous spirit.

"Yes, so when the caterers let me down... and then your mother told me that you run a tearoom known for the best scones in Oxfordshire... well, I was absolutely delighted."

I gave an embarrassed laugh. "Thanks. Yes, our scones are our signature dish and they are very popular. I have to confess, though, I can't take any credit for them. I don't do any of the baking myself. There's a wonderful woman who lives in the village, who does all the baking for my tearoom."

"So you can help?" Annabel looked at me hopefully.

I smiled at her. "I'd love to. I'll have to double-check with Dora—can you let me know the number of guests you're expecting?—but I think we should be able to manage it." I thought for a moment, then added, "Do you need anything that is Christmas-related? We have been offering some seasonal items on the menu, like mince pies, but we haven't made any plum pudding—"

"Oh, homemade mince pies would be wonderful! And don't worry about the Christmas pudding. I'll take care of that," said Annabel. "In any case, I wonder if these more 'traditional' treats appeal more to the grown-ups than the children. They probably just want candy canes and chocolate! Oh, speaking of which—perhaps you could do a chocolate mousse? I think the children might prefer that to a traditional plum pudding."

"Yes, that should be easy enough. I know Dora has a special chocolate mousse recipe and she could probably give it a festive twist." I smiled. "I'm sure she'd enjoy the challenge."

Several minutes later, we were tucking into a lavish afternoon tea similar to the one I had seen on the neighbouring table. I was particularly interested to taste the scones, served with little pots of strawberry preserve, lemon curd, and clotted cream. They were light, fluffy, and delicious, but I was pleased to conclude that those served in my own tearoom were definitely better. The tea menu was impressive, though, each variety served loose-leaf in a white china pot and carefully poured through individual strainers.

As the waitress went around the table, pouring each of us a cup, Annabel smiled at me and said:

"I can't tell you what a load it is off my mind. One does try to be organised but no matter how one plans, things always seem to go wrong at the last moment. And it has been one thing after another this week. First the central heating went on the blink, then the caterers let me down, then my housekeeper told me that she had to give notice and leave immediately. She's been with us for years; I don't know how I'm going to replace her. It's the absolute *worst* time to be without a housekeeper! We have additional staff who come to do the cleaning and garden maintenance, of course, but I've always relied on Mrs Simms to manage the household, oversee the kitchen and pantry supplies, prepare the meals, and help with the entertaining. Especially now at Christmas, when we have this tea party, and then guests coming to stay—"

"Surely she can't leave so suddenly?" asked my mother, looking rather disapproving.

"Well, she *had* been talking for some time of leaving and finding a position closer to her elderly mother, who lives in Yorkshire. But I had been hoping that it might not be for another year at least. Then her mother had a stroke last week and it seems that she will need full-time nursing while she makes a recovery. So Mrs Simms decided that she might as well make the permanent move now. She's keen to spend Christmas with her mother and I felt obliged to let her go. She's leaving later today, in fact." Annabel sighed. "I don't know how I'm going to manage."

"What about an employment agency?" my mother suggested. "They should be able to help you find someone."

"Oh, I rang them almost immediately. The problem is, this is a difficult time of year... Most people want Christmas off to spend with their families. The few that were available seemed frightfully *young*. Girls in their twenties. I was really hoping to get someone older—you know, who might be more mature and reliable." Annabel sighed again. "Anyway, the woman promised to ring me as soon as she has any new applicants."

"I'd be happy to give you a hand with things at the tea party," I offered. "I'll have to come and deliver the food anyway. I can stay behind afterwards and help with the clearing up."

"Oh, that's very kind—thank you," said Annabel.

"I'll just have to ask Cassie to take Muesli home with her..." I mused.

"Muesli?"

"My cat," I explained. "She normally comes to the tearoom each day and then goes home with me in the evenings. But if I'm going to be at your tea party all afternoon and evening, then I'll need to ask my friend to drop her back at my place or keep her overnight."

"Why don't you take Muesli to Thurlby Hall with you, darling?" suggested my mother. She turned to Annabel and added proudly, "Muesli is a certified therapy cat, you know. She would be so good with the children."

"Really? That would be fantastic!" cried Annabel, her face lighting up. "I'm sure the children would love to have a cat to cuddle and play with." She gave a self-deprecating laugh. "Come to that, I'd love you to bring her just for myself. I absolutely adore cats. I wish I could have one but my husband detests them."

"Er... the thing is, Muesli can be very naughty," I said. "She's very confident and inquisitive and is always getting into places she shouldn't—"

"Oh, I'm sure she'll be fine," said Annabel, waving a hand. "Please don't worry about it. The place will be a mess anyway with all the children running about. I'm sure she'd be a wonderful addition to the party."

"Well... if you're sure," I said doubtfully.

"Yes, absolutely! You must bring Muesli," Annabel insisted. She smiled in anticipation. "I'm so looking forward to meeting her."

CHAPTER FOUR

It was with a certain amount of misgiving that I arrived on the doorstep of Thurlby Hall two days later, with Muesli in tow. Annabel herself opened the door and her face broke into a delighted smile when she saw the cat carrier I was holding.

"Gemma! Lovely to see you... and you've brought your little cat. How wonderful!" She bent to peer through the bars of the cat carrier. "Oh, she's gorgeous... Look at those big green eyes with the black around them like eyeliner... and that little pink nose," she gushed.

I looked at Annabel with some surprise. This was the most animated I had ever seen her—a far cry from the subdued, rigidly controlled woman I'd met at tea two days ago. It seemed a shame that she couldn't have a cat if feline company made such a difference.

"*Meorrw?*" said Muesli cheekily and Annabel laughed again.

"Oh, the children are going to love her!" she said. Then she wrapped her arms around herself and shivered, her breath coming out in a cloud of steam. "Do come into the house—it's freezing outside! It looks like that snow they've been predicting is arriving at last."

I cast a look over my shoulder at the sky, which was a strange pink hue, with low ominous clouds gathering on the horizon. The air had a biting quality and I could see a few flakes of white beginning to drift down from the heavens.

"Yes, it's already causing havoc on the roads. I hate to see what happens when it gets heavier," I said, making a face. "That's why we're late, actually—we took a wrong turn and ended up on the ring road outside Oxford and there had been an accident earlier, so there was a terrible pile-up."

"Where's Evelyn?" asked Annabel, peering over my shoulder.

I indicated the car being reversed into a space in front of the manor house. "She's just parking the car. I don't have my own car so it's great that my mother was able to give me a lift. I thought I'd bring Muesli into the house first, then go out to get the food."

"Oh, of course, come in... come in..." Annabel led me into the warmth of the house. "Oh dear, I hope the weather isn't going to prevent any of our children from coming. They all live locally, so hopefully they won't have too much trouble getting here—as long as the road through the gates is clear, that is. It's the only route in and out of the estate."

I followed her into an enormous foyer and entrance hall—almost the size of a small hotel lobby—and I stopped, slightly over awed. There was an expanse of black-and-white chequered flooring, a carved wooden staircase sweeping up to the second storey, a huge crystal chandelier and matching wall sconces, a grandfather clock with a majestically swinging pendulum, and a mounted stag's head glowering down from the far wall. Everything seemed to be lavish and grand and reeking of history. The only incongruous thing was a minimalist, stainless steel Henning Koppel clock on the wall next to the front door. Annabel saw me looking and gave a sheepish smile.

"Yes, I know—it doesn't quite go with the décor. The previous clock was ancient and when it needed to be repaired, I decided that I'd rather have something modern. I do love Georg Jensen things, and this is so beautiful in its simplicity," she said, indicating the white clock face and the lack of numbers. "I... I live in this house too and it's nice to have a bit of *my* personality in the place," she added in a slightly defiant tone, which made me wonder.

"Oh, it's still very elegant so it doesn't stand out too much," I assured her. Then I turned towards the door on my right, from which I could hear the sound of excited young voices. "Have the children arrived already?"

"Some of them have come early. I think they were too excited to wait," said Annabel with a smile. "I've settled them in the library; there's a tree in there and most of the Christmas decorations." She gestured around the entrance hall, which was only decorated with simple garlands of holly and ivy on the bannister of the main staircase. "My father forbade me from putting up too many gaudy things in here but he said I could make the library as festive as I like."

I looked at her curiously. I had assumed that Annabel was the mistress of the household, and yet she sounded almost like a teenager dependent on her parents' permission and approval.

"I hope I didn't overdo it," Annabel continued, laughing self-consciously as she led me towards the library. "I wouldn't want it to look too much like a Santa's Grotto in a shopping centre, but I thought the children would enjoy having all the traditional trimmings. We should probably lay out the tea in the dining room, though, which is across the hall."

"Right, I'll bring the food in and put it in there." I held up the cat carrier. "Actually, if you don't mind watching Muesli for a moment, I'll just pop back outside and unload the car..."

"Of course," said Annabel, taking the cat carrier eagerly. "And do ask Mrs Holmes to give you a hand. She's my new housekeeper. You should find her in the kitchen."

"Oh, did you manage to find someone then?"

"Yes, thank goodness. After our tea at The Randolph, I had a phone call from the agency that evening. They'd just had a new application come in. It's not a permanent contract, though—Ellen Holmes was just looking for a short-term position over the holidays—but I'm hoping to speak to her in the new year and persuade her to stay on. I can see already that she would make a wonderful replacement for Mrs Simms."

We were interrupted by a chorus of excited cries as we entered the library and the children saw the cat carrier.

"Oh! Is it a kitty cat?"

"I want to stroke it!"

"Me too! Me too!"

In a minute, Annabel was surrounded by children all clamouring to hold Muesli, whilst their accompanying parents looked on, smiling. She opened the cage and my little tabby cat strolled out, her whiskers quivering with excitement as she eyed all the new faces around her. Before long, she was obscured by a dozen little hands eagerly reaching out to pat her as she went around the circle, enjoying the attention.

"Oh, she's a natural!" said Annabel, watching with delight.

I laughed. "Yes, there's nothing Muesli loves

more than being made a fuss of."

I looked around the library, at the beautifully decorated Christmas tree by the door, the tinsel draped across the bookshelves and artfully looped across the ceiling, the large-scale Nativity scene set up in the corner, and the pile of brightly wrapped presents and stuffed stockings beside the fireplace. "This room looks amazing! You've done a fantastic job."

Annabel flushed with pleasure, although her voice, when she spoke, was back to that controlled, modulated tone which betrayed little emotion. "Thank you."

"It's really wonderful, everything you're doing for these children," I added warmly.

Annabel gave a wistful smile. "Actually, it's lovely to hear the sound of children's voices and laughter in the house. I always feel that the holiday season isn't the same without children. We do make an effort to celebrate Christmas every year with all the traditional customs—my father is very particular about that—but with just a few adults, it always seems a bit quiet and empty, even... a bit silly, really. For example, my father insists that we hang stockings up for every member of the family, and I've always done that to keep him happy, but it does seem faintly ridiculous..."

I followed her gaze to where five stockings in red velvet were hanging from the mantelpiece. Each had a name embroidered across the front: *Hugh,*

Edward, Annabel, Julian, and *Richard.*

"Do you have four brothers?" I asked.

She shook her head. "Hugh is my father and Richard is my husband. He always gets a stocking, even though he sneers at it every year."

"Ah. And do your brothers Edward and Julian also—"

"Julian is my cousin. He's arriving today to stay for Christmas, so you'll meet him. I've sent the car to get him; he lives in Oxford—he's a don at one of the colleges there—but he always spends Christmas with us. He's a bachelor, you see, and we were quite close as children. Well, when I say 'close', I mean that he spent a lot of time here at Thurlby Hall when we were all growing up. We didn't necessarily play together—Julian was always quite aloof and mature for his age," said Annabel with a wry smile. "But he is part of the family. In fact, with the baronetcy and estate entailed to the male line, he's my father's heir."

"Oh? But I thought nowadays an estate owner is allowed to pass the entailed land to anyone he chooses simply by a deed or a will?"

"Yes, but my father is very old-fashioned and conservative. He passionately supports male primogeniture and believes that it's important to uphold the ancient English laws. Besides, he likes Julian and, I have to admit, my cousin would be an ideal person to take over the estate. He shares my father's love of pomp and ceremony, his sense of the family status and title, and the importance of upholding centuries of tradition..."

I looked at the woman next to me curiously, wondering how she felt about losing her home and inheritance simply because her father refused to pass it to his own daughter. As usual, Annabel's face betrayed no emotion. Then I remembered the last stocking on the mantelpiece.

"What about your brother? Wouldn't he inherit the estate first—"

"Edward is dead," said Annabel quietly. "Father always insists that I still hang up his stocking every year." Something crossed her face as she said this, but it was gone so quickly that I thought I might have imagined it.

"Oh. Um... and I suppose you don't have any sons who could inherit?" I said, more to fill the awkward silence than anything else.

"I don't have any children at all." Annabel's eyes strayed to the laughing kids across the room and she gave a strained smile. "We tried. But it wasn't meant to be..."

"Oh." I cursed myself for my thoughtless insensitivity. *Of course.* If she'd had children, surely their stockings would be hanging from the mantelpiece too?

As I groped around for another subject, we were distracted by the sound of laughter and we turned to see the children and their parents clustered around the Nativity scene in the corner, talking and pointing excitedly. We went over to find them staring at the almost life-sized, straw-filled model stable, where a cow and sheep and donkey were gazing tenderly down... at a grey tabby cat curled up in the manger, lying on top of the ceramic swaddled infant.

"Muesli!" I cried, mortified. "What are you doing?"

"She's squashing the Baby Jesus," said one of the children.

I lifted my cat out and set her on the floor but she gave a little chirrup and instantly jumped back in the manger again. I tried again but Muesli was back in the wooden makeshift crib in a flash, wriggling and pushing the ceramic baby aside so that she could curl up more comfortably. The children giggled and I flushed with embarrassed annoyance.

"I'm so sorry," I said to Annabel as I reached down to lift Muesli out again.

"Oh, leave her," said Annabel, chuckling. "She looks so sweet in there... and I know enough about cats to know that they can be very determined when they want something."

"You can say that again," I muttered, giving Muesli a dirty look.

She gave me a flick of her tail in reply and began purring smugly. Rolling my eyes, I gave up and headed out of the library to get the food. Annabel followed me, saying:

"Actually, don't bother Mrs Holmes. I'll come and give you a hand. I'm not doing anything anyway—just waiting for the rest of the guests to arrive..."

There were quite a few bowls and platters to bring in and it took us several trips but we soon had everything laid out on the long mahogany table in the formal dining room. I surveyed the table with pride: Dora had outdone herself—as well as our famous signature scones, there were also Victoria sponge cakes and finger sandwiches, Chelsea buns and fruit tarts, and a pyramid of homemade mince pies, each golden brown and beautifully dusted with icing sugar. There was also a bowl of chocolate mousse, decorated with whipped cream and candy canes, which Annabel set next to a platter containing an enormous Christmas pudding.

"Wow," I said, eyeing the plum pudding, dark, rich, and moist, with the customary sprig of holly at the top. "That looks incredible."

"Yes, I was lucky that Mrs Simms likes to follow tradition and always makes plum puddings on the Sunday before the start of Advent, to give them time to mature... so she has left several for us to enjoy. My father loves plum pudding, so we don't just save it for the lunch on Christmas Day—we have some in the days leading up to Christmas too." Annabel turned to a side table and lifted a box filled with clusters of fake holly berries and frosted pinecones, twines of ivy, short sections of tinsel, and gold foil stars. "I saved some of the Christmas decorations to go on the table."

"That's a great idea!"

Together, we arranged the decorations around the plates of food, and soon the table had a wonderfully festive look.

"Hmm... what we really need are some tealights amongst the plates, to give everything a lovely glow," Annabel mused, eyeing the table. "There should be some in the cabinet in the antechamber next door; we keep a supply of candles in different sizes. If you'll help me fetch some..."

She led the way to a closed door on the other side of the dining room. I followed and was just about to step through when Annabel jerked to a stop in front of me and I heard a gasp escape her lips. Looking over her shoulder, I saw a man and woman in the antechamber, locked in a passionate embrace. Her skirt was hitched up in a lewd fashion and his hand was inside her unbuttoned shirt. They sprang apart and faced us, their cheeks flushed and their eyes wary.

Annabel stared at them, her face ashen. For a moment, she seemed to have been turned to stone. Then she said, in that carefully modulated voice, devoid of emotion:

"Gemma—this is my husband, Richard Floyd."

CHAPTER FIVE

There was a long, horrible silence. I stood at a loss, not sure where to look, what to do. Was I supposed to walk over and shake hands with the man as if we'd just been introduced at a cocktail party and pretend that I hadn't walked in and caught him *in flagrante*?

It would almost have been better if Annabel had screamed and made a scene—and basically behaved like someone who had just found her husband groping another woman. The fact that he'd had the audacity to carry on with his wife so close by was an even worse insult. But she stood, as still and remote as a statue, her face rigidly under control. I cast her an incredulous look. Surely this was carrying the British tradition of "stiff upper lip" a bit too far?

It was the other woman who finally broke the

silence. She emitted a nervous giggle and said, "I was just about to come and look for you, Annabel, darling, to see if you needed any help with the food." She straightened her clothes and fluffed out her hair. "But it looks like you have someone helping you already. Well, I'll just pop upstairs, then, and see if Hugh needs anything. Maybe he'd like to come downstairs and join the party? The poor darling was looking a bit peaky this morning. I'm sure a bit of time with the children would do him good."

With a cool smile, she sashayed past us and out of a side door, which led from the antechamber directly into the hallway. I watched her go, staggered at her *chutzpah*, and wondered who on earth she was. She spoke with the confident familiarity of someone important in the family, and yet Annabel hadn't mentioned another woman in the household. She was much younger—somewhere in her early or mid-thirties—with a hard face overlaid by a superficial prettiness. Her hair was blonde, expertly tinted, her nails beautifully manicured, and her clothes looked as if they had come straight from Paris... and yet there was something coarse and cheap in her manner. Still, I admired the smooth way she had extricated herself from an awkward situation and I was just about to try and follow her example when Richard Floyd gave a humourless laugh and said, in a jeering tone:

"Still the ice queen, eh?"

Then, without a word to his wife, he strode across the room and disappeared through the same door that the blonde woman had used.

There was another uncomfortable silence and, for a moment, I thought that Annabel was going to crack at last. Then she took a deep breath, straightened her shoulders, and went across to the cabinets by the wall where she fumbled for a moment before pulling out a packet of tealights. She marched back into the dining room, her head held high, and I followed, watching uncertainly as she lit the tealights, put them into holders, then began systematically placing them amongst the plates. Her silence and unnatural calm were beginning to worry me. I felt like I ought to say something, to offer some gesture of moral support, but at the same time, her attitude made me hesitate. After all, she was a client, not a friend, and maybe commenting on her humiliation might have been even worse than having witnessed it.

Annabel set the last tealight down, then walked unsteadily to the drinks cabinet in the corner.

"Shall... shall we have a drink?" she asked with forced brightness. Without waiting for me to answer, she grabbed a bottle of whisky and sloshed a generous measure into a tumbler, then downed it in one gulp. She poured herself another, then turned to look at me expectantly.

"I... er..." I hesitated. I knew that I was a lightweight when it came to alcohol, but still...

wasn't this too early in the day to be drinking hard spirits? "I think I'll just grab a soft drink from the kitchen, thanks. Got to keep a clear head for washing up later," I said, with a weak attempt at humour.

Annabel seemed almost not to hear me. She threw back her second glass of whisky and began pouring herself another. I started to protest but, before I could speak, a bell rang out imperiously somewhere in the house. Annabel jumped.

"That's Daddy," she said in a breathless voice. "He must want something. I... I must go to him."

Without waiting for me to reply, she left the room and practically ran up the staircase, disappearing from sight. I stared after her in bemusement for a moment, then—after a last look at the dining table—I returned to the main hall. There, I found that the rest of the children and their parents had arrived and the place seemed to suddenly be full of noise and laughter. I was also surprised to see that my mother was standing with four little old ladies I recognised: Mabel Cooke, Glenda Bailey, Florence Doyle, and Ethel Webb—affectionately called the "Old Biddies" (though not to their faces!).

"Hello!" I said, going over to join them and blinking as I got a proper look at their attire. The Old Biddies looked like they'd got dressed in the dark, in a Christmas reject shop. They were wearing hideous Christmas jumpers in gaudy red and green, mismatched Christmas socks, over-sized Santa hats, and to top it all off, they had huge Christmas bauble earrings swinging from their ears.

"Hello, Gemma, dear," said Mabel in her booming voice. "Your mother told us that you're catering the tea party. I know you don't have any Christmas puddings to offer, since Dora decided not to make any for the tearoom—even though I *did* tell her that plum puddings are essential on a Christmas menu, but of course, *some* people just do not appreciate well-meaning advice..."

She sniffed with great disapproval and I had to hide a smile. As the bossiest of the Old Biddies, Mabel was used to being "top hen" and she hadn't taken kindly to Dora usurping her position at the tearoom when the latter had been hired as the baking chef. Since then, the two women had been locked in a perpetual battle of passive-aggressive "one-upmanship", with me caught unwittingly in the middle.

"Anyway, I've brought you one of my own Christmas puddings, so you can serve it with the rest of the tea."

Mabel thrust a plate at me. I stared at the large mound covered with silver foil.

"Oh... er... thank you," I said, taking the plate. Carefully, I lifted the foil to peek underneath, then reeled back from the alcoholic fumes wafting out. *Bloody hell! How much brandy had Mabel put in this thing?* I coughed and hastily replaced the foil. "Um... That's really kind of you, Mabel. The thing is... Annabel has some Christmas puddings prepared already. Her previous housekeeper made them before she left, so there's plenty to go around."

"I'm sure Annabel's housekeeper is a very capable woman, but *my* plum puddings are different," said Mabel.

Yeah, they'll put everyone in a coma, I thought. Thankfully, my mother spoke up at that moment:

"If Gemma doesn't need the pudding, Mabel, I'd be delighted to take it. We have relatives arriving from the States and I'm sure they'd be keen to taste some traditional English Christmas treats. I hadn't got around to organising a pudding yet for the Christmas Day lunch so this will be perfect."

Mabel looked mollified and I passed the plate to my mother with relief. Then I glanced at the Old Biddies' outrageous attire again and ventured to ask:

"What are you doing here?"

"We're here to sing carols!" squealed Ethel.

Glenda nodded excitedly, her wrinkled cheeks glowing almost neon pink from all the blusher she had applied. "Yes, Annabel invited the 'Twelve Greys of Christmas' to come and entertain the children at the tea party—"

"Although the others couldn't make it, so it's really just the 'Four Greys of Christmas' today," added Florence, her plump face slightly anxious.

"It doesn't matter," said Mabel, waving a hand. "We are the founders of the group, and therefore the most important. And I'm sure Gemma can step in and help with the singing if—"

"*Me?* Oh no... no..." I protested. "I can't sing to save my life."

"We'd have to call ourselves 'The Four Greys and One Brown of Christmas' though," said Florence, frowning as she eyed my boyish pixie cut.

"And Gemma isn't festively dressed. She needs a Christmas jumper and some bauble earrings too," added Glenda, looking at my clothes with disapproval.

"I have some extra jumpers that I knitted back home, although I don't suppose there's enough time to go back and fetch them now?" Ethel said. "What a shame. The one with the two snowmen kissing would have fitted you perfectly, dear... or the one with the reindeer face on the front."

"Er... they sound lovely but... um... I don't need a Christmas jumper, thank you very much," I said hastily. "Um... so what are you singing?"

"Good, old-fashioned Christmas hymns," said Mabel stoutly. "None of this seeing your mother kissing Santa Claus and blue Christmas nonsense. We'll be doing 'Joy to the World', 'Deck the Halls', 'Hark the Herald Angels Sing'—"

"Surely no carolling would be complete without a rousing rendition of 'Good King Wenceslas'," said an amused voice.

We turned to see a distinguished-looking man in his early fifties standing next to us. He was taking off his hat and gloves, and had obviously just arrived. Behind him, I could see a young man in a chauffeur's uniform coming through the front door, carrying an overnight case.

"Ah, Julian... how nice to see you."

Annabel came gracefully down the stairs, as cool and composed as ever, as if her earlier distress had never occurred, and came over to join us. She leaned towards the man to receive a peck on the cheek, then turned and said to us:

"This is my cousin, Professor Julian Morecombe."

"Oh, I believe I've heard my husband mention you. Parnell College, isn't it?" said my mother with a smile. "I'm Evelyn Rose. I gather you met my husband recently when he took part in a debate at the Oxford Union. He says you had a stimulating discussion over drinks in the Members' Bar afterwards, about the role that music might have played in inspiring revolutions throughout history."

The man raised his eyebrows. "Yes, indeed. Professor Philip Rose... So you are his lovely wife? What a pleasure to meet you, Evelyn! The old dog—Philip never told me that his wife was so young and attractive," he added, arching an eyebrow and giving her an exaggerated look of admiration.

My mother twittered like a young girl. "Oh, don't be silly. I have a daughter grown, you know. This is Gemma," she added, gesturing to me.

"Ah... well, they do say that a child is a mirror of

the parent, Evelyn, and I can certainly see that your daughter is a testament to your charm and beauty!"

Oh, for goodness sake... I stifled the urge to roll my eyes. I know, I know—it was silly and ageist of me to think that life ended at forty, but there was something cringeworthy about watching your parents and their middle-aged friends flirting, especially in such an ostentatious manner.

Julian Morecombe took my hand and, for a horrifying moment, I thought he was going to kiss the back of it, but he only clasped it tightly whilst looking deep into my eyes. I shifted uncomfortably. Then, to my relief, the ageing playboy released me and turned to the Old Biddies.

"My goodness, Annabel, you *are* spoiling me this Christmas—I had no idea I was going to be surrounded by so many lovely ladies!" he cried with another exaggerated look of admiration.

Glenda simpered, Ethel went bright pink, Florence smiled shyly, and even Mabel flushed with pleasure.

"And I believe that you are going to entertain us with some Christmas carols?" continued Julian smoothly.

"Oh yes, perhaps it would be a good idea to have those now, Mrs Cooke," Annabel spoke up. "Then the children can have their tea before opening their presents."

She raised her voice and began calling people into the main hall. A few minutes later, everyone was gathered in a semicircle facing the Old Biddies, who had taken up the traditional carollers' position, just outside the front door. It was after five o'clock; the sun had set and snow was falling harder. A chill wind swept in through the open door, stinging our cheeks, but no one seemed to mind. Somehow, the cold seemed to add to the atmosphere.

Mabel had produced an antique metal lantern whilst the other three Old Biddies shared a hymnbook between them. In spite of their ridiculous Christmas costumes, they made a cosy picture as they stood, lit by the gold glow of the lantern and framed in the doorway, with the inky-blue sky behind them and snow swirling in drifts around their heads. They began to sing and, as the familiar words rose in the air, I felt the hairs prickle at the back of my neck.

"On the first day of Christmas
My true love gave to me
A partridge in a pear tree..."

I glanced at the crowd, pleased to see that everyone really had assembled in the hall. The children were rapt, their eyes shining, whilst their parents watched with nostalgic smiles. Beside them, Annabel and my mother stood listening in identical poses of ladylike poise, whilst Julian Morecombe nodded in time to the tune next to them. A little bit beyond them, Richard Floyd was watching sullenly with his arms crossed, and on the other side of the hall, the blonde woman I'd seen earlier was leaning against the staircase bannister, a bored expression on her face. She was standing with a stolid, grey-haired woman wearing an apron, whom I guessed to be the new housekeeper.

> *"...Eight maids a-milking,*
> *Seven swans a-swimming,*
> *Six geese a-laying,*
> *Five... gold... rings,*
> *Four calling birds,*
> *Three French hens,*
> *Two turtledoves,*
> *And a partridge in a pear tree!"*

As the last words of the carol died away, there came the sound of loud clapping and a male voice called out:

"Bravo! Bravo! Now *that* is a welcome worth coming home to!"

A handsome man with salt-and-pepper hair appeared suddenly in the doorway beside the Old Biddies. He swept them a bow, then stepped into the house, brushing the snow from his coat. My eyes widened as I recognised the man I had met at the train station.

There was a loud gasp next to me. It was Annabel; she was staring at the newcomer, her face deathly pale. She raised a shaking hand to her mouth and took a step forwards, but before she could speak, a new voice rang out. It was a thin, quavering voice, but there was no mistaking the joy and delight in the tone:

"Edward! My dear boy! I knew you weren't dead! I knew you would come home one day!"

I turned to see an old man halfway down the staircase, leaning heavily on the bannister for support. He was dressed in a Victorian-style, burgundy velvet smoking jacket, which hung loosely on his thin frame. His white hair, which would once have probably been described as "leonine", was now sparse and limp, and his aquiline nose and strong eyebrows, which must have once dominated an arrogantly handsome face, now looked too prominent amongst his haggard features. Still, as he hobbled down the remaining steps, I could see the resemblance to the man who had just arrived.

Annabel made an indeterminate noise and tried to put a hand on the old man's arm as he passed her, but he shrugged her off impatiently as he rushed towards the newcomer.

"Hello, Dad," drawled Ned, flashing his white teeth in a mocking smile. "As you can see, the prodigal son has come home."

CHAPTER SIX

The crowd had fallen back in a respectful silence and now everyone watched agog as the rest of the family came to greet Ned. Annabel stepped forwards first, offering a cool cheek to be kissed—a mirror of what she had done with Julian earlier—and I was stunned at the self-control which enabled her to greet a brother she had thought dead for years with the same aplomb as the cousin she saw regularly.

"Hello, Ned... I never thought... It's been so long that we'd given you up for lost..." she murmured.

"Ah... well, you know me, sis," said Ned, grinning. "Always turning up again like a bad penny. Besides, you didn't think you'd get rid of me that easily, did you?"

He said it jokingly but there was something of a sneer in his voice and I saw Annabel flush. For a moment, some violent emotion blazed at the back of her eyes, then she had herself rigidly under control again, her face wiped smooth. She stepped back to allow her husband to come forwards. Richard Floyd clasped his brother-in-law's hand and gave it a brief shake, saying with a frown:

"Ned... We thought you were dead."

"You thought... or you hoped?" said Ned, smirking.

Richard stiffened. "If that's supposed to be funny—"

Sir Hugh Morecombe laughed and clapped his son on the back. "I see you haven't lost your wicked sense of humour, my boy."

Ned turned to his cousin. "So, Julian... still coming to Thurlby Hall for Christmas every year, just like old times, eh?" He eyed the other man up and down, taking in the sharply tailored jacket with the brocade waistcoat, the Italian silk scarf draped artfully over the nape of the neck, and the pointy-toed tan leather shoes that completed the ensemble. "Bloody hell, Julian, I always thought you were a fop, but look at you now!"

Sir Hugh cackled with laughter again. "That's what I always say! That's what I always say!"

Julian affected a nonchalant air, although I could see a muscle ticking in his jaw. "I see you haven't lost your charm, Ned," he said blandly.

Ned gave him a wolfish smile. "We can discuss that more over dinner, if you like. Speaking of which, I hope you've prepared a fatted calf for me. Or perhaps I should say 'fatted goose' since it *is* Christmas. In fact, I'm looking forward to a Christmas feast just like the old days." He rubbed his hands in anticipation. "Roast potatoes, sage and onion stuffing, Yorkshire pudding, Brussels sprouts... and mince pies and plum pudding to finish, of course." He glanced at Annabel. "I hope Mrs Simms is still making her excellent Christmas puddings?"

"Mrs Simms has left us, actually," said Annabel. "But she made several puddings in advance, so we'll still have them for Christmas this year. And Mrs Holmes," she indicated the woman in the apron, standing at the rear of the crowd, "who has taken over the housekeeper position, is a fantastic cook. I think you'll find that her roast potatoes are even better than Mrs Simms's."

Ned glanced carelessly at the housekeeper, then his attention slid to the blonde woman next to Mrs Holmes. She had been eyeing him with bold interest and now she came forwards, thrusting a hand out and saying in a breathy voice:

"Hello... I'm Kelly." She gave him a coy smile. "I never realised when I became engaged to your father that I would end up with such a handsome stepson."

Ned's eyebrows shot up and he glanced at his father, obviously wondering at the forty-plus years' age difference between the old man and his fiancée.

"I see you've been busy, Dad, since I've been away."

The old man cackled again and took Ned's arm, leading him down the hallway. "Come with me, my boy. I have so much to say to you..."

There was a pregnant silence in the hall after they'd disappeared, then one of the children said, in a plaintive voice:

"Are there going to be more Christmas carols? Or can we go and open our presents now?"

Everyone laughed and the tension was broken. Soon, the hall was filled with the merry hubbub of conversation again and it was almost as if the recent dramatic arrival had never happened.

Annabel gave the Old Biddies an apologetic smile and said, "I think it's getting a bit cold now for more carols. Why don't we all go into the dining room for some tea and then the children can open their presents in the library?"

"Yay!"—"Presents!" —"Hurray!" cried several little voices.

The children and their parents trooped into the dining room, and I watched with pleasure as they exclaimed over the treats laid out on the table. The time seemed to fly as I went around helping to pour tea and serve the food. Before I knew it, the kids— their faces now liberally smeared with chocolate mousse—were back in the library and watching excitedly as Annabel began handing out stockings stuffed with gifts. The atmosphere in the room became manic as children began tearing open their presents, and whooping and yelling with delight.

"There will be tears soon, you'll see," said Mabel, surveying them with a practised eye.

"Tears?" I said with a disbelieving laugh. "What do you mean? They're having the time of their life!"

"Ah, but just you wait... What with all the sugary treats they've had and the over-excitement... well, things will start to get too much for them soon."

She was right. Within a few minutes, two children started squabbling over a toy in one corner whilst, in another, a little girl sat down on the floor and began kicking and screaming in a full-blown tantrum.

"Oh dear... time to go home, I think," observed one parent with a wry smile. She glanced out the window, where snow was falling heavily. "And it's probably a good idea with the weather too."

They all began collecting their little ones and soon the children were bundled up in their hats and coats and mittens, waving goodbye and thanking us for the party. In a few more minutes, they were all gone, the sound of their cars muffled by the falling snow.

"Well, I think your Christmas tea party was an unqualified success, Annabel!" said my mother. "Now I hope you don't mind, but I must dash as well. Our guests from the States are arriving tomorrow and I still have several things to prepare."

"Oh, not at all, Evelyn. Thank you so much for all your help." Annabel glanced at the Old Biddies.

"And you too, Mabel... Glenda... Ethel... Florence—the carol was delightful."

"I suppose I'd better go too, as I'm getting a lift with my mother," I said, biting my lip and casting a troubled glance back towards the dining room. "But I really wanted to stay and help clean up—"

"I'm sure we'll manage, but there's no need for you to rush off if you'd just like to stay a bit longer," said Annabel. "I can have Cole run you back into town later in our car. That's the benefit of having a private chauffeur." She smiled. "And you haven't had any tea yet—you must stay and have a cup with me before you go. You too," she turned to include the Old Biddies in her invitation. "You're all welcome to stay."

"Why don't you all go on first," I suggested. "I'm just going to take these platters to the kitchen and rinse them, so that the food doesn't dry and stick on them, otherwise it will be a nightmare to get off later."

"Oh, I'm sure Mrs Holmes would be happy to do that for you," said Annabel.

"No, no, I'd like to do it myself," I said firmly. "It's one of my policies. When I cater an event, I don't like to make any extra work for the clients or resident staff if I can help it. I'll only be a minute."

Going to the dining room, I stacked the large platters I'd brought and took them through to the spacious kitchen at the back of the manor house. Mrs Holmes was nowhere in sight, but I saw that she had already piled several of the used cups and plates next to the double sink by the window. Carrying my platters over, I was pleased to discover that they were both butler sinks—enormous, rectangular farmhouse-style sinks—which gave me ample room to turn the platters properly under the tap, so that I could rinse them thoroughly from all sides. I flicked on the hot tap and bent over the sink, directing the stream of water carefully over the edges of the platter.

A hand curved suddenly around my waist, the fingers caressing my hip.

I jumped and whirled around, splashing water everywhere. Ned stood behind me, smirking.

"What are you *doing*?" I hissed.

"Sorry. You looked so tempting there, bending over the sink..." He trailed off suggestively.

I stared at him. Was this man for real? Which century did he live in?

"I could report you for sexual harassment," I snapped.

He raised his hands, palms up, in a defensive gesture. "Hey... I was just fooling around, okay? No need to get your knickers in a twist. Bloody hell, I'd forgotten how frigid English girls can be."

"*What?* This isn't about me!" I said furiously. "*You're* the one who groped me!"

"So? Are you telling me that you *really* didn't enjoy it?" he asked with a leer. "Don't tell me that it didn't turn you on... just a bit?"

The man was unbelievable. I'd never met anyone with such an over-inflated ego; the idea that a woman might not find him attractive couldn't even enter his head. As if in confirmation of my thoughts, he stepped suddenly close and grabbed me around the waist again, pulling me towards him. I smelled the alcohol on his breath as he bent his head and tried to kiss me.

"How dare you!" I cried, twisting my head away.

"Aww... come on! It's Christmas! Season of goodwill and all that... just a little kiss, eh? We could be under the mistletoe—*OWW!*"

He flinched as I kicked him, then grinned. "You little tigress! Still, I like a woman with spirit..."

"Get your hands off me, you bastard! Let me go! *Let me go!*"

I began struggling in earnest but he was strong and I felt a flicker of fear. I opened my mouth to scream, but at that moment I heard footsteps approaching and, a second later, Mrs Holmes stepped into the kitchen. She stopped short at the sight of us and gasped, nearly dropping the stack of plates she was carrying. Ned's grip loosened and I took the chance to twist out of his arms, backing away from him and putting several feet between us.

There was silence, except for the sound of my panting and the drip of water from the tap. Mrs Holmes came slowly forwards and something in her scandalised expression must have pierced even that thick skin of his, because Ned scowled and, muttering under his breath, hurried out of the kitchen. I sat down quickly in one of the kitchen chairs. My legs felt shaky and I found that I was trembling.

"Are you okay?" Mrs Holmes asked anxiously, coming over to me. "Did he hurt you?"

"No, no... you came in before anything really happened—not that what happened wasn't enough," I added grimly. Now that the shock was over, I felt my temper rising. I was furious at what Ned had done but also furious at myself for not retaliating better, for being so helpless.

"I can't believe he did that..." said Mrs Holmes in a faint voice. "It's not as if he's a young man anymore—"

"Even if he were younger, it would be no excuse," I snapped. A mixture of anger and shame boiled inside me. "That slimy creep isn't going to get away with it. I don't care if he's related to a client, I don't care if he takes me to court... I'm going to report him to the police for sexual assault! And if he so much as touches me again, I'll *kill* him—"

I broke off as I saw the housekeeper staring at me, wide-eyed. She looked so shocked and upset that I forgot about my own outrage for a moment. Hastily, I put a reassuring hand on her arm.

"Hey... it's okay. I'm all right. He didn't really hurt me. He just surprised me while my back was turned at the sink and tried to grope me and kiss me. Not that it makes it right," I added quickly. "But

I'm not injured or anything, okay? And I'm not some naïve young thing either, so you don't have to worry about me. I'm going to make sure that Ned Morecombe pays for his actions. Wealth and status won't protect him!" I stood up and took a deep breath. "Anyway, I'd better finish rinsing my platters—"

"Are those them in the sink? Here, let me wash 'em for you."

Ignoring my protests, the housekeeper washed and dried the platters, then stacked them in a neat pile for me. By then, I'd calmed down, and when I finally joined Annabel and the Old Biddies in the drawing room, I found myself hesitating when they looked at me expectantly, obviously wondering why I had been so long.

I had been planning to blurt out the whole story and declare my intention to report Ned, but as I looked at Annabel's pale face, I felt a wave of compassion for the woman. I remembered her distress earlier and the heavy drinking, and suddenly I didn't want to add to her troubles. The catering job was finished, anyway, and I would be leaving Thurlby Hall soon, with no intention of returning or seeing Ned again. Maybe it would be better if I kept things to myself, at least until after Christmas.

So I plastered a bright smile on my face and said: "Sorry for taking so long. The platters took a bit longer to rinse than I expected and I had a bit of a... er... chat with Mrs Holmes."

"Oh, that's all right. I've been having a lovely chat myself with Mabel, Glenda, Ethel, and Florence... and your cat has been keeping me company," said Annabel with a smile, looking down at Muesli, who was curled up in her lap.

"You managed to prise her out of the manger?" I said, impressed.

Annabel laughed, looking relaxed and happy for a rare moment. "Yes, with the help of some ham from one of your finger sandwiches." She gestured to the teapot on the table in front of her. "Do sit down. The tea is still hot—"

"Actually..." I gave Annabel an apologetic look. "I think I'd better be making a move. It's nearly eight and I need to get back—"

"Gemma, haven't you seen the weather?" said Annabel, indicating the windows.

I followed her gaze and my heart sank as I saw the conditions outside. Somehow, a fierce snowstorm had whipped up in the time since the children had left, and now the view was completely obscured by a flurry of white.

"It's much too dangerous to drive in this," Annabel was saying. "There will be no visibility on the roads at all. You'll have to wait until the snow dies down a bit." She smiled. "And if it doesn't, then you can stay the night. Don't worry—it's no trouble at all. There are spare rooms prepared already, as we always have guests at this time of year. Mabel and the others have already accepted." She glanced at the clock on the mantelpiece. "Dinner will be served in half an hour, so you'll have time to freshen up, if you wish." She glanced at Muesli again. "I'll ask Mrs Holmes to make up a small dish for Muesli too. Would she be happy with roast chicken?"

I swallowed a sigh. It looked like I had no choice but to stay longer at Thurlby Hall.

CHAPTER SEVEN

The last thing I felt like doing was spending more time with the Morecombe family, but it would have been too rude to refuse Annabel's invitation, and besides, I had to admit that I was starving. So half an hour later, I found myself following the Old Biddies into the dining room and joining the rest of the family at the table. I made sure, though, that I sat as far away from Ned as possible and, to my relief, he seemed to be avoiding me too. It was too small a group, though, to avoid overhearing the conversation—even at the other end of the table— and I found that with the tea party over and the children and guests gone, the thin veneer of civility seemed to be cracking.

"...so what have you been doing with yourself, Julian? Last I knew, you were doing a DPhil or something at Oxford. You still haunting the cloisters?" Ned drawled, looking at his cousin.

Julian drew himself up importantly. "Yes, as a matter of fact, I am now a senior lecturer and the Tutor for Music at Parnell College."

Ned gave a mocking whistle. "So we have a real scholar in the family, eh?"

"It should have been you, Ned," said Sir Hugh, looking at his son fondly. "You know that's what I wanted for you. A professorship at Oxford, head of a department—"

"Oh no, not for me the life of a stuffy academic!" Ned shook his head and laughed. "Nope, I wanted to find my fortune in America—the land of promise and opportunity! Ah, what a wonderful place! So much—"

"If it was that wonderful, then why did you come back?" growled Richard Floyd suddenly.

Ned smirked. "Ah... well, the problem with the land of opportunity is that everyone else is there too, trying to grab what they can, and one gets tired of all that grabbing after a while."

"Why would you have needed to grab anything? You had your trust fund money, didn't you? You cleaned the account out when you ran away, and I would've thought that a few million pounds would be enough—even for someone like you," said Richard with a sneer.

"Well, perhaps I didn't quite have your business acumen," said Ned with an ironic smile. "I made a few... unwise investments, shall we say?"

"So you burned through your money and now you're back to grab some more again," said Richard with a dangerous glint in his eye.

Ned gave an insolent smile and leaned back in his chair to look around the room, his eyes lingering on the expensive porcelain displayed in the cabinets, the valuable oil paintings on the walls. "Well... I hardly think I will need to do much 'grabbing', when there's so much here simply for the taking."

Richard bristled. "Now, look here...! If you think you can just march back and claim everything as yours—"

"But it *is* mine," said Ned with a taunting smile. He turned to his father, who had turned away to talk to Kelly, and called out, "Isn't it, Dad? You always said that one day, everything would belong to me."

"That's right, that's right, my boy," said Sir Hugh, beaming as if his son had said something very clever. "As my heir, everything will belong to you. The title, the estate, the majority shares in the company, the position of CEO—"

"The CEO position!" Richard Floyd rounded on the old man, white lines of anger around his mouth. "But you said—"

"*Gentlemen!*" Annabel gave a nervous trill of laughter. She nodded at me and the Old Biddies. "Really... I think you're forgetting yourselves. We have company."

Ned shrugged and poured himself more wine. Richard Floyd eyed his brother-in-law with malevolence as he sat back in his seat, but he didn't say anything else.

"I think the thing you're forgetting is that *I'm* marrying your father," said Kelly with an arch smile. "And as his wife, I expect I'll be entitled to the estate—"

"The estate is entailed to the male line," said Julian stiffly. "That means only a male heir can inherit."

"And that would have been you, wouldn't it, before I showed up?" said Ned with a malicious smile. "I hope I didn't ruin your Christmas too much, cousin. After all, I know how much you've always wanted to be 'lord of the manor'."

Julian flushed a dull red. "I don't... That's certainly not... It... it would have been my duty to accept the title if you... if there had been no one else," he blustered.

"Well, I'm not dead yet, so you can all stop bickering," said Sir Hugh, chuckling.

Of all the people at the table, he was the only one who seemed to be in genuinely good spirits. In fact, as the meal dragged on, he seemed to get more and more jolly, talking and laughing with Ned, and ignoring almost everyone else. Richard Floyd sat in a sullen silence, rousing himself only to ask for more wine. Next to him, his wife remained as cool and composed as ever, although I noticed that her wine glass was refilled even more frequently than her husband's. Julian did seem to recover his aplomb and made an effort at gaiety, reverting to his previous playboy persona and flirting outrageously with Kelly. The blonde woman played along with him, although I noticed that her eyes were often on Ned and there was a speculative gleam in them which made me wonder if she was transferring her predatory inclinations from father to son. After all, if Ned was due to inherit everything, then marrying the younger man was a much more attractive prospect than tying herself to a septuagenarian.

I was surprised that the Old Biddies said very little during dinner. I had thought that Mabel—who normally had an opinion on everything—would be unable to resist commenting on the family drama, but she simply sat and concentrated on her food, as did her three friends. Well, it had been a long day and it was easy to forget, given their usual boundless energy and enthusiasm, that the Old Biddies were in their eighties. It was hardly surprising that they would be tired after all the activity and excitement.

When the meal was over, Sir Hugh insisted on following the archaic tradition of the men remaining in the dining room for port, whilst the women withdrew to the drawing room for coffee first. We followed Annabel obediently, but when she tried to pour the Old Biddies each a cup, they declined.

"No? Perhaps you would like tea instead? And how about some chocolates?" Annabel suggested, gesturing to the box of chocolate truffles on the coffee table.

"Oh no. No chocolate after 6 p.m. Did you know that cocoa can cause constipation? Yes, indeed!" said Mabel, warming to her favourite subject. "It can also cause tummy rumbling, intestinal cramps, and..." She paused dramatically. "Excessive *wind.*"

"My cousin says chocolate always gives her dreadful reflux," Glenda chimed in. "She burps horribly after she has anything with cocoa in it. And she says it gives her spots. Even though she's seventy-four."

"I read a book once on the history of chocolate when I was still working at the village library," said Ethel, her eyes wide. "It said that the Aztecs would give chocolate to their human sacrifices, just before they killed them!"

"Oh... er... right," said Annabel, obviously not quite sure how to respond to this catalogue of horrors.

"Well, I think chocolate is lovely," said Florence, crossing her plump arms and jutting her double chin out. "There's nothing like a cup of hot cocoa on a winter's day or a bit of chocolate fudge with your afternoon cuppa. But no, thank you..." she added as Annabel held the tray of truffles out to her. "I won't have any tonight. If you'll excuse me, I think

I'll be going up to a nice hot bath and to bed."

The other Old Biddies echoed her and, a few minutes later, they retired upstairs. I watched them go wistfully. I really wanted to follow their example—I was physically exhausted from the long day and emotionally drained from the earlier ordeal in the kitchen, as well the general undercurrents of tension in the house—but somehow it felt too rude to get up and leave straight after them. So I forced myself to accept a cup of tea and sat making desultory conversation with Kelly and Annabel.

To be honest, I wasn't feeling very charitable towards the former. It was really hard—after the sordid scene I had stumbled on earlier, and with the way she had behaved at dinner—not to just label Kelly a vain, immoral gold-digger. But I tried to remind myself not to fall into the judgemental trap of assuming that every young, attractive woman who tied herself to a much older man had to be a calculating fortune hunter, and I tried to keep an open mind as I chatted with her. After half an hour's conversation, though, I had to admit that Kelly hadn't done much to change my prejudices against her.

I was relieved when I felt that I had sat long enough for politeness and could rise at last and bid them goodnight. It was only when I got up to the guestroom that I remembered Muesli. *Bugger!* I had forgotten all about my cat. After polishing off the lavish dinner of kitchen scraps that Mrs Holmes had prepared for her, the little tabby had wandered off by herself. She hadn't been in the drawing room with us just now, but I had a sneaking suspicion I knew where she might be.

Returning quietly downstairs, I passed the dining room, where I could still hear the rumble of male conversation—perhaps Sir Hugh and the others lingering over their port—and made my way to the library. But as I was about to enter, I realised that there were harsh voices coming from within: Richard and Annabel. It sounded like I had stumbled into the middle of a domestic.

"...when are you going to grow a spine and stop being such a doormat? It's always 'Daddy says this'... 'Daddy wants that'... always bloody giving in to him, always doing what he wants!"

"He... he's an old man. He needs—"

"Ah, bollocks! You've always pandered to him. Even when you were a teenager and should have been out snogging boys and smoking dope, you were sitting at home, all prim and proper, being little Miss Perfect... and look where that's got you, eh? Your father still favours Ned—Ned, who got girls pregnant left, right, and centre; Ned, who always disobeyed the old man; Ned, who never did an honourable thing in his life!" Richard's voice took on a sneering tone. "But I suppose you still think you can win your father over with self-sacrifice? Get Daddy to love you by doing everything he wants?"

"You should be grateful for my compliance

because that's the only reason I married you!" said Annabel suddenly in a choked voice. "Yes! There was another man—a wonderful man—who loved me, and we were going to be so happy together... but I rejected his proposal because I knew Daddy wanted me to marry you, the rising young star in his company... and I have regretted it every single day since." Annabel's voice was thick with bitterness. "So don't you dare laugh at my love for my father. If it weren't for my 'self-sacrifice'—as you put it—you wouldn't be here now: enjoying the benefits of my father's estate, a senior partner in the company, a contender for the CEO position—"

"Which I'm not going to get now that Ned has come back," snarled Richard. "Well, I'm not going to let him muscle in on my position in the company, do you hear me? *You* might have no backbone with the old man but *I'm* not going to lie down and roll over just because he snaps his fingers. I've spent my life building up this company and that CEO position is mine by right! I'm not letting anyone take it from me!"

"What... what are you going to do?"

Richard's voice was grim. "Whatever I need to."

There was suddenly a rush of footsteps and, before I could react, the door to the library was flung open and I found myself face to face with Richard Floyd.

"What are you doing here?" He scowled.

"N-nothing... I mean... I'm... er... I'm looking for

my cat..." I stammered.

"I don't know what Annabel was thinking, letting you bring that mangy beast into the house! I had better not find a single cat hair on any of my clothes or I'll be sending you the bill for the dry cleaning!"

Without waiting for me to reply, he pushed past me and stalked away.

CHAPTER EIGHT

I stood for a moment, trying to regain my composure, then hesitated as I looked at the open library doorway. The last thing I wanted to do was face Annabel. Aside from my own embarrassment at having overheard the fight, I could just imagine her state after a row like that, and I didn't want to add to her humiliation by walking in on her crying.

Maybe I should just leave Muesli where she is for the night? But I couldn't—I was too worried about what she might do if she was left alone. Especially now that I'd seen Richard Floyd's hostility, the last thing I wanted was for Muesli to decide to use some of Thurlby Hall's priceless antique furniture as her new scratching post!

Taking a deep breath, I stepped into the room, bracing myself to find a distraught, tearful woman. Instead, I found Annabel standing gracefully by the mantelpiece, her face devoid of tears—or in fact, of any expression at all. I eyed her in amazement. I was almost beginning to question if the woman was human!

The only sign of any kind of distress was the wine glass full of dark red liquid in her hand and, as I went slowly across to her, I could see a decanter full of port on the mantelpiece behind her. She looked up at me enquiringly, a polite smile on her face.

"Ah Gemma... is there something you need?"

"No, er... I was just looking for Muesli, actually. I forgot to take her up to my room—ah, there she is! I thought she might be here."

Annabel followed as I walked over to the Nativity scene set up in the corner and looked down at my cat, who was curled up once more in the manger.

"She does like that spot, doesn't she?" said Annabel, a trace of life coming into her face as she gazed down at the little tabby. "Maybe you could get a manger for her to sleep in at home?"

I gave her a wry look. "Trust me, if I bought a manger especially for her to sleep in, Muesli would turn her nose up and never go near it. This is just typical cat behaviour. Part of the reason she wants to sleep in there is because she knows she's not supposed to."

I bent and scooped up Muesli, who meowed irritably, squirming in my arms. Annabel reached out to stroke my cat, a wistful look on her face, and

I felt a stab of pity for the woman. I thought of her outward appearance of wealth and prestige... and then the reality of the huge, empty house with no children or pets to love, the bully husband who humiliated her, and the tyrannical father who ignored her gestures of affection. I glanced at the glass in her hand again and began to see why Annabel drank so much.

She stiffened slightly and I realised that she had seen my face and probably guessed my thoughts. She flushed, but her chin came up and the expression in her eyes, when her gaze met mine, was proud and dignified. Embarrassed, I looked away and, mumbling a goodnight, hurried from the room.

Carrying a sulky Muesli, I climbed back up the stairs and made my way to the guest bedroom. I deposited my little cat at the foot of the bed. She looked around peevishly, obviously not pleased with her surroundings, and gave me a petulant meow. I ignored her and hurriedly undressed, then turned out the lights and climbed into the bed, shivering as I slid between the cold sheets. Like most big old houses, Thurlby Hall was poorly insulated and, without the warmth from the big fireplaces in the main living areas downstairs, the upstairs rooms were freezing. Outside the window, I could hear the wind howling; it didn't sound like the snowstorm was going to die down any time soon. Pulling the blanket up to my chin, I snuggled deeper into the bed and tried to go to sleep.

But sleep wouldn't come. In spite of how weary I felt, I found that my mind was racing, replaying the scenes I had witnessed earlier that evening, recalling conversations I had overheard. The strangeness of sleeping in an unfamiliar room didn't help either. Noises you barely noticed in your own home suddenly seemed to jump out at you: the distant rumbling of the pipes in the plumbing, the creak of floorboards and the shuffle of footsteps, the sound of muffled conversation from the rooms downstairs, the chime of the grandfather clock as it struck the half hour...

I closed my eyes and tried to relax, to ignore the sounds from the house and to empty my mind. But the sound of footsteps intruded again—this time much closer. My eyes flew open and I turned my head to look at my bedroom door. Light seeped in beneath it from the hallway outside. The floorboards creaked and a shadow fell across the sliver of light as footsteps crept softly past, heading to the room beyond mine. I heard the door open and voices whispering, a giggle—it sounded young and female—and then the soft thud of the door closing, muffling the voices so that I could hear them no longer.

I turned over in bed, my thoughts churning. My first thought was of Richard and Kelly having another sordid assignation—except that I knew that the room beyond mine belonged to Julian

Morecombe. We were the only two people in this wing of the house. Perhaps Julian had come up to his room first, while I was downstairs looking for Muesli, and then Kelly had crept up here to join him? I thought back to the way the two had been flirting at dinner. The blonde woman had already shown that she had the morals of an alley cat. *She'd probably have no hesitation shagging one man this afternoon, then climbing into the bed of another one tonight*, I thought with distaste.

Well, it's none of my business, I reminded myself. Turning over in bed again, I sighed and closed my eyes, and tried to go to sleep once more. Somehow I must have drifted off, because when I next opened my eyes, the house seemed different. *It's quiet*, I realised. The household seemed to have retired and even the wind outside had died down slightly. I sat up in bed and looked around, frowning. It wasn't just the quiet. Something else was bothering me, something else was—

I stared suddenly at the foot of my bed, where Muesli should have been curled up sleeping. The space among the folds of the blanket was empty. Quickly, I scanned the room, then froze as I saw that my bedroom door was slightly ajar. The little minx! She must have sneaked out and gone downstairs again. *Probably to sleep in that bloody manger*, I thought dourly.

Sighing, I got out of bed, hastily pulled on some clothes, and made my way downstairs. The house was in darkness and everything was still, except for the ticking of the grandfather clock in the main hall. The time showed that it was nearly half past midnight. Then I saw the light coming from the library and realised that perhaps one of the family was still up. I hoped fervently that it wasn't Richard Floyd. The last thing I wanted was to face the surly businessman again and explain that I was—once more—looking for my cat.

I approached the library doorway and hesitated on the threshold, peering in. The light was actually a glow from the fire, which was dying down now to a few burning coals. Most of the room was in shadow, and it didn't look like anyone was here after all.

I stepped inside and walked over to the corner beside the fireplace, where the Nativity scene had been set up. Sure enough, Muesli was curled up in the manger, alongside the ceramic model of the Baby Jesus.

"Muesli!" I whispered.

She raised her head and blinked sleepily at me, then deliberately rolled onto her back and gave me a cajoling look.

"*Meorrw?*" she said.

"Sorry," I muttered. "You can't sleep here. Come on..."

I bent down to scoop her out of the wooden crib, then stopped as I caught sight of someone in one of the leather wingback chairs facing the fireplace. The high back had hidden them from view before, but now, from this angle, I could see an arm flung out to one side. The light from the dying fire played over the expensive Tag Heuer watch on the wrist and I stiffened. It was Ned and, from the relaxed way the arm hung over the side of the chair, it looked like he had fallen into a drunken stupor. *Great.* The last thing I needed was for him to wake up and decide that he'd like to repeat his performance in the kitchen earlier.

Quickly, I reached for Muesli, but the little tabby was faster. She jumped out of the manger and darted away from me.

"Muesli!" I hissed, furious.

"*Meorrw!*" she retorted, trotting over to the fireplace.

She paused beside Ned's armchair and reached up to sniff his limp fingers. Her whiskers twitched, then she hissed and backed away, the fur on her back bristling.

I frowned and walked slowly over, rounding the side of the armchair, then gasped at the sight that met my eyes.

Ned was slumped over sideways, his head hanging down between his shoulders. At least, I guessed it was Ned. Someone had pulled a Christmas stocking upside down over his head—*his* Christmas stocking, I realised, as I saw the embroidered letters spelling "*Edward*" on the red velvet. I couldn't see his face and I hadn't reached down to check his pulse, but somehow I *knew* he was dead. I reached out with trembling hands and grasped the edge of the stocking, yanking it off his head.

His head came free, lolling back on his shoulders, and I stared at the rigid mask of his face... the bared teeth, mottled skin, and bloodshot eyes... the signs of a man who had been suffocated to death.

CHAPTER NINE

I stood frozen for a moment, just staring. Somewhere in the background, I heard the grandfather clock chiming the half hour again, the sound adding an eerie overtone to the scene in front of me, but otherwise my mind was blank. Then the shock hit me. I stumbled backwards and my hands flailed around, groping unconsciously for some support. My fingers brushed against the slippery smoothness of porcelain... felt it slide away from me... I gasped and whirled around, making a wild grab, but it was too late. An antique Chinese vase, which had been standing on the table next to the armchair, teetered sideways, then toppled over, smashing on the floor.

Muesli gave a high-pitched yowl and jumped clear of the broken pieces just in time. She leaped over the coal scuttle next to the fireplace and shot past the panelled fire screen, knocking it over. It fell with a loud clang of metal that seemed to echo through the whole house. Before I could react, I heard a staccato of footsteps in the hall outside and, a moment later, Mrs Holmes burst into the room.

"Miss? What happened? I heard the most dreadful racket and then I—" She broke off, her eyes bulging as she came around to where I was standing and saw Ned's body.

"Is... is he dead?"

I nodded.

"Oh my God..." She drew a rasping breath, then opened her mouth and screamed.

"Mrs Holmes. *Mrs Holmes!*" I shook her gently, trying to stop the rising tide of hysteria. "Stop it!"

She fell silent, although her eyes remained riveted on Ned's body. I looked around and spotted the decanter of port that Annabel had been helping herself from earlier. There were a few unused glasses on the tray next to the decanter. Quickly, I went over to the mantelpiece and poured a glass of the dark red liquid, then returned to the housekeeper.

"Here, drink this," I said, holding the glass out to her.

She took the port with shaking hands and drank a few gulps, then lowered the glass and took a shuddering breath.

"I'm... I'm sorry... It was such a shock—"

"It's okay. I understand."

More footsteps sounded outside—clattering down the stairs, hurrying across the hall—and the next moment, the room seemed to be filled with people, all talking at once.

"What the hell is going on? Who's making that infernal racket?" Richard Floyd demanded, striding into the room. I was surprised to see that he was still dressed in the suit he had been wearing earlier—had he not gone to bed?—and I noticed that the hem of his trousers was damp.

He was followed by Annabel, who *had* obviously undressed and gone to bed. She was wearing a dressing gown hastily belted around her waist and her face was bare of make-up, her hair loose around her shoulders. Pushing past her husband, she hurried over to where Mrs Holmes and I were standing, then gasped as she saw her brother. Her face went even paler and she put a hand to her mouth. For a moment, I thought she was going to scream too, but then I saw her spine stiffen, that familiar iron control settling over her like armour.

Richard Floyd had gone completely silent as he arrived next to us and stared down at his brother-in-law's body. Julian Morecombe, on the other hand, seemed to have gone the other way, gabbling in an almost hysterical manner:

"Oh my God, is he dead? What happened to him? Was there an accident? Did you check his pulse—

are you sure he's dead? Because sometimes people appear dead but, in fact, they are simply deeply unconscious and..." He trailed off, staring at the still figure in the armchair, then swallowed convulsively, pulling the edges of his dressing gown tighter around him.

It was a very elegant silk men's dressing gown—the kind of thing one might have seen in a Noel Coward play—with a maroon paisley pattern and a monogrammed breast pocket. It was long, almost to his ankles, but as Julian shifted slightly, the edges parted and I saw that his legs were bare. In fact, it looked like he was wearing nothing else under the dressing gown, which suggested that he had probably been naked in bed. *Alone?* I wondered, my eyes straying across to Kelly, who had come in last and was keeping her distance, as if afraid to come too close and see the body in the chair.

"He's been suffocated," I said quietly. "I found him with that on his head." I indicated the Christmas stocking lying on the floor, where I had dropped it. Everyone looked at it in horror.

"But how..." Julian said, shaking his head. "I don't understand—"

"Oh, Muesli!" said Annabel suddenly.

I followed her gaze and looked down to see that Muesli had trotted over to join us. She was now at our feet, sniffing around the base of the armchair where an overturned plate of plum pudding lay on the floor, next to a shattered glass of port. It looked like the two items had been on the small table next to the armchair and had been knocked to the floor in the struggle earlier. Muesli was eyeing the crumbs of plum pudding with interest and I saw her stick her little pink tongue out inquisitively.

"Mrs Holmes, you'd better clean that mess up," said Annabel quickly. "In case anything is poisonous to cats."

The housekeeper bent towards the floor but I put a hand on her arm, saying sharply:

"No, wait! Don't touch anything!"

She paused and looked at me in surprise.

"You mustn't touch or move anything in a crime scene," I explained, picking Muesli up so that she was out of harm's way.

Everyone turned astonished eyes on me.

"Crime scene?" spluttered Julian. "But surely... you're not suggesting that there's been... foul play?"

"What else can it be?"

"It could have been an accident."

"An accident?" I gestured to the body in front of us. "Ned was suffocated by a stocking over his head. How could that have happened by accident?"

"Well, I... I don't know..." blustered Julian. "But it's ludicrous to suggest that... that it was..."

"Murder," said Kelly, her voice unnaturally high.

Richard rounded on her. "Don't jump to conclusions!" he snapped. "Why would anyone want to kill Ned?"

I can think of someone with lots of reasons, I

thought, looking at him. Aloud, I said: "We need to call the police."

"I'll do it," Richard muttered, turning and leaving the room.

We were all silent after he left, standing awkwardly around the armchair, then Mrs Holmes said timidly:

"Would... would anyone like a cup of tea?"

Annabel gave her a grateful smile. "That's a good idea, Mrs Holmes. Perhaps you could—"

She broke off as we all heard a loud shuffling in the hall outside. It sounded like someone coming slowly down the staircase.

"Daddy!" Annabel gasped and rushed out to the hall.

I followed and saw Sir Hugh halfway down the staircase. He was wearing pyjamas and a dressing gown, and negotiating the steps with the help of his walking stick. He looked up as we ran into the hall and said petulantly:

"What on earth is happening? I heard the most awful noise up in my room... crashing and screaming..." He turned to his daughter, who had rushed up the steps to put a supportive hand under his arm. "Well?" he barked.

Annabel hesitated, then said, "Something has happened to Ned, Daddy."

"What's happened to him?"

"I... he... he's dead."

The old man reeled slightly. "Dead?" Then his

brows drew together. "What do you mean? How can he be dead?"

"We're... we're not sure yet," said Annabel. "Richard's gone to call the police."

Sir Hugh looked at the open door of the library, then started down the rest of the stairs.

"No... wait, Daddy... I don't think you should go in there..." Annabel tried to hold him back but her father pushed her roughly away.

"Leave me alone! I want to see—I have a right to see!" he snapped.

He reached the bottom of the stairs and hobbled with surprising speed into the library. The others backed away as he approached the armchair. There was a long silence as he stood and looked down at the body of his dead son. If I had expected some kind of dramatic collapse, I was disappointed. Sir Hugh passed a hand briefly over his eyes, then I saw his shoulders straighten and his back stiffen, as he drew himself up taller. I realised suddenly where Annabel had inherited her rigid self-control from as he turned around and I saw the impassivity in his face. Only his hoarse voice betrayed him slightly as he said:

"My son is dead. I have nothing now."

"No, Daddy, you have me!" cried Annabel, rushing forwards to take her father's hand.

He gave her a scornful look. "You? What's the use of having you?" Shaking her off, he said, "I'm going to bed. Nobody disturb me until the police arrive."

A spasm of pain had crossed Annabel's face at her father's words, but she quickly smoothed it away and stood watching expressionlessly as he shuffled out of the library. I glanced at Kelly. I would have thought, as the old man's fiancée, she would have been the first to rush to comfort him, but she seemed to have retreated into herself, huddling in the other armchair, staring blindly into the fireplace. Julian, on the other hand, couldn't seem to keep still; he was pacing nervously up and down, his restlessness even more apparent when compared to Annabel's unnatural stillness. Both of them, however, in their own ways, were making me uneasy. I walked over to the Nativity scene and deposited Muesli back in the manger. At least this way I knew she would stay put somewhere safe. Mrs Holmes was nowhere in sight and I hoped that she had gone to the kitchen to make tea. A hot drink might help to calm everyone's nerves.

When footsteps sounded a few minutes later, though, it wasn't the housekeeper, but Richard Floyd who entered the library.

I looked at him eagerly. "Are the police coming?"

He shook his head. "They can't. The access road is completely blocked. A tree came down in the storm, as well as several power lines. They're sending engineers and an emergency repair crew, but with the current road and weather conditions, and the lack of visibility... They think it could take all night. They might even have to wait until morning. It's still snowing, and apparently the wind is going to pick up again. The Met Office issued a warning earlier that wind speeds could exceed seventy miles an hour overnight, and to be careful of flying debris. They won't endanger men's lives by sending them out in severe weather conditions." Richard paused, then added, "Especially when—in this case—the situation isn't really an emergency. The victim is already dead."

"So what are we going to do?" asked Julian, fidgeting with the belt of his dressing gown.

Richard shrugged. "Go to sleep."

"What?"

"That's what the detective sergeant told me. He said that there was nothing for us to do and there's no point staying up when they probably won't arrive until morning. We should just all go to bed."

No one moved. I could see it in all their faces, even though no one had said a word. It was the same thought that had been going through my mind: if the manor house was cut off by the snowstorm, then that meant that no one could have come from the outside. The person who had attacked Ned and killed him had to have been someone in the house. We were going to sleep with a murderer here amongst us.

CHAPTER TEN

I must have been more tired than I realised because somehow, in spite of the events of the night and knowledge of a murderer on the loose, I fell into a deep sleep and awoke to find my bedroom curtains showing the soft light of morning. Pulling on a cardigan, I went over to the window and looked out. A winter wonderland met my eyes. Everything was covered in a pristine blanket of white, with the landscaped grounds of Thurlby Hall obscured by banks of snow and the trees lining the driveway standing like two rows of black skeletons silhouetted against the pale grey sky.

For a moment, I was filled with a sense of wonder and enchantment. Then I remembered the body downstairs, and suddenly the beautiful snowy landscape took on grim meaning. I remembered that I was trapped in a house where a murder had taken place. On an impulse, I rushed over to my handbag and fumbled inside until I found my phone, then dialled Devlin's number. It wasn't until he answered in a voice thick with sleep that I realised I probably should have waited until a bit later to call.

"Gemma?" he said groggily. "Is something wrong?"

"N-no... sorry, I forgot how early it was."

"Forgot?" Devlin sounded puzzled. "How do you *forget* how early it is? And what are you doing up anyway? You're not usually a morning person—"

"I couldn't sleep. Oh, Devlin, I'm at Thurlby Hall—you know, that place I was telling you about, where I was catering the tea party? Well, the snowstorm got so bad last night that I had to stay here overnight and then... there was... there's been a murder," I said in a rush.

"*What?*" Devlin sounded thoroughly awake now.

"Yes, it's the son of Sir Hugh Morecombe, who's the owner of Thurlby Hall... he turned up yesterday, just out of the blue—the son, I mean, Ned Morecombe... actually, I'd met him before, just by chance, on the day you left... I bumped into him as I was leaving the station, and then afterwards at The Randolph, and he was a bit obnoxious... although he was far worse yesterday—in fact, I'm not surprised that he was murdered—he was a total creep... and his brother-in-law is a miserable

97

enough git to have done—"

"Gemma... *Gemma!*" Devlin cut in. "I don't know what you're talking about!"

I checked myself and took a deep breath, then I began to slowly recount everything that had happened. When I got to the part about Ned assaulting me in the kitchen, Devlin exploded in a violent curse.

"He did *what*? The bloody bastard—if he wasn't dead, I'd be coming down right now to kill him myself!"

I couldn't help a small smile. I might have been a modern, independent woman, more than capable of looking after herself, but there was still something nice about Devlin's caveman protectiveness.

"Are you sure he didn't hurt you?" he asked urgently.

"Yes, yes... it was more a shock than anything else," I assured him. "It was nothing I haven't had to cope with at drunken office Christmas parties in the past."

"Who's been groping you at office Christmas parties?" demanded Devlin in a dangerous voice.

I laughed. Okay, maybe it was time to show him *my* inner cavewoman. "Nobody. I'm fine, Devlin. Honestly. Calm down. You're forgetting that there's something much more important—there's been a murder."

I told him the rest of the events that had occurred. When I'd finished, he said in a mock-stern voice:

"Gemma, what did I tell you about staying out of trouble?"

"Well, I didn't find a dead body on purpose," I said indignantly.

He sighed. "I know, sweetheart. But like I said, trouble seems to follow you... Anyway, hopefully the police will arrive this morning and you'll be able to go home and forget all about it." He paused, then added, "I don't like the thought of you alone in a house with a possible murderer—"

"Oh, I'm not alone. I mean, aside from the other members of the family, the Old Biddies are here too."

"You're joking."

"No, they came over to sing carols at the tea party and then got snowed in with me, so they spent the night here too. I didn't see them last night though; I suppose they must have somehow slept through everything, although I'm not sure how... But I'll see them this morning."

"Well, make sure you stay together," said Devlin. "Don't go wandering around the house alone. There's safety in numbers. And whatever you do, *don't* start snooping around and trying to get involved in the investigation!"

"I don't intend to," I reassured him. "I'm just looking forward to getting out of here and going home... How about you?" I asked, changing the subject. "How's it going so far? We only had a brief chat when you arrived and you didn't really say much. Is it nice to catch up with your mother?"

He hesitated. "Yes, it's good to see her. She seems very well." He paused, then added, "She's got a new boyfriend."

"Ah... right," I said, not sure how to respond.

Even though Devlin and his mother weren't very close, I could imagine that it would be uncomfortable for him to meet another man in the potential role of "stepfather". Besides, with Devlin's mother having had him in her teens, she was only in her late forties herself and any man she was with would probably not be that much older than Devlin.

"Um... what's he like?" I asked hesitantly.

"He seems nice enough," said Devlin in a non-committal voice. "Mum seems happy, which is what's important, I suppose."

"I'm sure she's happy because you're spending Christmas with her," I insisted. "It must be wonderful for her to have you back home again and to be able to spend quality time with you."

"Mmm..." said Devlin, still in that non-committal tone.

I frowned. Somehow I had a feeling that things weren't going very well, but it was obvious that Devlin didn't want to talk about it. I remembered that the subject of his mother was one he always struggled with—in fact, it was only recently that he would even talk about her at all. So I knew that there was no point pressing the issue. Instead, we talked a bit longer about the weather and the prospect of a "white Christmas" in Oxford before saying goodbye.

When I got downstairs twenty minutes later, carrying Muesli in my arms, I found that my guess was right: the Old Biddies were already up and gossiping with Mrs Holmes in the kitchen. They pounced on me as soon as I entered and insisted that I recount everything again in detail.

"I can't believe you didn't hear anything," I said as I finished.

"Well, we had taken our hearing aids out, dear," Florence explained as the other Old Biddies nodded.

"Oh... I never realised you wore hearing aids," I said, peering at their ears where I couldn't see any obvious device.

"My goodness, I thought it was exciting enough when Sir Hugh asked us to witness his new will... and now there's a murder!" said Glenda with a delicious shiver.

I stared at her. "Sir Hugh asked you to do what? What new will? When was this?"

"After dinner, when you remained with Annabel and Kelly in the drawing room. We were just going up to bed when Ellen here," Mabel nodded at the housekeeper, "told us that Sir Hugh wished to see us in his upstairs sitting room."

"He had just finished writing a new will," Ethel explained. "And he needed two witnesses. He asked me to be one of them," she added proudly.

"And I was the other," said Florence, beaming.

I stared at them. "Did you see... did you get to read the will?"

They shook their heads. "We were just told that it was his new will and asked to witness him signing it, and then write our own names."

"Did anyone else know about this new will?" I asked, glancing at Mrs Holmes, who was listening avidly.

"Well, Mabel and Glenda, of course, since they were in the room with us," Florence said.

"And that other gentleman—Annabel's husband—he might have known," Ethel spoke up. "He was standing outside Sir Hugh's bedroom door. He jumped when I came out and mumbled something, then hurried away. It reminded me of the naughty boys in the village library who used to chew gum and then try to stick it on things when the librarians weren't looking. They made a dreadful mess. I remember catching one of them once in the act. Mr Floyd looked just like that... Didn't you see him?" she asked in surprise as the other three looked at her blankly.

"No, we were still talking to Sir Hugh. You went out first," Florence reminded her.

"Are you saying that Richard Floyd might have been eavesdropping?" I asked Ethel excitedly. "If he knew that Sir Hugh had made a new will which favoured Ned, he might have had reason to—" I broke off as I suddenly realised that Mrs Holmes was still listening agog to everything we were saying. Whatever my feelings were towards Richard Floyd, it seemed wrong to badmouth him in front of his staff—especially if I were accusing him of murder! Clearing my throat, I said, "Um... well, anyway... I suppose a will is hardly a state secret. Sir Hugh himself might have made an announcement about it at the next family gathering."

"I wish we *had* got a proper look at it," said Florence wistfully.

"Yes, it's very likely that it has something to do with Ned's death," said Mabel, nodding emphatically.

"Well, the police—" I broke off as the internal phone rang in the kitchen.

Mrs Holmes hurried to answer and, after speaking for a moment, she hung up and turned to me: "That was Sir Hugh. He asked me to find you— he'd like to speak to you and he asked if you could please go up to see him in his room."

"Me?" I stared at her in surprise. "Um... sure... I'll go up right away. Do you mind giving Muesli some breakfast?"

I placed the little tabby cat down on the floor and she trotted expectantly over to Mrs Holmes. The housekeeper laughed and bent to pat Muesli.

"Of course. I've saved some roast chicken especially for her."

Leaving the Old Biddies eyeing me enviously, I

followed the housekeeper's instructions and made my way back up the staircase and along a different corridor to the other wing of the house, where Sir Hugh's suite of rooms was situated. I knocked and stepped into a spacious sitting room with connecting doors to a master bedroom and en suite. Sir Hugh was sitting in an armchair, talking on the phone, and he waved me impatiently in when he saw me.

"...yes, yes... that's right, she discovered the body... told everyone not to touch anything... yes, that's what I thought... Hmm... that's all very well, Jeffrey, but when are they going to get here? Yes, I know, but my son has been murdered, for God's sake! All right... yes, well... I'm not going to just sit around waiting, I can tell you... You get your men here and, in the meantime, I'm doing things my way. Goodbye."

Sir Hugh put the phone down and looked at me. "That was Detective Superintendent Jeffrey Kendall. He's a personal friend. He tells me that your boyfriend is a detective with the Oxfordshire CID?"

I nodded, wondering where he was going with this. The Superintendent was Devlin's boss and I had met him a few times at police social functions that Devlin had taken me to. I had found Kendall to be an austere man who didn't take kindly to any challenges to his authority. From the one-sided conversation I had overheard just now, though, it sounded like he might have met his match in Sir

Hugh.

"He also tells me that you're practically an honorary member of the CID yourself."

"Oh no, nothing like that," I said hastily. "It's just that I've... er... assisted the police on a few murder cases—"

"More than just assisted—you solved several of them! Yes, I know about you, young lady," said Sir Hugh, nodding. "I read about you in the papers. You're that girl they call the 'Tearoom Sleuth'; the one who solved several murders that had the police completely stumped. There was the May morning stabbing in Oxford... and the cat show poisoning at the Meadowford village fête... and that American who was killed with a scone...." He leaned back and narrowed his eyes, eyeing me speculatively. "And you've got a good brain on you. Oxford graduate, that's what the papers said... and you used to have a high-flying corporate job overseas before you returned to England, isn't that right?"

I was taken aback at how much he knew about me. I knew that there had been some press in the papers, especially after each case, but I usually avoided looking at it. It was too embarrassing reading about myself. As long as it gave good publicity to my tearoom, I hadn't minded too much. Now, though, I was beginning to feel distinctly uncomfortable at the way the media seemed to be representing me.

"No, no, Sir Hugh—I think you're reading too

much into what the papers are saying. You've got completely the wrong impression of me. I don't—"

"And you knew exactly what to do last night," the old man continued as if I hadn't spoken. "Mrs Holmes told me how you made sure no one touched anything and that the library door was locked last night. I told Jeffrey just now—he was very impressed, I can tell you. In fact, I'm sure he'd agree with me when I say that since the police can't get here, *you* need to take over the case."

CHAPTER ELEVEN

"What?" I said, so surprised that I forgot about being rude.

Sir Hugh nodded grimly. "I'm not going to rest until we find out who killed Ned. But it's going to take them hours to unblock the road, neutralise the power lines, and restore access to Thurlby Hall. Jeffrey told me that the earliest his men could get here was probably this afternoon, but it might not be until tomorrow. That's another whole day! I can't just sit here doing nothing. The murderer could be getting away!"

"Er... actually, no one can go anywhere at the moment; that's the whole point," I pointed out. "By the time anyone can leave Thurlby Hall, the police will be here too."

He shook his head impatiently. "No! No!

Everyone knows that the most important thing after a crime is to get statements from all witnesses and suspects, before people's memories get hazy... or before they've had time to cook up an alibi! So you've got to get everyone's account of their movements last night. I want to know where they were, and what they were doing at the time of the murder." He leaned forwards and pointed a finger at me. "You have experience questioning suspects, you'll know what to look out for... and you can tell everyone that the police have assigned you as their representative."

"But they haven't!" I cried. "That's a complete lie and it's probably against the law, impersonating the police—"

"Who said anything about impersonating? You're just helping to get statements."

Sir Hugh turned to look at some framed photos on the side table next to him. I saw that they were almost exclusively of Ned as a much younger man: riding a horse without a saddle, lounging in an armchair with a book, standing with a pretty girl beside a tree, leaning out of the driver's seat of a convertible, flashing his brilliant white smile... Sir Hugh picked up the last one and looked down at it pensively.

"I know everyone thinks Ned was a complete cad, and yes, I agree, he didn't always behave as a gentleman should have," he said quietly. "Ned always breaking hearts and being careless with money and I suppose he was a bit too arrogant for his own good... *but he was my son!*" His voice broke. "And you don't know how many years I have been waiting for him to come home!"

The raw emotion in his voice made me uncomfortable and I sat, not knowing what to say.

"They told me he was dead, you know," Sir Hugh continued after a moment. "When Ned disappeared, I hired a private detective and they traced him to the United States. But then the trail went cold. I kept them looking for years—whatever it cost, I just wanted him to be found—but the most they could dig up in the end was a report of a tour bus accident, with Ned listed as one of the victims. They said it was proof that he was dead... but I never believed them! Never!" He looked me in the eye. "I have never been a religious man, you know, but I started praying then. I prayed every night for my son to be returned to me. And then... and then yesterday, when I saw him standing in the foyer..." Sir Hugh broke off, breathing heavily. "It looked as if this Christmas, my prayers were finally being answered: I got Ned back at last... *and now he's been taken from me again!*" He clenched his fist, his face anguished. "Do you realise what that feels like? And I'm supposed to just sit here and wait? Without knowing who might have done it and why?" He reached out and gripped my hand. "Please... I can't just sit here waiting for the police... I'm... I'm going out of my mind! I need to know that something is being done, that the investigation is started in some way."

I stared at him, not knowing what to say. Yes, I had "questioned" suspects before, but it had always been in the guise of an informal chat. Sitting each of the other members of the house down to a formal interview seemed like a completely different proposition, one I wasn't comfortable with. On the other hand, I was moved by Sir Hugh's plea—I knew that such a show of emotion must have been very difficult for such a proud, aloof man. And I could understand his anger and helplessness, and why he felt such a desperate need to be proactive.

I opened my mouth to reply but, before I could say anything, the door burst open and four little old ladies toddled in.

"Of course Gemma would be delighted to help you, Sir Hugh," said Mabel in her booming voice. "And how lucky that we should be here too! You know, Gemma could never have solved all those cases without our help. Young people might think they know everything but there's nothing like the wisdom that comes with age, wouldn't you agree, Sir Hugh?" She rubbed her hands. "Now, when do we begin?"

I stared at the Old Biddies in exasperation. *Grrr...* They must have been eavesdropping outside the door! Now they surrounded Sir Hugh, who looked slightly befuddled at being confronted by four nosy old ladies, all talking at once.

"Right, shall we start with you, Sir Hugh?" said Mabel briskly. "Did Ned have any enemies?"

"Hang on, hang on," I protested. "You can't... we're not—"

"I suppose Ned had loads of enemies. The boy was a real rascal," said Sir Hugh, leaning back with a sad, fond smile. "Always mixed up in something or other, running with the fast crowd, playing around with the girls... Ah, he was just a chip off the old block, really."

Mabel leaned forwards. "But do you think any of them would have wanted to kill him?"

"Well, it's hard to say..."

I looked helplessly from one to the other as they continued, completely oblivious to my protests. Sighing, I gave in. *If you can't beat 'em, you might as well join 'em.*

I spoke up: "Wait, listen... there's no point talking about Ned's enemies, really. Because of the snowstorm, we know that no one from the outside could have come to Thurlby Hall last night—which means that the murderer had to have been someone in the house." I turned to Sir Hugh and added gently, "Possibly someone in your family."

The old man gave a grim nod. "I have thought of that."

"Can you tell us when was the last time you saw Ned last night?" I asked.

"It was after dinner. I called him up here and told him that I was changing my will, in his favour.

I thought he would be grateful, but no, the young devil just laughed in my face and told me that I could do whatever I liked." He gave a ghost of a smile. "I liked that. No begging or grovelling or being sickeningly unctuous. Anyway, he told me he didn't want the title or the estate—he was happy for me to hand that to Julian—he only wanted the money. I gave him a good talking-to for not doing his duty, but he just laughed again and said that if I were looking for a dutiful child, he would call Annabel. Insolent pup," Sir Hugh said, his mouth curving in an appreciative smile. "Anyway, then he said goodnight and left. That was the last time I saw him."

"We saw him when we were coming up to witness the will," Glenda spoke up. "He was heading to the library."

"Ah... probably gone to have some vintage port and plum pudding in front of the fire. It was always Ned's favourite thing to do every Christmas," said Sir Hugh with another fond smile. "When he was a boy, we started a tradition of leaving a glass of port and a plate of plum pudding beside the fireplace for Father Christmas, and Ned quickly developed a taste for vintage port himself. He used to wangle some off me every Christmas—even before he was officially allowed to drink—and then sit in front of the fireplace with a plate of pudding and say that he was waiting for Father Christmas."

I cleared my throat as he seemed to lapse into a

brooding reminiscence. "There's something I don't understand: if you were convinced that Ned was still alive, wouldn't he still have been in your will? Why did you need to change it back to favour him?"

Sir Hugh shrugged. "Kelly convinced me to write a new will when we got engaged. She said it was stupid leaving everything to a man who had been officially declared dead for over fifteen years and I... well, I suppose a part of me felt that perhaps she was right. Here I was, considering marrying again and possibly fathering new sons... it seemed like it was time I gave up the ridiculous hope that Ned might return to claim his inheritance."

"So who benefited in that new will?"

"Well, the estate and title would have still gone to Julian, unless a new male heir was born, Richard would have had majority shares in the company, as well as taking over my position as CEO... and as my wife, Kelly would have received most of my personal wealth that wasn't tied to the estate."

"Oh... and Annabel?"

Sir Hugh waved a dismissive hand. "She's married to Richard, isn't she? But yes, I did make a small allowance for her."

I felt a stab of pity for Annabel and the way her father treated her like an afterthought, but I tried to keep my personal feelings out of the way and focus on the case. "So... then you called Mabel, Glenda, Ethel, and Florence up to witness your second new will—the one favouring Ned. Did you tell anyone else about it?"

"No. I was planning to announce it on Christmas Day, but until then, nobody else knew except Ned and your friends here." He hobbled over to the opposite side of the room to a large oil painting of a nude woman on the wall. It was slightly askew and Sir Hugh straightened it as he said, "I put the will in the safe behind this painting as soon as your friends left. And I'm the only person who knows the combination." He turned back to give me a sharp look. "Why do you ask? Do you think someone else knew about it?"

I nodded. "I think your son-in-law might have known as well."

He frowned. "Richard?"

Ethel told him about finding Richard Floyd listening outside the door, and the old man scowled.

"I knew Richard wouldn't like it. He's had his eye on the CEO position for a long time. Fancies himself the 'big boss', eh? Well, it's still my company," said the old man, jutting his chin out. "*I* founded it and *I* was the one who built it up—no matter what Richard thinks—and if I want to give it to my son, then it's my bloody right! Oh yes, I know it's unfair—Ned never did a day's work for the company—but he *is* my son, my own flesh and blood, and if I want to give it to him, that's my business and Richard has no right to object! He's got his own shares and he's done well enough out of the company. In fact, I know he's used our client network and industry contacts to start a few side ventures of his own. So he has nothing to complain about!"

"Did anyone else come to see you after we left, Sir Hugh?" asked Glenda.

"Kelly came to wish me goodnight. She goes to bed after me, but she usually comes to see me before I retire. I knew she would come last night— she'd been angling after some diamond necklace she'd seen and I knew she wanted to ask me to buy it for her... the little gold-digger," he said with a chuckle.

I looked at him in surprise. Most men wouldn't have been so blasé if their future wife had a mercenary attitude. Sir Hugh saw my expression and gave a bark of laughter.

"Do you think I'm stupid? Of course I know Kelly is only with me for the money. But it works both ways." He grinned lasciviously. "It's not often that a man my age gets to have a pretty little thing fussing over him and her nubile, young body warming his bed..."

I drew back in distaste. Suddenly, I could see where Ned got his "charming manners" from. "Did *Kelly* ask about the will?" I said.

"No, although she asked lots of questions about Ned."

"What sort of questions?"

The older man shrugged. "Just... what kind of things he liked, his favourite activities, his pet hates... Is that significant?"

I hesitated. I certainly wasn't going to tell Sir Hugh that I thought his fiancée might have been transferring her sights from father to son. "Not necessarily... but everything needs to be noted. It could be relevant later."

"There, you see?" said Sir Hugh suddenly, with a triumphant smile. "You sound just like a detective!"

CHAPTER TWELVE

"This is so exciting! It's like being in a real-life country house murder mystery—the kind you read about in an Agatha Christie novel," gushed Glenda as the Old Biddies preceded me down the staircase.

"Ooh yes, those were always my favourite," agreed Ethel. "Especially the ones where everyone is marooned in the house where the crime takes place... just like us!"

I eyed her askance, not sure what there was to celebrate about being trapped in a house with a murderer.

Mabel smiled complacently. "I've always wanted to find a body in a library."

"Except that it was Gemma who actually found it," Florence pointed out. "You were snoring in bed."

"Well, I was there in spirit," said Mabel. "Anyway,

the important thing is that we're helping her now. And the first thing we need to do is look for footprints," she added authoritatively.

I laughed. "What?"

"There are always footprints," Ethel said, as if explaining something to a small child.

"In mystery novels, not in real life!" I said impatiently.

"Books are based on real life," Florence argued.

"Aww, come on! You don't seriously think there's going to be a set of footprints in the snow, conveniently leading away from the library to the murderer's hideout or something?"

"How do you know until you've looked?" asked Mabel. She shook her head and made a tutting sound. "Young people nowadays! Always so ready to give up and cry failure before they've even really tried... Always expecting results instantly... In my day, young lady, we believed in persistence and—"

I heaved a sigh of exasperation. "Fine. You can go and search if you like, but I'm not going to traipse around looking for imaginary footprints! I'm going to do what Sir Hugh asked me to and get the others' statements of where they were at the time of the murder."

***

I found Mrs Holmes in the kitchen. As I stepped in, she seemed suddenly familiar, and I frowned for a moment, trying to place her, before I realised where I must have seen her before: on the front of a dozen greeting cards depicting Mrs Claus in a cosy Christmas scene. With her round, wire-rimmed glasses perched on the end of her nose, her bun of grey hair, and her plump, comfortable figure, Mrs Holmes looked just like Santa's kindly, motherly wife as she sat working at the wooden table in front of the kitchen fire. In fact, I half expected to see her baking Christmas cookies or making toys, and it was a bit of a let-down to see that she was only doing something as mundane as peeling potatoes.

Her movements were mechanical and her mind seemed to be far away. She jumped when I came in and put a hand to her chest, saying, "Oh! You startled me, miss."

I smiled apologetically. "Sorry. I didn't mean to scare you."

She sighed. "It's all right. I've just been jumpy all morning. It's the thought of what happened last night and that man's body in the library..." She shuddered. "Lord, when I signed on for a temporary job over Christmas, I didn't think I'd be getting involved in a murder!"

I made a sympathetic noise, then said hesitantly, "I know it was a horrible shock, but would you mind if I asked you a few questions about last night? Sir Hugh has asked me to get preliminary statements from everyone, since the police have been delayed and might not get here for another day."

"Oh... of course." She eyed me curiously, obviously wondering why I had the authority to question everyone, but she answered readily enough when I began asking about her movements the night before.

"After dinner, I served tea and coffee in the drawing room, and then I went back to the kitchen to clear up. Everything was such a mess—there were still things from the tea party that hadn't been washed, and I also needed to prepare some things for the next day's meals... so I was here until nearly midnight."

"Did you see anyone in the family?"

"Well, Mrs Floyd popped in for a minute on her way up to bed, just to check a couple of things on the menu for the next day."

"When was that?"

The housekeeper frowned. "Around eleven thirty, I think... no, it must have been just before that because I remember hearing the clock chime the half-hour in the main hall after she left."

"And no one else?"

"No... oh, wait, I saw Mr Floyd as well. It was after Mrs Floyd had gone up; in fact, everyone seemed to have gone to bed. The house was very quiet. I heard a noise out in the hall. It sounded like the front door, which was odd at that time of night. So I went over there," she pointed to the kitchen doorway, "and stuck my head out. I saw Mr Floyd coming in the front door."

"Really? What time was that?"

"Just before midnight."

"Are you sure?"

She nodded. "Yes, I could see the clock by the front door. It was eleven fifty."

"And you're sure Mr Floyd was coming into the house, not going out?"

"Oh yes, he was taking off his coat. I think he might have gone out to have a smoke—he was holding a cigar in his hand."

"In that weather?" I said disbelievingly.

She shrugged, her expression implying that she'd stopped wondering about the eccentric habits of the wealthy clients she worked for.

"Did you see where Mr Floyd went after he came in?"

"I think he went upstairs."

"Not to the library?"

Her eyes widened. "The library? You mean, you think he might have..."

I didn't answer.

"No, I'm pretty sure he went upstairs," said Mrs Holmes. "Although I have to admit, I didn't actually *see* him go up the staircase. I just peeked out for a moment, really, then when I saw that it was him, I came back in here. But he looked like he was heading for the stairs."

"Were you still working when you heard me knock over the vase in the library?" I asked, recalling that she had still been dressed and wearing her apron.

"Well, I'd actually finished and was about to take off my apron and get ready for bed, then I remembered that one of the pans from dinner had some burnt sauce stuck on the bottom." She rolled her eyes. "I've had one of those before and if you don't soak it overnight, it'll never come off. I was just about to take it over to the sink when I heard the crash in the library." She gave me an embarrassed look. "I'm sorry again about screaming and all that. It's just that it was such a shock—"

"No, no, it's perfectly understandable," I said. "It would have been strange if you *hadn't* screamed. Everyone expects you to freak out when you see a dead body." I glanced at the huge pile of potatoes she was peeling and added sympathetically, "I suppose you'll be relieved when all the holiday entertaining and festivities are done, and things quieten down again in January. Are you going to stay on at Thurlby Hall?"

"I don't know yet. Mrs Floyd has been terribly nice to me and it *is* a very well-paid position, but..." She glanced around and made a face.

I smiled at her. "Maybe you'll feel differently after you've had a bit of time off. Do your children live nearby or—"

"I don't have any children. In fact, it's actually 'Miss Holmes'," she confessed, blushing slightly. "It's just that I use 'Mrs' as a sort of official title for work because that always sounds more dependable, doesn't it? Especially in a housekeeper. People seem to just naturally call you that too, especially once you pass a certain age. Everyone assumes that you must be married and have children."

I gave her a rueful look. "Yes, I just did that—I'm so sorry! I made the same mistake with Annabel—I mean, Mrs Floyd—when I first arrived at the tea party. I just assumed that she had kids and the stockings on the mantelpiece were for them... I felt terrible when she told me that she was childless. She looked so sad. I wanted to kick myself for not being more tactful."

"Ah well, everyone makes mistakes, and I'm sure Mrs Floyd didn't take it to heart. She's a lovely lady. I sometimes wonder how she could be Sir Hugh's daught—oh!" Mrs Holmes broke off, flushing. "Sorry, forget I said that."

As I left the kitchen, though, I couldn't help thinking that I agreed wholeheartedly with the housekeeper. Sir Hugh didn't deserve Annabel as a daughter.

CHAPTER THIRTEEN

I found Annabel, Richard, Julian, and Kelly in the dining room having their breakfast, and I hesitantly explained what Sir Hugh had asked me to do. I had been dreading their reactions—whatever Sir Hugh might have said, and however accepting Mrs Holmes had been, I didn't think the others would take as kindly to my questioning. Just as I expected, Richard Floyd exploded:

"What? That's the most ludicrous idea I've ever heard! You're nothing but a stupid tearoom waitress—who are you to take the police's place? Well, I'm not speaking to you! You have no right to question me as a suspect—you should just bloody get back in the kitchen where you belong!"

"Richard!" cried Annabel, looking shocked. She gave me an apologetic look. "I think my father's right and it's a great idea for you to help the police. I'm sure we'd all be very happy to answer any questions, especially if it would help to find Ned's murderer. In fact, I'd be happy to go first."

I glanced warily at her husband and asked, "Is there somewhere we can go that's more private?"

"Yes, of course. This way…" Annabel rose and led me across the hall, to a small sitting room with large bay windows overlooking the gardens and an antique piano in the corner. She shut the door and gestured to the sofa. "This used to be the music room. We don't tend to use it much now. We won't be disturbed in here."

I observed her as she came over to sit next to me. Her face was pale and there were dark circles under her eyes, but they seemed to be more the result of a disturbed night than sleepless grief. In fact, I couldn't detect any sign of mourning for her dead brother—although that didn't necessarily mean anything, I reminded myself, given Annabel's self-control and extreme composure.

"Can you tell me what you did last night—and specifically the last time you saw Ned?"

"Well, as you know, after dinner we ladies all retired to the drawing room—except your elderly friends who went to bed first. We had a cup of tea together, then you left. I thought the men would arrive, but it seems that my father had gone straight upstairs and Ned had gone with him, so only Julian joined us in the drawing room."

"What about your husband?"

Annabel shrugged. "I don't know where he was. He might have gone out to smoke one of his horrible cigars. I hate the smell of them and I've asked him to go outside if he wants to smoke one."

No, he wasn't out smoking, I thought. He was lurking around outside Sir Hugh's bedroom, eavesdropping on the conversation about the new will.

"Anyway, Julian had a cup of tea, then he said that he was really tired and was going up to bed. Kelly got up soon after and said that she was very tired too and was going to have an early night."

"Oh?" I perked my ears up. It was interesting that they had both gone to bed so close to each other. I couldn't help thinking of the footsteps and whispering that I'd heard outside my bedroom door last night, and that high-pitched, feminine giggle that I'd been sure was Kelly's. "Um... are Julian and Kelly quite... er... friendly?"

Annabel gave me a sidelong look, obviously guessing my thoughts. "Kelly is *friendly* with many people," she said, compressing her lips.

Belatedly, I remembered the sordid scene we'd walked into yesterday afternoon, with Kelly getting *very* "friendly" with Annabel's husband. Hastily, I changed the subject.

"Um... when I came downstairs last night to look for Muesli, I couldn't help overhearing you and Richard in the library. You seemed to be having a row. It sounded like you were talking about Ned?"

Annabel shifted uncomfortably. "Yes. After Kelly left, I decided to move into the library instead of sitting in the drawing room by myself. Then Richard came into the library; he was in a foul mood. When I asked him what the matter was, he started complaining about Daddy favouring Ned."

"Did your husband and your brother not get on?"

She hesitated. "Richard never liked Ned. He always resented him and, although he was careful not to show it, I got the impression that he was pleased when Ned disappeared. But surely you're not suggesting that Richard might have—" Annabel broke off, staring at me.

"Did you see Ned again last night?" I asked, not answering her.

"Yes, in fact, he came into the library after you left. He... we... we had a bit of a chat," she said, flushing

I looked at her reddened cheeks curiously. It was the most emotion she had shown so far. I wondered what the "chat" with her brother had been about.

"Then I left Ned in the library and popped in to see Mrs Holmes in the kitchen. I wanted to ask her something about tomorrow's—I mean, today's menu, and then I took myself off to bed."

"Did Ned seem okay when you left him in the library?" I asked.

She hesitated for a fraction of a second. "Yes. He'd got some plum pudding from the kitchen and was going to have it with a glass of port. That was always his favourite treat at Christmas."

"And that was the last time you saw him alive?"

She nodded.

"What time was that? When you left him in the library, I mean."

She frowned. "It must have been around eleven fifteen? I only stopped in the kitchen for a minute or so, and I know that it was around half past eleven when I got into bed. I remember hearing the grandfather clock downstairs chiming the half-hour."

Yes, I heard that too, I recalled. It was just before I'd heard the whispering and footsteps outside my door. Then I'd drifted off, and when I'd woken up again, it was after midnight. I also remembered being vaguely aware of the grandfather clock striking twelve thirty just as I discovered Ned's body.

So during that hour—between the time Annabel had left Ned in the library and the time I'd found him—someone had sneaked up on him and overpowered him...

"Were you asleep when the commotion happened?"

"Yes, I jolted awake when I heard the screaming. It gave me a dreadful fright. I jumped out of bed, grabbed my dressing gown, and came running downstairs."

"What about your husband?" I asked,

remembering the way Richard Floyd had still been fully dressed.

"I don't know. The bed was empty next to me when I awoke... although I remember seeing him on the landing when I rushed out, and he went ahead of me down the stairs..." Annabel rubbed her temples. "I'm sorry, there was so much confusion and I'd just woken up, so I wasn't really paying much attention."

"Does Richard often come to bed late?"

Annabel shrugged. "Perhaps. I don't really pay much attention... I just go to bed when it suits me. Richard does often stay up later, probably for work."

Or for assignations with your future stepmother, I thought cynically. Still, it seemed unlikely that Richard had been with Kelly last night, since I'd heard her going into Julian's room. So, where *had* he been?

It was a question I intended to ask him, I decided grimly—whether he wanted to be questioned or not.

CHAPTER FOURTEEN

"Why should I tell you anything? You're not the police. I haven't got my lawyer here. I don't have to answer any of your questions!"

I regarded the belligerent man in front of me. Everything he said was true, and yet somehow I got the impression the real reason he was making such a fuss was because he was scared. *Richard Floyd is a bully*, I reminded myself. And the only way to deal with bullies was to call their bluff.

"You're right," I said calmly. "You don't have to answer my questions. But since everyone else seems happy to give me a preliminary statement, it's going to look very suspicious to the police that you refused. But that's fine. I'll simply make a note that you were reluctant to explain your whereabouts on the night of the murder. I'm sure the police can draw their own conclusions and—"

"Wait a minute, wait a minute..." said Richard, scowling. "Who said I was reluctant? You're making it sound like I have something to hide! I just don't like being treated as a suspect."

"Well, if you can tell me about your movements last night, maybe you can be eliminated as a suspect," I said in a reasonable tone.

He gave an exaggerated sigh. "Fine. There's nothing much to tell anyway. I hung around in the dining room with Julian after dinner—Ned had gone up with Sir Hugh to his rooms—and then I joined Annabel in the library. That's when I... er... met you looking for your cat. And then I went to the billiards room and had a game by myself. After that, I fancied a cigar so I went out."

"At that time of night?" I said, raising my eyebrows.

"Why not? I wanted a bit of fresh air. Besides, Annabel hates my cigars; she's always whinging about their smell—"

"But it was snowing!"

He shrugged. "A bit of cold doesn't bother me. I had my coat on. Besides, if you stand by the wall on the lee of the house, you hardly feel the wind. It's very sheltered on that side. I just went out the front door, around the corner, and stood under the eaves."

I thought of the layout of the manor house. "Isn't

that near the library window?"

Richard looked wary. "Yeah, the library window is just beyond the corner where I was standing."

"Did you look through? Could you see Ned in the library?" I asked.

"No, it was a bit far from where I was standing; plus there's a huge holly bush just outside the window, which blocks the view."

"When did you come back in?"

"Just after midnight. Ten past twelve? Something like that."

I narrowed my eyes. According to Mrs Holmes, it was just *before* midnight when she'd seen Richard come in. But I decided not to challenge him at the moment. Instead, I asked:

"And after you came in, you went straight to bed?"

He hesitated almost imperceptibly. "Y-yes. I went upstairs."

"But Annabel said that you weren't in bed when she was woken by the screaming—she said you never came to the bedroom last night."

"What? Of course I went to the bedroom."

"She says she saw you out on the landing when she rushed out to go downstairs."

"Well, I—Annabel must have remembered wrong," he blustered. "There was so much confusion last night and she was probably still half-asleep. I... uh... might not have actually been *in* bed when she woke up... I was probably still getting undressed and about to get into bed—yes, that's right, I remember now. I'd come to the bedroom and I was trying to keep quiet so as not to wake her, so I was tiptoeing around. But then just as I was about to get undressed, I heard the racket downstairs so I rushed back out. By the time she got out of bed, I was already out there on the landing." He leaned back, looking pleased with his account.

I didn't believe a word of it. For a man who normally showed so little consideration for his wife, it seemed completely out of character that Richard Floyd would start "tiptoeing around" so as not to wake her. No, I was sure he was lying.

"What time did you go out to have your cigar?" I asked suddenly.

"I don't know," he said irritably. "I wasn't keeping track, okay? It was sometime before midnight— maybe a quarter to twelve? Something like that?"

"And you said you didn't come back in until ten past twelve... and yet Mrs Holmes says that she saw you return to the house just *before* midnight."

"What? That's rubbish! Mrs Holmes must be wrong—"

"Just like your wife was wrong about you not being in the bedroom when the screaming started?"

"I... what's that got to do with this?" he snarled. "I explained that already, and as for this, I'm telling you, I definitely came back in after midnight—"

"No, I think you're lying," I said, leaning forwards and looking him straight in the eye. "You don't want to admit that you came in earlier because then you would have to account for an extra twenty minutes... and why would you be covering up unless you were doing something in that time which you didn't want anyone to know about? Like perhaps... murdering your brother-in-law?"

"What?" He stared at me aghast. "That's a load of bollocks! I didn't murder Ned! I never went into the bloody library after I came in the house. I told you, I came straight upstairs—"

"But you didn't go to your bedroom. Your wife confirms that. So what were you doing?" I shot back. "I know you were eavesdropping outside Sir Hugh's room earlier in the evening—yes, my elderly friend told me that she caught you outside the door—and you probably heard about your father-in-law's new will and guessed that he would be changing everything in Ned's favour. Everyone knows you resented your brother-in-law, and suddenly he was back, taunting you, muscling in on your territory, and reaping the rewards of all the hard work *you* put into the company... You couldn't bear it. You're a hard-nosed businessman, used to ruthless tactics to gain an advantage. So you decided to kill him—"

"NO!" Richard surged to his feet, his face flushed and angry. "Being ruthless in business dealings is totally different to committing murder. Okay, yes... I admit to being outside Sir Hugh's rooms and overhearing him talk about the will... and yes... I was...I was angry... but that doesn't mean I killed Ned!" He leaned forwards suddenly, thrusting his face close to mine. "If you really want someone with reason to kill my brother-in-law, then the person you should be speaking to is Julian."

"Julian?"

"Yeah. He's been desperate to inherit the estate for years—Annabel told me that when she and Ned were kids, he used to make them call him 'Sir Julian' when they were playing. He loves all that 'lord of the manor' nonsense. It's all he's been waiting for: for the old man to die so he can inherit the baronetcy and the estate. With Ned gone, Julian would be back in position as Sir Hugh's only male heir." Richard nodded grimly. "If anyone had a good reason for getting rid of Ned, it's Julian."

CHAPTER FIFTEEN

Unlike the others, Julian Morecombe looked well rested and at ease when he came into the music room. In fact, he seemed almost jolly.

"So... we're playing murder mysteries, are we?" he asked with a dry smile. "How perfect for Christmas. Oh, I beg your pardon, it does seem to be bad taste, doesn't it? To be making jokes like this when my poor cousin is lying dead. But one has to maintain a sense of humour, doesn't one?"

"You don't seem very upset about Ned's death."

He shrugged. "I'm not going to pretend something I don't feel. Of course, I'm sorry about what happened to Ned, but we were never close, and I can't say I'm going to miss him either, since he hasn't been a part of my life at all for the past twenty-five years. In fact, I'd already got used to thinking that he was dead."

It might have sounded heartless but, in a way, I found that I appreciated his blunt honesty, rather than a fake show of grief.

"Can you think of anyone who would have wished him harm?" I asked.

He gave a humourless laugh. "Oh, any number of ex-girlfriends, I should imagine. Ned was always breaking hearts, picking up women, playing around with them then... 'dumping them', I believe, is the phrase? He certainly excelled at treating them badly... I remember my aunt—Ned's mother—having a fit when Ned came back from Eton for the holidays one summer. He'd been messing around with a couple of girls in the village—simultaneously, I might add—and even got one of them pregnant! And he was just seventeen at the time. He became even worse after my aunt died; her influence used to restrain him, I think, but with her gone, Ned had no one to check him at all. Sir Hugh would just laugh and call Ned a chip off the old block." Julian pulled a face. "My uncle was a terrible womaniser in his younger days and is a dreadful male chauvinist still, so Ned's outrageous behaviour fitted with his idea of being a 'man's man'. In fact, he made excuses even during the terrible scandal after Ned disappeared."

"What scandal?" I asked curiously.

"Oh, didn't you know? Ned was engaged to some socialite or other in London. Daughter of one of Sir

Hugh's business associates, in fact. Jessica, I think her name was. Neville Smythe's daughter. They weren't to be married until after his twenty-first birthday, but they'd already had a lavish engagement party and everyone was talking about the wedding. It was going to be the society event of the year and the match would have united two great empires. Then, a week after he turned twenty-one—and he was able to access his trust fund—Ned took the money and disappeared. My God, you should have seen the uproar! His fiancée was in hysterics, her father was threatening to kill Ned, the society papers were having a field day..."

Julian shook his head at the memory. "And it just kept getting worse. It came to light that Ned had been visiting some pretty dodgy gambling dens and had racked up huge debts; he'd been messing with one of the maids here during his engagement and got her up the spout, *and* he'd taken some jewellery from the safe—heirlooms that had been in the Morecombe family for generations. Talk about leaving a trail of destruction in your wake..." Julian shook his head again and laughed. "Of course, no one realised about the jewellery at first—Sir Hugh thought that it had been stolen and he raised hell, calling his superintendent friend in the CID and insisting that they launch a full-scale investigation... until we received a postcard from Ned saying he'd taken the jewels and that he was starting a new life and not to bother looking for him. And that was the last we heard of him... until he showed up on the doorstep yesterday afternoon!"

"Wow..." I said, thinking that the whole thing sounded like something straight out of a melodramatic TV drama.

"Yes, it sounds like some dreadful soap opera, doesn't it?" said Julian, reading my thoughts. "And I can imagine that Ned wouldn't have changed his ways once he started his new life in the States. I'm sure he left a trail of broken hearts and other carnage behind him wherever he went. So really, I think it would be easier to look for who *wouldn't* want to do him harm... otherwise, you'll be wading through a pretty big pool of suspects!"

Except that they weren't all at Thurlby Hall, I thought. Regardless of how many enemies Ned might have had, none of them had been snowed in, here in the house with him last night. Only the people currently in the household had had the opportunity to murder him. I glanced at Julian Morecombe again. *And whatever he might say, this man is one of them.*

I cleared my throat. "Would you mind telling me about your own movements last night?"

He gave that dry smile again. "Ah... seeing if I have an alibi? Well, I can tell you from the outset that I don't. I was upstairs sleeping at the time of the murder but I can't prove that."

"When did you go up?

"Oh, about eleven, I think. I had coffee with

Annabel and Kelly in the drawing room, and then took myself off to bed."

"Alone?"

He frowned. "What do you mean?"

I hesitated, then asked: "Was anyone in your room with you?"

"What kind of question is that?" he snapped. "Now, look here—I've agreed to answer some questions in good faith, but that does not give you the right to pry into my personal affairs!"

I sat back in surprise. "You're awfully defensive."

"I'm not defensive!" he spluttered angrily. "I...I just resent the invasion of privacy. Besides, I don't see how this has any bearing on Ned's murder."

"It might, if the person who was with you could give you an alibi."

He paused and I could see his eyes shifting, as if he was thinking rapidly. Then he said stiffly, "Well, not that it's any of your business, but—for the record—yes, I *was* alone last night. And now, if you'll excuse me, I've had all the interrogating I can stomach for one day!"

I watched thoughtfully as he stormed out of the room. Julian Morecombe had been blasé and relaxed, even joking about being a murder suspect. It was only when I'd asked about his sleeping arrangements that he had become touchy. What did that mean? The obvious conclusion was that he *hadn't* been alone in bed last night and was afraid to let anyone know.

I thought of the footsteps I'd heard, the whispering, the feminine giggle... There was a certain young woman who had been flirting with Julian the whole evening—a young woman who was Sir Hugh's fiancée. If Julian had been having an affair with Kelly, that was certainly something he would want to keep secret—especially if he was hoping to stay in his uncle's good graces and inherit the estate.

Well, Kelly was the one person I hadn't spoken to yet. It would be interesting to hear what *she* had to say about her whereabouts last night...

***

"Isn't this just awful? Oh my God, I never thought I'd get involved in a murder!" Kelly gave a delicious shiver. "To think that Ned was being killed downstairs and I was up in my room fast asleep."

I pounced on that. "You went to bed early last night?"

"Well, not super early. Around eleven, I think. Right after Julian went up." She wrinkled her nose. "I didn't want to sit around with Annabel any longer. She's such a miserable cow. She was still fuming about seeing me with Richard yesterday afternoon, but of course—typical—she wouldn't talk about it. She was just being all icily polite... it made me want to scream! Honestly, I would have preferred it if she had started yelling and calling me a slut. At least she would have seemed more human—*what?*" she said, as she saw my expression. "Don't look at me like that. We're all consenting adults here. If Annabel wasn't such a cold fish, maybe Richard wouldn't be looking for consolation elsewhere. You can't blame a man for trying to get a bit of nookie where he can."

I hadn't wanted to comment but her callous words provoked me into saying: "And what about you? You're an engaged woman."

"Me?" She gave a coy smile. "Well, a girl's got to have some fun, hasn't she? Stuck here in this mausoleum with a man who doesn't even have his own teeth anymore!" She waved a hand. "Yeah, yeah, I know... you're going to say I knew what I was taking on when I got involved with Hugh, but still, there's got to be some compensation. Besides, Hugh doesn't mind me amusing myself, as long as I make myself available for him when he wants me," she added crudely.

I drew back, feeling disgusted. She caught the movement and gave me a contemptuous look.

"Oh, I know what you're thinking, sitting there, all holier than thou," she sneered. "But we're not all like you, lucky enough to be born into an upper-middle-class family, with money and privilege and an Oxbridge education. Some of us have to take what we can grab with our own hands—and I'm not ashamed of that!" She sat back and smoothed down her dress, running her hands over her hips with a complacent smile. "It was my lucky day when I got a job as one of Neville Smythe's secretaries last year, and that gave me the chance to meet Hugh. I made damned sure that he noticed me whenever he came for business meetings—"

"Sir Hugh is still doing business with Neville Smythe?" I said in surprise. "But I thought... after what happened between Ned and Jessica..."

Kelly shrugged. "Business is business. I'm not saying that the two of them are the best of friends but there were too many links between their companies—too much money to be lost—if they cut all ties. Besides, the broken engagement was years ago and Jessica soon got some other poor sod following her around, with his ring on her finger."

"So she was married?"

"Yeah, and then divorced, I think. I remember Hugh saying that he'd dodged a bullet; at least the maintenance payments were someone else's problem now." She laughed. "That just shows how naïve he is... He assumed that he would only ever be paying maintenance to his son's ex-wife—he never thought that he might be paying money to his own!"

"You're planning to divorce Sir Hugh?" I asked quickly.

She gave me a cool look. "No. But a girl has to be prepared. As I said, I haven't had anyone looking out for me—I've learned to fend for myself."

"Are you alone then? No family?"

Her expression became guarded. "I'm an orphan. I was given up for adoption and brought up in foster homes."

"Oh. I'm sorry," I said lamely.

She grinned. "What are you sorry for? I've done all right for myself, haven't I?" She gestured around the room. "I'm going to be the mistress of all this soon—just you wait and see!"

I took a deep breath, realising that we were going off track, and made an effort to bring the conversation back to Ned's murder.

"So were you... 'amusing yourself' with anyone last night?" I asked.

"No. I would have been up for it, but Richard seemed to be in a foul mood. I passed him as I was going upstairs—he asked me where Annabel was and looked like he was spoiling for a fight, so I made myself scarce." She smirked. "I let their wives deal with all that crap."

This time I refused to let her goad me. "What about Julian?" I asked.

"Julian?" She laughed and gave me a sly look, as if enjoying a private joke. "No, I wasn't with Julian. I went back to my own room and had a facial and did my nails..." She held her hand out and admired the gleaming pink talons at the tips of her fingers, then looked back up at me and smiled. "And after that, I went to bed."

I stared at her. I knew I'd heard her going to Julian's room, so why was she lying? She'd just shown that she had no problem talking about her sexual exploits, so it couldn't be due to modesty or embarrassment... Was she protecting Julian? Perhaps he had made her promise not to reveal their affair?

Or is there some ulterior motive that I haven't figured out yet? I wondered as I sat by myself in the music room after the blonde woman had left. Sir Hugh had said that Kelly would have inherited his personal assets if Ned hadn't been around... that could have been motive enough.

CHAPTER SIXTEEN

I left the music room with my notes from each of the interviews and suddenly felt a great burden of responsibility as I looked at the sheaf of papers in my hand. I would be glad when the police arrived and I could hand the investigation over to them. Still, in the meantime, I had to agree with Sir Hugh that doing something proactive was better than just sitting helplessly around, waiting for aid to arrive.

I wondered what the Old Biddies had been doing during the time I was speaking to everyone and went in search of them.

"Oh, I believe they went outside," said Annabel when I encountered her in the main hall. "They were talking about looking for something under the library window."

Oh God. They're not still obsessing over

footprints...? I thought with an internal groan. Leaving my notes in a safe place, I put on my coat and stepped out of the house. The cold air hit me like a slap in the face and my breath rose in a cloud of steam. It had stopped snowing, but there was a sense of expectation—as if this was just a pause—and there was still a stiff wind blowing. I shivered and drew my coat closer, scanning the bleak snowy landscape which no longer looked like such a winter wonderland.

Turning, I made my way carefully around to the lee of the house. *Richard Floyd was right,* I thought, as I turned the corner and found that the wind instantly died down. This side of the building was very sheltered and if you stood very close to the wall, right under the eaves, you wouldn't even get hit by rain or snow—unless the wind changed direction.

That had obviously happened at some point in the night, I noted, as I saw snow banked up against the side of the house. But now the wind was blowing the other way and the collected snow formed a smooth unmarked slope. I almost felt bad walking through it and marring the pristine whiteness. I'd seen the Old Biddies though—they were huddled together further down this side of the house, beside a window and a large holly bush—so I took a deep breath and started ploughing across.

"What are you doing out here?" I asked breathlessly as I arrived next to them. "It's freezing!

And it looks like it's going to start snowing again soon. Surely you're not still thinking—"

I broke off, staring in disbelief at the ground. There, in the smooth white snow banked up beneath the eaves, was a set of perfectly outlined footprints. They were just outside the window—the library window, I realised, as I peered in through the glass panes and saw the Christmas tree and the Nativity scene in the far corner. The trail of footprints curved away from the window and led away from us, further down the side of the house.

"We told you there would be footprints," said Mabel smugly.

I noticed suddenly that Glenda and Ethel were crouched down next to one of the footprints. Glenda was holding a steaming pot filled with dark, golden liquid and Ethel was carefully spooning some of the liquid from the pot into the depression, whilst Florence leaned over them, watching anxiously.

"What on earth are you doing?" I asked.

"We're making a cast," Florence said.

I looked at her blankly. "A cast?"

"Of the footprints, dear," Ethel explained. "They always do that in the books. It's very important."

"Ooh yes, you can tell if the man was short or tall, thin or fat, and whether he walked with a limp," said Glenda enthusiastically.

"Shouldn't you let the forensics team do that when the police arrive?" I asked, watching them sceptically.

"What if the wind changes and blows the snow under the eaves? It will cover all the footprints and they'll be gone," said Mabel.

"Well... okay, but surely you need special equipment to make a cast—"

"We didn't have that so we just improvised," said Mabel airily. "We're using maple syrup."

"You're what?" I gaped at her.

Ethel nodded eagerly. "Like in the *Little House on the Prairie* books by Laura Ingalls Wilder! Do you remember? Laura and her sister made their own snow candy in winter, using molasses and sugar, and fresh snow. They poured hot syrup onto the snow and it cooled into solid candy in special shapes."

"They do it in Canada too with maple syrup," said Florence. "My neighbour Cora is from Ontario—although she's been living in the U.K. now for years, you know, ever since she married Gordon, who's English—anyway, she showed me how to make maple syrup taffy once, using pure maple syrup and fresh snow." She smacked her lips at the memory. "Mmm, it was delicious!"

"And they just happened to have a bottle of pure maple syrup in the kitchen here," added Glenda. "Wasn't that lucky?"

I looked at them in exasperation. "You can't use maple syrup as a cast for footprints! It will melt the snow before it has any chance of taking the imprint..." I trailed off as I realised that the Old

Biddies weren't listening to me. They were all bent over, eagerly watching the maple syrup which had been spooned into one of the footprints. The golden liquid flowed around the depression and slowly hardened. A few minutes later, Glenda carefully prised the frozen orange mass out of the snow.

"Aha! There, you see?" said Mabel triumphantly, holding up the piece of hardened maple syrup. I looked askance at the long, flattened blob. It looked nothing like a footprint to me.

Great. The police are going to be delighted with that... But seeing the Old Biddies' proud, flushed faces, I kept my sarcastic thoughts to myself and instead looked down at the trail of prints again. I followed it with my eye as it curved away from the window and into the distance, where it seemed to end abruptly. I frowned and began to follow the trail, and the Old Biddies shuffled after me. The footprints hugged the wall, staying close to the side of the house, under the eaves, until they reached a section of wall covered by ivy. The Old Biddies looked around in confusion.

"It doesn't make sense," Glenda cried. "Why did they suddenly stop? It's as if the person just vanished into thin air."

"Maybe they climbed into a window," Ethel suggested.

Florence surveyed the wall. "But there aren't any windows on the ground floor here."

Mabel had been looking up the wall and now

pointed to the thick mass of ivy covering the exterior of the house. "Aha! I know what happened. Look, there are stems broken and patches where leaves are missing. The murderer must have escaped out of the library window, run along the side of the house, and then climbed up the ivy."

"No, wait—the footprints are facing the other way," I said, pointing down at the snow. "See? The person wasn't coming from the library to here. It looks like they did the reverse: they climbed *down* the ivy and went towards the library."

"Of course, that's what I meant," said Mabel, blithely doing a one-eighty. "The murderer got into the library from the outside. They probably didn't want anyone in the house seeing them enter the library, so they sneaked around this way through the library window."

"They must have climbed down from there," said Ethel, pointing upwards.

We all looked up, following the direction of her finger. The mass of ivy snaked up the wall and spread out around a window on the second storey. I leaned back to get a better view, then I drew a sharp breath. I had noticed something on the sill of the window *beyond* the one we were looking at

"I wonder what room that is?" asked Florence, still looking at the first window.

"I think I know," I said slowly. "That's Julian Morecombe's bedroom."

CHAPTER SEVENTEEN

I found myself facing four pairs of surprised old eyes.

"How do you know, Gemma?"

I pointed to the window beyond. "See that window there? That's my bedroom. You can see my handbag on the windowsill. And Julian's room is the one next to mine. We're the only two people staying on this side of the house."

"Does that mean Julian murdered his cousin?" asked Glenda in an excited whisper.

"I knew it!" said Mabel, nodding. "I always said, didn't I, that he looked shifty?"

"No, you said he looked constipated," Florence reminded her.

Mabel waved a dismissive hand. "Constipated... shifty... same thing."

"But... I don't think Julian Morecombe looks like the kind of man who would climb out of a window," protested Ethel.

I glanced up at the window again. Hmm... she had a point. The suave Oxford don, with his silk kerchiefs and bespoke tailored suits, looked like the last person on earth who would climb down an ivied wall. Besides, while Julian wasn't fat, he had the usual stoutness that came with good living and middle age. I eyed the ivy branches again. Could they have held his weight?

"Murder makes you do desperate things," declared Mabel.

"No, Ethel is right... It doesn't quite fit," I said. "Also, if Julian *had* climbed out of his bedroom and sneaked in the library window to murder Ned, why aren't there any tracks of him returning?" I asked. "These only show him going to the library window— shouldn't there be a set of tracks showing him coming back? It doesn't make any sense."

"Maybe he returned to his bedroom the normal way, through the house," said Florence.

"But if he could do that, why didn't he just go into the library that way too? Why go to all the effort of climbing out of his bedroom window? It would have been freezing and pitch dark last night." I shook my head. "It just doesn't add up. Also, I've just remembered something else: Julian had a dressing gown on when he rushed downstairs last night, but I'm pretty sure that he wasn't wearing anything underneath."

The Old Biddies looked at me blankly.

"Well, doesn't that mean that he was in bed?" I asked. "He must have jumped up and only had time to fling his dressing gown on before coming downstairs."

"You mean, he was sleeping in the nude?" squeaked Ethel, slightly shocked.

"Some men do, dear," said Glenda, with a fond smile of reminiscence. "I remember meeting a lovely gentleman a few years ago, when I was on a cruise with my friend Barbara... Diego, I think his name was... and he always slept without a single stitch on! He said it was his hot Spanish blood. He did have wonderful chest hair. Even though it was going quite grey, but it was still so thick and crinkly, and he liked me to run my hand through—"

"Er—right! So about the murder..." I interrupted hastily.

"Well, I don't see how Julian being naked under his dressing gown means anything," said Mabel. "Maybe it shows that he was actually dressed for going outside and he didn't have time to change back into his pyjamas, so he just put his dressing gown on, to pretend that he was in bed."

"Perhaps we ought to go and look in his bedroom, and see whether he wears pyjamas?" suggested Glenda hopefully.

"Oh no, we're not sneaking into anybody's bedroom to check what they wear to bed," I said before they got any ideas. "Besides, does Julian really have a motive to murder Ned? He seems to enjoy a comfortable bachelor life in academia, and from the way he dresses, I don't think he wants for money—"

"Well, you can always have more money, dear," said Glenda. "And some people are just greedy, even if they have all they need. They'd still like more."

"I suppose so... but it seems to me that the only thing Julian might have wanted is the estate and the title—and according to Sir Hugh, Ned was happy to relinquish those anyway."

"But perhaps Julian didn't know that," Florence pointed out.

"Maybe..." I still wasn't convinced. "Personally, I think if anyone had a motive to kill Ned, it wasn't Julian; it was Richard Floyd."

I told them about the heated conversation I had overheard between Richard and Annabel, and then the discrepancies in his account of his movements the night before.

"I'm sure he's lying about the time he came back into the house," I said as I finished. "And if he came in just before midnight, as Mrs Holmes said, instead of *after* twelve, as he insists, then there's a good amount of extra time unaccounted for—more than enough for him to have gone to the library and killed Ned. And he would have had no trouble overpowering his brother-in-law either," I added, thinking of the heavyset businessman.

I paused as I noticed that it was starting to snow again and the wind was changing direction. This side of the house was still more protected, but I could feel the lash of the wind getting stronger. I glanced down at the tracks beside us. If the wind got fiercer still, it might blow fresh snow sideways under the eaves and the footprints would be obscured.

I should have taken a photo, I thought, berating myself for not having my phone. I'd been so pre-occupied that morning, I'd left it on my bedside table when I came downstairs. If I'd had it with me, I could have at least tried to get a picture of the footprints—which would have been better than the maple syrup blob that Glenda was so proudly clutching. *Oh well, it's too late now*, I thought as we started back towards the front door. In any case, with the sky darkening again and the ambient light fading, I consoled myself with the thought that there probably wasn't enough contrast in the white snow for the phone camera to pick out details in the footprints.

We returned to the welcome warmth of the drawing room to find everyone except Sir Hugh there. Annabel was sipping a cup of tea, with Muesli happily purring on her lap, whilst Kelly sat on the sofa next to her, flipping through a fashion magazine in a bored manner. Julian and Richard sat on the opposite settee, the former fastidiously eating a slice of fruit cake, the latter staring out of the window in a sullen silence.

Annabel looked up as we entered and said:

"Oh my goodness, you all look frozen! Do sit down and I'll ask Mrs Holmes to bring a fresh pot of tea."

Ten minutes later, warmed by the hot drink and a large chunk of moist fruit cake, I sat cradling my teacup and eyeing the various family members. Richard Floyd seemed like the obvious suspect but I couldn't completely discount Julian Morecombe either. The footprints didn't quite make sense but it was undeniable that they led to—or rather from—his bedroom window. Plus, I knew for a fact that Julian had been lying about his activities last night. My gaze drifted over to the young, blonde woman who I was sure had been with him. *Could* Kelly *be the person who had climbed out of Julian's window?* I wondered. *She's certainly petite enough to climb down the ivy... although whether she would ever do such a thing is another question,* I thought, eyeing the woman's manicured nails and perfectly styled hair.

It seemed that I wasn't the only one brooding about Ned's murder and everyone's potential as suspects. The atmosphere in the drawing room was nervous and strained, and it didn't improve when Sir Hugh came downstairs to join us. I'd thought he might want some kind of progress report from me, but he seemed to have lost his enthusiasm from the morning. He sat brooding in an armchair and barely responded to Annabel's solicitous remarks, other than to mutter irritably every so often:

"Where are the police? Why are they taking so bloody long?"

It was a relief when Annabel rose at last and said: "Well... it's nearly two o'clock. Perhaps we ought to make our way to the dining room for lunch? Mrs Holmes has prepared some cold meats and we can—"

She broke off as we heard the distinct sound of car engines outside. I sprang up and ran to the window, and felt a rush of relief as I saw several white cars with the traditional Battenberg livery of blue and yellow checks approaching up the snowy driveway. The police had arrived.

CHAPTER EIGHTEEN

"About time!" growled Sir Hugh, grabbing his walking stick and hobbling out into the main hall.

Eagerly, I followed him, but my heart sank when the front door opened and a flashily dressed young man in plain clothes marched in, accompanied by several uniformed police officers. It was Inspector Dylan Pratt, the arrogant, young CID officer who had been transferred from London earlier in the year and who had an overinflated opinion of his own abilities. I would have loved to have nothing to do with him and slink quietly home, but I remembered my sheaf of notes and knew that I had to at least hand them over with an explanation of what I had been doing all morning.

"You did *what*?" Pratt snapped when I'd taken him aside, out of hearing of the others, and handed him the notes I'd collected. "What the hell did you think you were playing at? You had no right to question anybody! You're not a trained police officer, you're not CID—just because you're O'Connor's girlfriend, you think you get special privileges, do you? Well, your boyfriend isn't here to protect you and I'm going to report you to the Superintendent. He's not going to stand for civilians sticking their nose in—"

"He probably already knows," I said tartly. "He's a personal friend of Sir Hugh's and it was actually Sir Hugh's idea that I should get preliminary statements from everyone. He was very insistent and—"

"So what? You could have said no, couldn't you? You agreed to do it because you *wanted* to stick your nose in! Because you're a little Miss Know-It-All who thinks she's better than the police and wanted to play at being detective!"

I bristled at his words, but I knew I couldn't argue. He was right in that I wasn't a police officer and I could have—and probably *should* have—refused, no matter how much Sir Hugh had pushed. Wishing now that I'd never let myself be swayed by the old man, I thrust the sheaf of notes at Pratt and said:

"I'm sorry. I was just trying to help. Anyway, here are my notes—for what they're worth. You can read them or chuck them; I don't care. I know you won't believe me but leading a murder investigation is *not* what I had planned for Christmas. You can have the whole thing with my blessing!"

I turned to go but he stopped me.

"Hang on, hang on... you haven't been questioned yet."

"Me? You think I might be a suspect?" I asked incredulously.

"You were here in the house, just like the others—you have to account for your movements too, just like them. I'm not going to give you special treatment."

"I'm not asking for special treatment!" I said through gritted teeth. "I've written a detailed account of my own movements last night. It's included with the other notes." I gestured to the papers in his hand. "But if you want to question me again, go ahead."

Before he could answer, a booming voice rang out suddenly behind us.

"Inspector Pratt! Haven't seen you for a long time... Your trousers, young man, are still falling down. Has your generation never heard of a belt? And what on earth have you done to your hair? It looks like an otter's backside."

Pratt watched with horror as Mabel advanced towards us, followed by the rest of the Old Biddies. "I... I didn't realise that your old friends were here," he said in a faint voice.

I grinned. "Yes, they were snowed in at Thurlby Hall with me. In fact, they've been helping with the preliminary investigation. I assume that you'll be wanting to question them too? I'm sure they'll be delighted to talk to you. Mabel Cooke, especially, has a lot of theories about the murder."

Pratt gulped, his Adam's apple bobbing up and down. "Er... actually, that's not necessary. I'm sure... er... that you've given a good account in your notes and I'll... I'll speak to you tomorrow if I have further questions. I know where to find you. Now, I've got to go and... um... check the... parking of the police cars!" He bolted out of the front door.

I laughed and went upstairs to collect my things. I was in good spirits: the police were here, the investigation was no longer my responsibility, and I was looking forward to a quiet Christmas, stuffing my face with delicious food and festive treats. Twenty minutes later, I was back in the main hall, waiting with the Old Biddies, for the Morecombes' chauffeur to bring the car around. I had found Muesli in her usual favourite spot—curled up in the manger of the Nativity scene—and, ignoring her disgruntled meows, had managed to wrestle her into the cat carrier. Now she was pressing her pink nose against the bars of the carrier door and protesting loudly.

"*Meorrw! Meee-orrw! MEEEEE-ORRW!*" she wailed.

"Aww, poor thing..." said Annabel, looking at the little tabby in concern. "She sounds so upset. Do you think she's all right? Perhaps she got injured when you put her in the carrier? Or maybe she's hungry?"

I shot my cat a sardonic look. "Oh, she's fine. She's just miffed because she didn't want to be moved from the manger and now she's having a tantrum. She always carries on like a drama queen when she doesn't want to be in the carrier."

Annabel sighed wistfully. "I do wish she could stay a bit longer... It's been so lovely having her around... I don't suppose you could leave her for a few—" Her face clouded over. "Oh... I forgot. Richard hates cats. He'd never agree." She sighed again—a deep, anguished sigh. "I so wish I could have a cat. The house wouldn't feel so big and empty then—"

I reached out impulsively and grabbed her hand. "You know, Annabel, there are many rescue cats desperately needing a home, especially at this time of the year... Why don't you go and adopt one? Your happiness is important too and if it's something that matters to you, then your husband should compromise. After all, it's not as if you're living in a small flat where the cat would be on top of him all the time. This house is more than big enough for him to have some space that's cat-free and—" I broke off suddenly and let her hand go, giving her a sheepish smile. "Sorry... that was forward of me. I just... well, you deserve to be happy too."

She gave me a tremulous smile, that chilly mask dropping for a second. "You're a nice girl, Gemma." Then she stepped back, the cool reserve back in place as she continued in a polite voice: "Thank you again for providing all the wonderful food for the tea party yesterday. I will certainly be calling you for the next event that the charity is hosting." She glanced towards the front door with a frown. "I wonder what's keeping Cole? It shouldn't take him so long to bring the car around."

An enormous luxury SUV pulled up in front of the manor house at last, with a slightly harassed-looking young man at the wheel. He sprang out and came up the front steps, saying:

"Sorry for taking so long, Mrs Floyd! The car needed a top-up of antifreeze—took me a while to find the bottle."

He hurried to help me with the platters, stowing them in the boot, and I smiled to myself as I saw Glenda flutter her eyelashes at him. She might have been in her eighties, but in her heart, Glenda was still eighteen and the Morecombes' chauffeur, with his clean-cut, boyish good looks, was just her type. She hurriedly claimed the front passenger seat, and sat giggling and simpering like a little girl as we glided smoothly down the driveway from Thurlby Hall. Cole obviously didn't mind flirting with little old ladies; he sat laughing and bantering with Glenda until her cheeks were flushed bright pink.

"...and where did you learn to drive a car so well?" Glenda twittered.

"I've always been mad about cars," said Cole with a laugh. "Wanted to be a mechanic, actually, but didn't get enough GCSEs to qualify for an advanced apprenticeship. Then a mate told me about chauffeur jobs and it sounded just the ticket. He's with a company and rotates around different clients, but I was lucky: I got a full-time chauffeur position driving for a private client down in London. I was there a couple of years and I learned a lot. Then this job with the Morecombes came up and it was an even better deal." He caressed the merino leather upholstery and brushed-steel finish of the dashboard. "It's not everyone who gets to drive a premium model BMW X7! This thing has a twin-power, turbo six-cylinder diesel engine with 400 horsepower and 760 Newton-metre of torque—it can accelerate from nought to sixty in five point four seconds!—and it's got a Bowers and Wilkins 3D surround sound system... and a panorama sunroof... and massage in the seats... And I even get accommodation with the job! My mate was dead jealous, I can tell you!"

"So what does a full-time chauffeur do?" I asked curiously. "Do you just wait around until a member of the family needs to go somewhere?"

"Yeah, but there's not much 'waiting around'. I keep busy most days. Mrs Floyd often goes into town... and Kelly too... Sometimes I drive Mr Floyd to work if he doesn't want to take his own car. And Sir Hugh, of course—he doesn't drive at all anymore, so I take him wherever he needs to go."

"It was very good of you to bring us yesterday,"

gushed Glenda.

"Oh, that was no problem. I had to go into Oxford anyway to bring Julian—Professor Morecombe from one of the colleges."

"You didn't happen to see Ned Morecombe arriving yesterday afternoon, did you?" I asked, unable to stop myself despite vowing not to get involved in the murder investigation anymore.

"Yeah, I did, actually. I was just putting the car in the garage when I saw this taxi pull up and he got out."

"Was he alone?"

Cole nodded. "Yeah, it was just him in the taxi. He paid the driver, and then walked up to the front door—" He glanced at Glenda next to him. "—where you were singing carols. I didn't see what happened when he went in but I heard from Mrs Holmes later that there was a real fuss."

"Yes, his arrival was a great shock to the family... although I daresay not as much as his murder last night," said Mabel grimly.

"Bloody hell, yes! You could have knocked me down with a feather when I came over this morning and heard that he'd been murdered!" cried Cole.

"You don't live in the house?" I asked.

He shook his head. "I live above the garage."

"Does it have a view of the house? Can you see the library window from there?"

"Yeah, although there wasn't much of a view last night, what with all the wind and snow."

"So you didn't notice anything odd?"

"What d'you mean by odd?"

"Like somebody lurking outside the library window," said Mabel eagerly.

"Or someone climbing up the ivy," Ethel piped up.

The car bumped on the road. "Someone *what?*" said Cole.

"We think the murderer got in through the library window," Florence informed him. "We found foo—*ow!*" She yelped and looked at me reproachfully. "Gemma! You stepped on my foot."

"Sorry. Must have been the car bumping," I mumbled. I caught Cole's eye in the rear-view mirror and said: "Er, Cole... listen... this thing about the murderer climbing in the library window... well, it's just a theory. The police haven't confirmed anything and I'm not sure we should even be talking about it—or repeating it to anyone else," I added quickly, not wanting him to start spreading rumours among his "mates". The last thing I needed was for Inspector Pratt to accuse me of leaking confidential information about the investigation to the public!

He grinned. "Okay. Mum's the word. Anyway, I didn't see anything. Not that I was standing at the window the whole night, of course. I went to bed pretty early. Too bloody cold."

"Did you know much about Ned?" asked Glenda.

"Yeah, Sir Hugh talked about him all the time.

He'd go on and on, especially when we had long journeys... But I always thought that Ned was dead." He gave a lopsided smile. "Well, I suppose that's true now."

CHAPTER NINETEEN

By the time I got back to Oxford, it was late afternoon. Cole had dropped the Old Biddies off first at their respective homes, then driven me back to my little modern cottage in a development beside Folly Bridge, on the south side of the university city. I sighed with pleasure as I stepped into my front hallway and let Muesli out of her carrier. She strutted around, rubbing her chin on various bits of furniture and meowing loudly. I smiled to myself. For once, I was in total agreement with my cat: it was good to be home.

Then I remembered that I was supposed to be going over to my parents' this afternoon and staying there until after Boxing Day, so there wouldn't be much time to enjoy being home—I would have to leave again in a few hours. *At least I don't need to check in at the tearoom though,* I thought with a flash relief. The Little Stables had officially closed yesterday for the holiday season and would not be reopening until after New Year's Day.

I filled Muesli's bowl with fresh cat food but she sniffed it disdainfully, then looked up at me.

"*Meorrw!*"

"What is it? Your food is there." I pointed to the bowl.

"*Meorrw... Meorrw!*" Muesli lashed her tail, then looked hopefully towards the fridge.

I put my hands on my hips. "Oh ho! Expecting some roast turkey and smoked salmon, are you? Well, this isn't Thurlby Hall and you're not getting luxury table scraps anymore."

"*Meoooorrw?*" Muesli said forlornly.

"No. You've got perfectly good cat food. Very expensive, specially formulated cat food, that I have to make a special trip to the pet shop to buy," I added, looking at her sternly. "And that's all you're going to get."

Muesli gave an irritable twitch of her whiskers, then turned and stalked huffily out of the kitchen. A minute later, I could hear her in the sitting room, yowling piteously, like a stray who hadn't been fed for days.

Grrrrr... Cats!

Ignoring her histrionics, I went upstairs. I was looking forward to getting out of my grimy clothes and into a hot shower. As I stood under the spray, it felt a bit like I was symbolically washing off all the tensions and dramas of the past day. I stepped out at last, pink and glowing, and feeling refreshed and rejuvenated. As I was towelling myself dry, I glanced at the vanity unit and realised that I'd run out of my favourite moisturiser. There was enough time to pop into town and buy a bottle, I decided. One of the great benefits of where I lived was how close it was to the centre of Oxford. It would take me ten minutes to walk up to the high street where all the shops were. I would be back in under an hour, with still plenty of time to spare.

Fifteen minutes later, I found myself on Cornmarket Street, the main pedestrianised strip in the centre of the university city. Melting snow lay in patches along the sides of the street and I could see debris that had been blown around by the strong winds was littering the pavement, but overall the centre of town seemed to have escaped the worst of the snowstorm and the shops were all open, keen to make the most of the last trading hours before Christmas.

It was even more crowded than the last time I'd been there, with hordes of people rushing around in a panicked fashion, trying to do their last-minute shopping before Christmas Eve. *Which is tomorrow!* I realised with a jolt. It was hard to believe that at this time yesterday, I hadn't even arrived at Thurlby Hall... so much had happened in the last twenty-four hours!

I turned to head into Boots, the big chain pharmacy, then paused in delight as I recognised the bespectacled young man standing on the corner. It was Seth Browning, one of my closest friends. I'd met Seth in my first year at college, and while most of us had headed off to graduate trainee positions after finishing our degrees, Seth had opted to remain in the bosom of academia. He was now a Senior Research Fellow in Chemistry at Gloucester College and the comfortable routine of tutorials, lectures, and research conferences suited his shy, studious personality. He looked very different today, though: instead of the black academic gowns and brown tweed jackets that were his usual attire, he was wearing a green elf costume and a lurid red Santa hat on his head.

"Seth!" I cried, rushing over to him. "What are you doing here?"

He pushed his glasses up his nose in a gesture I knew well and gave me a sheepish grin, holding up a collecting tin.

"Raising money for the Domus Trust," he said. "We always come out on the streets at this time of year."

"Oh, of course," I said, remembering Seth's involvement with the local charity which supported homeless people in and around Oxford. I dug into my pockets and pulled out some change, dropping it into the tin.

"Thanks. Everyone's been very generous," said

Seth, nodding gratefully at a man who passed by and dropped some money into the tin as well. "We've been out collecting since the start of December and we've raised far more than we expected."

"That's brilliant!"

He nodded, beaming. "We've organised a big feast on Christmas Day, plus gifts for everyone... We'd like to make it really special this year, so that even those who have no homes or families don't miss out on all the things the rest of us take for granted." He looked at me with interest. "I hear you've been involved with a similar event for the Sinterklaas Foundation?"

"Yes, they had a Christmas tea party for the kids at Thurlby Hall yesterday and I was catering for that."

"How did that go?"

"Oh, the party was great—the children had a fantastic time and it was wonderful to see their faces. It was what happened afterwards..." I grimaced.

"What do you mean?"

I gave him a brief summary of what had happened since yesterday and he burst out laughing.

"Gemma! Only *you* could go to a Christmas tea party and end up stumbling on a murder."

"I didn't do it on purpose!" I said indignantly. "Trust me, the last thing I wanted was to find a dead body... and then to get dragged into the murder investigation too..."

"Come off it, Gemma. I'll bet you secretly love playing detective," said Seth, chuckling. "And I'll bet that the Old Biddies were in seventh heaven!"

"Yes, being marooned in a country house where a murder has taken place... I think it was the best Christmas present you could have given them," I said with a laugh. "You should have seen them, Seth—they were running around looking for footprints and poking their noses into everything."

"So... who are the suspects?"

"Everyone who was at the house, really—well, aside from Sir Hugh, of course. I doubt he murdered his own son. In fact, he was the only person who seemed to genuinely mourn Ned. The rest of the family all seem to hate him, or at least be completely apathetic about his death. Even his own sister doesn't seem that upset. Although I have to say, Ned Morecombe was a complete tosser," I added darkly. "I'm not surprised that nobody misses him and I also wouldn't be surprised if he had a lot of enemies."

"But if you were snowed in, then it's unlikely that his murderer was an outsider—regardless of how many enemies he had," Seth pointed out.

"Hmm... I can see why you have an IQ of 190," I said, giving him a teasing look. "Yes, that's what I thought too. Which means that the murderer is likely to have been someone in the family.

Personally, I think it's most likely to be Richard Floyd—he's the brother-in-law, and he's a thoroughly unpleasant character. He's got the most motive too. But then there's an odd thing going on with footprints outside the library window, which are somehow connected to the cousin, Julian Morecombe—"

"Wait, did you say Julian Morecombe?"

"Yes."

"Julian Morecombe, who's the Tutor for Music at Parnell College?"

"Yes, why?"

"I know him," said Seth. "I've played against him in OUCCC cricket matches."

"What's he like? Is there any university gossip about him?"

Seth shrugged. "You know, the usual..."

"What usual?"

Seth rolled his eyes. "They say he's an old roué who gets a bit too friendly with students—always the same type: young, attractive, and blonde..."

I thought of Kelly, who certainly fit those criteria. "There's Sir Hugh's fiancée as well."

"Fiancée? But... I thought you said Sir Hugh is in his mid-seventies?"

"He is," I said dryly. "But having a lot of money seems to trump having a lot of wrinkles."

Seth laughed. "And that's it? There's no one else staying there?"

"Well, there's the housekeeper and the chauffeur,

but they're both highly unlikely to be the murderer. For one thing, neither of them have any motive to kill Ned; they barely knew him..." I frowned. "Although... Cole the chauffeur drove us back this afternoon and something's been niggling me about the conversation we had with him—"

"Something he said?"

"No... I don't know... maybe... I can't quite put my finger on it..."

"What about the sister?"

I looked at Seth in surprise. "Annabel?"

"Yes, you haven't mentioned her at all, and earlier you said she didn't seem upset about her brother's death."

"Well, that's probably more because she's very aloof and controlled. Seriously, Seth, she doesn't just have a 'stiff upper lip'—she has a 'stiff entire face'! But she couldn't have been the murderer."

"Why not?"

"Because... because she's just too *nice*! In fact, she's a bit of a doormat, really—she seems to let her husband humiliate her and treat her horribly, and her own father is really abusive to her... but she's still desperately trying to please him."

Seth smiled sadly. "That's classic abused wife syndrome. But you know, Gemma, I've come across several cases of domestic abuse while working with the Domus Trust and there's one thing I'll tell you: when those women finally snap, they *really* lose it. Maybe Ned's return was the straw that broke the camel's back... Does Annabel have an alibi?"

"Well, she said she was sleeping."

"Can anyone confirm that? Her husband?"

"No, Richard Floyd wasn't in their bedroom at the time—although he told me that he saw Annabel on the landing before they rushed downstairs together."

"She could have simply been pretending to come from the bedroom."

"I suppose so," I agreed reluctantly. "But honestly, Seth, she can't be the murderer. She's a victim, not an attacker! Really, if you'd met her, you'd know what I mean. Plus, I don't see how she could have done it—physically, I mean. Ned was a big, tall guy and it would have taken someone pretty strong to hold him down and suffocate him... Annabel is tall but she's very slim; almost too thin, actually. She just wouldn't have the strength to do it."

"Well, the police are on the case now, aren't they? So you can leave it all in their hands—"

"Oh God, but do you know who's been assigned to the investigation? Dylan Pratt! That idiot couldn't detect his way out of a paper bag!"

"He *is* the police though and he's got the resources—the forensics team and access to databases and everything to support the investigation properly."

"I suppose so..." I muttered.

"Gemma, let it go," said Seth with a smile. "It's

Christmas! You shouldn't be worrying about a murder."

I returned his smile and pulled my mind away with an effort. "You're right, you're right. Helping my mother get ready for Christmas Day is what I should be worrying about. She's getting into a real tizz about it."

"Have you got a lot of people coming?"

"Well, in the past, my mother would make a big lunch and all the relatives would come—you know, aunts, uncles, cousins, old family friends... and my grandparents too, when they were alive. But they've passed away now... and several of my aunts and uncles have left the country—one's emigrated to Canada, another's gone to France... and the few relatives who are still in England seem to mostly have other plans this year. So I think it's actually going to be a fairly small party on Christmas Day."

Seth frowned. "I don't understand—if it's only a few people, why is your mother getting so anxious about it?"

I smiled. "Because the few people who *are* coming are very important! It's a distant cousin of my father's and his family. They're American but relocating to the UK because Hank—that's my father's cousin—has been headhunted for a job with a company in London. Anyway, my mother seems to have suddenly decided that it's her responsibility to provide them with a proper 'traditional British Christmas' experience and she's gone a bit crazy!

She's planned a magnificent feast for Christmas Day and wants everything perfect for them..." I shook my head. "I just don't understand why she cares so much—it's not as if they're close relatives. I've never even met them before. So I don't know why she's so desperate to make a good impression."

"People can get like that," said Seth with a smile. "I've seen my parents do it too, especially with friends who are visiting the UK for the first time. It's as if they feel like they're representing their country and it's up to them to ensure that the visitor has a positive view of Britain. They'll go to ridiculous lengths and put themselves at great discomfort, just to make sure that they 'show their visitors a good time'."

"Anyway... I know you can't make it to the lunch but you'll be coming over for tea later in the day, won't you?"

"Of course! I'm really looking forward to it." He hesitated, then asked: "Um... Gemma, I don't suppose you know if Cassie has a proper jewellery box?"

"A jewellery box? No, I don't think so... I think she just keeps her bits and pieces in old chocolate trays. Why?"

"Oh... only because I was thinking of getting her one for Christmas," said Seth shyly. "I saw a Victorian teak-and-brass jewellery box in an antique shop and I thought she might like it."

"That's a great idea. I'm sure she'd love it."

"You think so?" he asked eagerly. "She told me we shouldn't get each other anything for Christmas this year, that we should just each make a donation to a charity instead—you know, she's so practical and sensible that way... but I still wanted to give her something a bit personal."

I smiled at him and thought sadly that what Seth really wanted for Christmas was for Cassie to say that she returned his feelings. That's probably what he'd wanted for Christmas every year, since the first year we all met as freshers at the same college here in Oxford. Seth had fallen head over heels for my best friend from the moment he laid eyes on her, but he had always been too shy to say anything. Sometimes, I wished I could just force him to confess his feelings, but I knew it wasn't my place to interfere.

Still, I thought with a smile, *it won't hurt to provide a "perfect opportunity" with a conveniently placed piece of mistletoe!*

CHAPTER TWENTY

"Darling, what kind of underwear does Devlin wear?"

I glanced up from where I was perched at the kitchen counter, finishing off a late breakfast the next morning, and gave my mother a suspicious look. "Why?"

"I was going to buy him some underpants for Christmas when I was in Debenhams the other day, but then I held off as I wanted to check with you to make sure I purchased the right kind. Your father likes white Y-fronts—in a baggy style—and I thought perhaps Devlin would like some too?"

Trying to push away the disturbing image of my father in baggy white Y-fronts, I said: "No, no, definitely not! Devlin hates Y-fronts or briefs or whatever you call them. He wears boxers. The classic kind. But Mother—"

"Oh wonderful, darling. I saw some lovely one hundred percent cotton ones when I was in Debenhams. I'm going to pop into town later to pick up some last-minute things and I can buy them then. The shops will be open late for Christmas Eve… What size does Devlin wear?"

"Mother, you can't buy Devlin underpants for Christmas!"

"Why ever not?"

"Because… because it's just too weird! Why don't you get him a pen or a bottle of aftershave—"

"Those things are so boring. Besides, I want to get him something he really needs, and I know men never think of replacing the essentials until the fabric is threadbare and the elastic is all gone."

"Yes, but… well… underwear is just a bit personal—"

"Oh, don't be silly, darling. I'm old enough to be Devlin's mother and I could easily have been changing his nappies and seen his willy—"

"*Mother!*"

"Well, never mind. I have Devlin's number—I can ring and ask him myself."

"No, no, don't do that," I said hastily, imagining a horror scene with my mother discussing "willies" with my boyfriend. "Um… Devlin takes medium."

"Ah good… now, I just need to make up some mincemeat for tomorrow's mince pies, then I can pop into town." My mother smoothed down her apron, then began taking various items out of the pantry and refrigerator.

"You make it yourself? I thought people just bought mincemeat from the shops."

"Homemade mincemeat, with fresh fruit added, is always nicer."

"But I thought mincemeat had to marinate for months to develop the flavours."

"It does have richer flavours when it's had time to sit for a bit, but the fresh version is nice too, in a different way. This is a recipe your grandmother used to make, except I don't use suet nowadays—I replace it with butter."

I stood up and pulled another apron off the hook on the wall, tying it around my waist. "Shall I give you a hand?"

"That would be lovely, darling. You can start by grating an orange and lemon—there are some in the fruit bowl there—oh, and also a Bramley apple. No, not the ones in the fridge; the Bramleys are there on the counter." My mother shook her head at me. "Really, Gemma, I would have thought you'd know the difference between a cooking apple and an eating one by now."

"Do they really taste that different once they're cooked?" I asked sceptically.

"Of course they do. The Bramley is a sour apple and cooks down to a pulp... much better in recipes. Right, now the grated zest and grated apple can go in the bowl here..." My mother pointed to a large mixing bowl.

"What have you got inside already?" I asked, peering in.

"Raisins, sultanas, currants, and candied orange and lemon peel." My mother waited for me to pour the grated zest and fresh apple in, then added a generous amount of dark brown muscovado sugar, grated butter, and the juices from the deskinned lemon and orange.

"Oops, almost forgot the mixed spice," she said. "Can you fetch it, darling? There should be a jar in the spice rack in the pantry. Not the 'allspice', mind—that's a different thing. Make sure it's 'mixed spice'."

I brought back the little bottle and unscrewed the cap. A warm, sweet-and-spicy aroma rose up, instantly enveloping me in a cocoon of cosiness and nostalgia. "Mmmm... that smells gorgeous!" I said, inhaling deeply. "It's cinnamon, isn't it?"

"Yes, and nutmeg, ginger, and cloves, plus a bit of allspice too. The essential combination for Christmas baking!" my mother declared. "Can you give everything a good stir, darling?"

I took the bowl and began working the mixture with a wooden spatula. It smelled heavenly and I said thoughtfully as I stirred: "I wish they weren't called 'mince pies'. It puts so many people off eating them, because they think there's meat in the filling. It's such a shame because they're missing out on something delicious."

"Well, they did used to include meat, darling—
that's why the filling is called mincemeat," my
mother reminded me. "When it was made in
medieval times, they included minced mutton as
well as dried fruits, nuts, and spices... But surely
everyone knows that they're just made with fruit
nowadays?"

"Not if they're not British or from Australia or
New Zealand," I pointed out. "Most Americans, for
example, aren't familiar with mince pies—nor are
the Japanese or a lot of other tourists. Ever since
Dora added mince pies to the tearoom menu, Cassie
and I seem to be explaining ten times a day that
they don't contain meat," I added, rolling my eyes.

"You should mention it on the menu," my mother
said. "Just write 'no meat included' in brackets."

"That's a good idea," I mused. "It's too late for
this year but maybe next Christmas..." I looked
down again at the mixture I was stirring. "Why are
you making more mince pies anyway?"

"Well, I thought I'd baked enough for everyone
but now I'm not sure. I think I'd better make an
extra batch tomorrow morning, just in case...
especially as I've just heard from Uncle Ronnie and
he might be coming to lunch too."

I groaned and stared at my mother in dismay.
"Uncle Ronnie? I thought he was dead!"

"Oh no, he's very much alive. He's only in his
late seventies—just a few years older than your
father, you know. In fact, although they're the two

oldest cousins on that side of the family, they've actually outlived a lot of the younger siblings. Poor Gerald died of cancer a few years ago… and Thomas suffered a stroke and ended up in hospital, where he died of pneumonia… There's only Agnes now and she's been nervous about travelling ever since she broke her hip, so she's spending a quiet Christmas at home this year, and her children are staying with her."

"I don't know why we call him *Uncle* Ronnie anyway," I grumbled. "He's not really my uncle. He's Dad's first cousin and my second cousin."

"Because he's much older and it's respectful," said my mother, giving me a severe look. "And we've always called him Uncle Ronnie, ever since you were a little girl."

"What about my *actual* aunts and uncles?" I asked. "Aren't they coming this year?"

"Well, you know Stanley passed away last year and your father's sister is in Canada now, with her family, and they're not planning to make a trip back to England this year. And *my* sister has decided to spend Christmas on a cruise in the Caribbean, while her boys have gone to Dubai for a break from the winter weather." My mother pursed her lips and made a tutting sound. "I'd hoped to have a nice big family reunion this year, but everyone seems to be leaving England and going away for Christmas these days! Even Helen Green isn't around—Lincoln has treated his parents and taken them away on a holiday to Prague, to see the Christmas markets."

Great. So we're just left with Uncle Ronnie, I thought with an inward sigh.

My mother clucked her tongue. "Still, I suppose we ought to count our blessings. At least we haven't had a tragedy in our family, like poor Annabel. I wonder if they'll still go ahead with their traditional Christmas Day lunch? I don't suppose anybody will be in a celebratory mood... although I have to say, I doubt Ned Morecombe will be missed much. He was such a horrid man."

I looked at my mother in surprise. "You didn't even know him."

"Well, I saw enough when I was at the tea party. He seemed like a very arrogant character—and so unpleasant to his own family! I heard him being very insolent to Annabel and he was downright nasty to Julian."

"What do you mean, Mother? How did you know—"

"I overheard them, darling. It was when you were in the dining room serving all the children tea and cakes. I went to look for some extra napkins and I happened to pass the music room. Ned and Julian were inside, and it was obvious that they were having a row. Well, Julian was trying to remain calm and polite but Ned was being abominably rude, calling Julian all sorts of names and speaking in a horrible, jeering tone... I really can't believe they're cousins! Julian is *such* a gentleman; so gallant and with lovely manners—he's not bent in the least. I really don't know why Ned was calling him that."

I froze. "Wait a minute, Mother—what did you say? What did Ned call Julian?"

She looked at me blankly. "He called Julian corrupt and laughed at him in a nasty way—"

"No, no, you said he called Julian 'bent'—was that the word Ned used? He didn't actually say crooked or corrupt or dishonest—"

"No, he said Julian was bent. In fact, he said he was going to tell Sir Hugh that Julian was bent."

"Oh my God..." I leaned back as it dawned on me. "Bent" did mean corrupt and dishonest, as my mother had assumed, but it had another slang meaning: calling a man "bent" could also mean that he was gay.

Suddenly, the sounds I had overheard outside my bedroom that night at Thurlby Hall took on a new meaning. I also realised what had been niggling me about the conversation in the BMW yesterday, when the Old Biddies and I were being driven home. It wasn't anything that Cole had said—it was the way he had *laughed*: a high-pitched, almost feminine chortle. Like a *giggle*. It must have struck me when I was listening absently to him and Glenda bantering, but I hadn't put two and two together... because I had been convinced that I had overheard a *woman* giggling that night. I'd assumed that Julian Morecombe had been entertaining a young lady in his room. It had never occurred to me that he might have been entertaining a young *man*.

And I realised that I'd made the same assumption yesterday afternoon when Seth had told me the gossip about Julian Morecombe: he'd said that the Oxford don had a reputation for getting too friendly with "young, attractive, and blonde" students—I'd automatically assumed that he had been talking about *female* students, but I had been wrong and it had been "blond" students.

Now I realised, too, why Kelly had had that sly smile and looked like she'd been enjoying a private joke when I'd asked if she'd spent the night with Julian... if she'd known that he was gay, she would have been amused at my ignorance.

If Ned had been taunting Julian that day at the tea party and threatening to reveal his sexuality, the Oxford don might have felt compelled to silence him. After all, Sir Hugh was conservative and old-fashioned, and could have been homophobic enough to cut his nephew from his will if he found out the truth.

Which meant that Julian Morecombe could've had a motive for murder too.

***

"If you wait there, Inspector Pratt will be with you in a minute."

I sat down on one of the chairs by the table in

the interview room and wondered if Pratt already knew about Julian Morecombe's homosexuality. Perhaps I was wasting my time coming to the police station. But whatever I might think of Pratt's abilities—or lack thereof!—I had a duty to report any information which might be helpful to the investigation.

When he finally came, however, Pratt barely listened to my account before waving a hand and saying dismissively:

"All right. I'll tell my men to confirm that and update his file."

"That's it? You're not going to do anything about it?"

"Like what?"

"I don't know! Like... like speak to the chauffeur? Or question Julian again, maybe?"

"Why should I?"

I took a deep breath, holding on to my temper. "Because it changes everything! It gives Julian a strong motive for murdering Ned."

He shrugged. "Maybe. Right now, I'm more interested in *your* motives."

I drew back in surprise. "*My* motives?"

"Yes, I'm pleased you came into the station. I was planning to come and find you this afternoon to question you, but this has saved me a trip."

"Question me about what?"

He leaned back and regarded me smugly. "You didn't mention in your statement that you had a run-in with Ned yourself. *Aha...* thought you could hide that, did you? You didn't think I would question the others and check on you, eh?"

"I... I wasn't trying to hide anything," I spluttered. "Of course I expected you to question everybody again. And I didn't think my... my encounter with Ned was relevant to the investigation."

"Not relevant to the investigation?" He raised his eyebrows in an exaggerated manner. "You were assaulted by the victim earlier that evening and you threatened violence if he tried anything again... Oh yes, I spoke to Mrs Holmes and she told me what happened. She said you were *very* angry and upset... so upset that you said you would—quote: 'kill him if he so much as touched me again'— unquote... Now, I would say that's very relevant, don't you?"

I stared at him. "That's... that's just stuff you say when you're worked up. You don't really mean you would kill anyone—"

"And it's interesting that you're the person who discovered Ned's body. I mean, who's to say that you didn't simply *pretend* to find the body in the library? Nobody saw you go in; we only have your word that you came down from your room... searching for your cat, did you say?" His voice dripped sarcasm.

"I *was* searching for my cat!" I snapped. "And it's preposterous, what you're suggesting! You think I might have murdered Ned Morecombe just because he groped me?"

"Ah, well, with all the fuss about women's rights and sexual abuse these days... you probably felt entitled to kill him. In fact, Mrs Holmes also told me that you said you were going to make Ned pay for his actions—"

"I meant legally! I meant that he would have to face official charges of sexual harassment—"

"Come on, admit it: you went back into the library—maybe you really were searching for your cat, but just at an earlier time than you said in your statement—and you bumped into Ned there. He'd been drinking, he was feeling horny, and he tried it on with you again: grabbed you and tried to kiss you, maybe even tried to do more. So you lashed out. You could even say it was self-defence," he added persuasively. "I'd be happy to accept that."

"What? Don't put words in my mouth! It never happened like that. Ned didn't try to assault me again—I never saw him at all after dinner. And I didn't go down to the library until *after* Ned was killed!" I stood up, furious. "If you're going to keep making these ridiculous accusations, I'm not going to talk to you anymore without a lawyer present."

CHAPTER TWENTY-ONE

I was seething when I came out of the police station. My bad mood changed to one of surprise, though, when I bumped into Mabel and the other Old Biddies on the front steps. They looked even more irate than I felt, their wrinkled cheeks flushed and their backs stiff with offended dignity as they tottered out of the station.

"Hello!" I said, falling into step beside them. "What are you doing here?"

"We came to ask the police if they'd found any leads from our important piece of evidence," said Mabel, drawing herself up.

"But they didn't seem to appreciate it very much," said Ethel sadly.

Glenda held up a flattened orange blob. "They didn't even want our maple syrup cast anymore."

"They had the cheek to laugh and call it useless!" said Florence.

"Never mind," said Mabel briskly. "If the police are too ignorant to make use of good evidence, we shall simply have to do things ourselves."

"Er... what do you mean?" I asked, giving her a wary look.

"Well, the obvious thing is to compare our maple syrup cast with the sole on one of Julian Morecombe's shoes," said Mabel.

She gave a satisfied nod. "And how lucky that Parnell College should be fairly close to here. Julian is a bachelor who lives at the college. We simply have to find a way to get into his rooms and take a look at his shoes—"

"Wait—*what*? You can't—"

"Miss Rose!"

I turned to see that a police constable had come out of the station and was holding a piece of paper out at me.

"Miss Rose, Inspector Pratt asked if you could please double-check this amendment to your statement and sign it..."

I sighed and threw an agonised look after the Old Biddies, who were already trotting off down the street, then quickly went back into the station. By the time I'd read the section, scrawled a signature, then come back outside, my four geriatric friends were no longer in sight.

"Bugger!" I muttered and started jogging down

the street.

I headed for Parnell College, sure that that was where the Old Biddies had gone. As I arrived at the college's huge medieval front gate, I noticed a familiar car parked on the opposite side of the road: a gleaming black BMW X7.

Is that the Morecombes' car? I wondered, glancing around for any sign of Cole the chauffeur. He was nowhere in sight and, after another look around, I went through the gate. While some of the colleges were open to visitors for certain hours each day, allowing tourists to catch a glimpse of Oxford college life, many were closed to the public and could only be entered by students and other academic members of the university. I pulled out my alumni card and brandished it at the college porter who leaned his head out of the Porter's Lodge window. I wondered how the Old Biddies had managed to get past—assuming that they had come in here.

"Um... I don't suppose you saw four elderly ladies come in here a short while ago?" I asked tentatively.

The porter brightened. "Oh, you mean Professor Morecombe's aunts."

"Professor Morecombe's *aunts*?"

He nodded. "Never realised he had so many aunts! They came to give him some homemade fudge for Christmas. Wish I had aunts like that." He grinned. "Mine just knit me ugly sweaters. Anyway,

I told 'em they could simply leave it with me and I'd give it to the Prof later, but they said no, they wanted to take it to his rooms themselves and leave it outside his door. Surprise him, like. Really sweet, don't you think?"

"So you gave them directions to his rooms?" I guessed, marvelling at the Old Biddies' improvisation.

He nodded. "I wouldn't normally allow non-members into the college, but seeing as it's Christmas and the college is pretty empty anyway..." Then, as if belatedly remembering, he looked at me curiously and asked: "Why are you looking for 'em?"

"Oh, I'm... er... Professor Morecombe's cousin," I said, giving him a bright smile. "It's a big Morecombe family reunion. Anyway, I said I'd meet up with them here at the college... um... Did you say that Julian's room is that way?" I pointed across the main quadrangle.

"Yes, first staircase on the right in the Rear Quad, through that arch there. But you can't—"

"Thanks! I'll find my way!" I gave him a cheery wave and hurried away before he could think of an objection.

Once across the main quad and through the arch, I found myself in a much smaller quad—more of a courtyard, really—enclosed by tall stone walls on four sides, each with a door to a staircase. Each staircase probably led up to student dormitories or tutors' rooms and I was glad that the porter had given me directions, as I wouldn't have known which one to tackle first. Turning towards the first door on my right, I realised what I had forgotten: that the doors to each staircase were locked and I didn't know the code for the keypad. How had the Old Biddies got in? Surely even their resourcefulness didn't extend to hacking a digital keypad?

Then, as the wooden door opened and a young girl stepped out, I saw the answer. Quickly, I grabbed the door as it started to swing shut behind her and, acting as nonchalantly as I could, I stepped inside. I found myself in a narrow stairwell with wooden steps zigzagging upwards. Hearing a murmur of voices above my head, I peered up and caught a glimpse of four white helmets of hair on a landing above.

For a moment, I had a terrible sense of *déjà vu* that reminded me of when I'd first returned to Oxford and just opened my tearoom: I'd somehow become embroiled in a murder investigation after an American tourist was mysteriously killed with one of my scones, and I had stood in a college staircase just like this one, searching for the Old Biddies, who had decided to do a bit of their own sleuthing.

Not much has changed in a year, I thought wryly as I started up the wooden staircase.

I found the Old Biddies on the second landing. They had moved towards one of the doors leading off from the landing and were huddled around it, arguing amongst themselves. They jumped visibly when I came up behind them.

"Oh, it's you, Gemma—thank goodness! We thought you might have been Julian Morecombe," said Florence, putting a plump hand to her chest.

"Hush! I need to concentrate..." said Glenda, bending over the doorknob.

"Why don't we ask Gemma to do it?" suggested Ethel. "She's younger, with more flexible fingers..."

"Do what?" I asked suspiciously.

"Unlock the door," said Mabel, taking something from Glenda and handing it to me.

I looked down at the metal tool in my hand. "What's this?"

"It's the Super Pick—'opens any door in under sixty seconds'," said Glenda proudly. "My great-nephew, Mike, gave it to me for Christmas. He said it came from a shipment which had fallen off the back of a lorry..." She frowned. "Although I'm not sure how he managed to catch them just as they were falling off. It must have been a great stroke of luck. And I don't know why he didn't try to stop the lorry driver to tell him that some of his cargo had fallen out. I suppose it was going too fast and was gone before Mike could notify him?"

I rolled my eyes. Mike Bailey was a notoriously shady character; a young man who seemed to be involved in a lot of dodgy deals and probably petty crime. He had even been a suspect in a murder investigation the first time I'd met him. But Glenda doted on her great-nephew and I didn't have the heart to tell her that "fallen off the back of a lorry" was a euphemism for "stolen goods".

"I'm not picking the lock—and I can't believe that you were trying to," I said, handing the tool back to Glenda and giving them a stern look. "You'd be arrested if anyone saw you!"

"Nonsense," said Mabel stoutly. "We're on the tail of a suspect—we're doing important police work."

"Yes, but you're *not actually* the police! And even if you were... well, even the police would need a search warrant before they could enter private premises—"

"Oh, tosh!" said Mabel, waving a hand. "Anyone would think that we were breaking and entering."

"But... but you *are* breaking and entering!" I said, my voice becoming shrill with exasperation. "You can't—"

"I did it!" cried Glenda triumphantly.

She pushed the door open and, before I could protest, the Old Biddies trotted into the room. I bit back a growl of irritation and followed them. We found ourselves in a large room—the size of a studio flat—filled with an abundance of books, papers, half-drunk cups of coffee, and coats, hats, and scarves tossed carelessly over the backs of armchairs. It was so *not* what I was expecting that I made an exclamation of surprise.

"What is it, dear?" The Old Biddies stopped and

turned to look at me.

"N-nothing... it's just..." I gave a sheepish smile. "I suppose it was stupid of me to automatically assume the stereotype that all gay people are neat and fastidious."

They looked at me blankly. "What are you talking about, dear?"

"Oh sorry—I hadn't told you," I said, remembering. "I just found out this morning: Julian Morecombe is gay. My mother overheard them talking, that day at the tea party. Or rather, Ned was taunting Julian and threatening to reveal the truth about his homosexuality. With Sir Hugh being so conservative, if he had found out, Julian could have been cut from the will... which gives Julian a good reason to want to kill Ned and silence him."

"Aha! I said he was guilty, didn't I?" said Mabel smugly. "Now we just need to match his shoes to the footprints outside the window and we will have solved the case!"

"No, that's not—"

Mabel ignored my protest and continued talking to the others. "I'll go and check his shoes. You have a look around for any other clues."

"Wait, you can't—"

I was roundly ignored again as—with expressions of glee—Ethel, Glenda, and Florence began poking and prying around the room, whilst Mabel marched to the wardrobe beside the bed.

I threw a nervous look over my shoulder at the

front door. It seemed quiet out on the landing and all I could hope for was that the Old Biddies would get tired of snooping before anyone came. Turning back, I saw that they were now heading through a connecting door on the other side of the room. I hurried after them and was momentarily distracted to find myself in a spacious en suite.

Wow... things have changed at Oxford since I was a student. I could remember my college room at the top of a draughty staircase, with one bathroom on the landing below, shared between sixteen students. It had nothing more than a utilitarian sink and bathtub (no shower) and it had been a scramble to nab the bathroom during the morning rush when everyone was heading off to lectures. Now I looked at the gleaming fittings and spacious shower cubicle in front of me with envy.

Meanwhile, the Old Biddies were busily poking through the male toiletries on the vanity unit, picking up each bottle and examining it with interest.

"Ooh, this smells lovely," said Glenda, spritzing some aftershave in the air and sniffing noisily.

Florence wrinkled her nose. "It's very citrusy, isn't it? Don't you think the spicy scents are much nicer, like cinnamon and myrrh—"

"Sandalwood," said Mabel authoritatively. "That's the best smell for a man. I always buy my Henry a bottle every Christmas."

"I think men smell nicest when they smell clean

and fresh," squeaked Ethel. She blushed and added, "There was a gentleman who used to come to the library and he always had lovely minty breath when he leaned over the counter to ask me about a book..." She fanned herself, her cheeks pink. "I still think of him every time I open a new tube of toothpaste!"

"Try spritzing some on your wrist," said Glenda to Florence. "They say fragrances smell different when they react with your skin—"

"Oh, for heaven's sake! This isn't the fragrance section of a department store!" I said in exasperation, snatching the bottle out of her hands and replacing it on the vanity unit. "We're in somebody's room! Someone could come any minute. We need to leave—"

I broke off as my ears caught a sound in the room outside. My heart lurched. The bathroom door hinges creaked and I whirled around to find a man standing in the doorway, staring at us.

CHAPTER TWENTY-TWO

It wasn't Julian Morecombe. It was a complete stranger and he was eyeing us in utter bewilderment.

"What on earth...?"

I groped desperately for a feasible explanation of why we would be standing in his bathroom, but before I could think of anything, Mabel surged forwards and said in her booming voice:

"Ah! Perfect timing! We've been waiting for you. Now, my dears..." She turned to the other Old Biddies and waved a hand like a conductor. The four old ladies took a deep breath, then burst into song, warbling like drunken nightingales as they sang:

"Deck the halls with boughs of holly,
Fa la la la la, la la la la!

Tis the season to be jolly,
Fa la la la la, la la la la!"

I stared at them open-mouthed, until Mabel elbowed me and hissed: "Sing!" Glancing at the man in front of us, who was looking even more dumbfounded than I felt, I began to join in weakly.

"Don we now our gay apparel... Fa la la, la la la, la la la!"

I can't believe I'm doing this, I thought as I stood and sang the whole carol with the Old Biddies, who bobbed and swayed enthusiastically next to me. When we'd finished, Mabel advanced on the man and shook his hand.

"Merry Christmas, sir! I hope you've enjoyed this bit of festive cheer."

"But... what..." he stammered. "Who...?"

"Oh, we're part of a special granny carolling group called the 'The Twelve Greys of Christmas' and this is a new service we're offering," said Mabel, beaming. "You see, traditionally, carols are always sung at the front door, but that is so predictable and boring. So we've decided to bring carol singing to your most private moments! In your kitchen, in your sitting room, in your toilet! So you can feel that Christmas really *is* all around." She patted his shoulder then turned away, saying briskly: "Righto! Must be off now. Many other bathrooms to do today..."

She marched out, her head held high, with Glenda and Florence trailing after her. Ethel paused next to the man and produced a tin from her coat pocket.

"Would you like to make a donation?" she asked brightly.

I made a choked noise and grabbed her arm, hauling her out of the room after the others. Out on the landing, I released her and glowered at the Old Biddies.

"You're unbelievable! 'Christmas carols in the bathroom'? I don't know how—" I broke off as a noise caught my ears again. But this time, it was something that was very familiar: a high-pitched giggle. I whirled around and found that the sound was emanating from a door on the opposite side of the landing. Forgetting myself, I hurried over and pressed my ear to the door. To my surprise, the door moved as I leaned against it, swinging open. *The latch mechanism must not have caught properly*, I realised, remembering a similar problem with my own college room door, which always needed a firm push to click into place.

Mabel pushed past me and marched in, with the other Old Biddies toddling behind her. I hurried in their wake and we walked into a room with a similar layout to the one we had just left. Except that the bed in this one wasn't empty: a good-looking young man I recognised was lounging amongst the sheets, and beside him, dressed only in a black scholar's gown and mortarboard, was Julian Morecombe.

"What... what is the meaning of this?" blustered Julian, springing up. His face was beetroot-red and he looked furious and panicked and scared. "How dare you...! These are my private quarters and you have no right barging in here like this!"

I averted my eyes and would have slunk away in embarrassment, but Mabel stepped forwards, unabashed, and pointed at Cole, who had jerked upright in bed.

"Young man, you were the one who climbed down the ivy on the night of the murder, weren't you?"

The chauffeur glanced uneasily at Julian and hesitated for a moment, then muttered, "Yeah, that was me. Julian told me to come to his room after dinner. He said I could sneak in the back door—no one would see me—and come up the old servants' staircase. He would be waiting for me in his room and open the door for me. And then after... afterwards, we were joking around and he dared me to climb down the ivy. So that's what I did. I got out of his room that way and went back to my flat above the garage."

"But your footprints led to the library window," I pointed out.

"Well, it was snowing, so when I got down the ivy, I walked along the side of the house, under the eaves, because it's more sheltered there. And then, just as I got to the library window, I saw someone come around the corner from the front of the house.

It was Mr Floyd; he'd come out to smoke one of his cigars. I didn't want him to see me so I ducked down behind the holly bush." Cole grimaced. "It was bloody freezing and I thought he was going to stay out smoking forever! It must have been something like ten minutes... Anyway, he finally went back in and I legged it back to the garage." He lifted his chin. "But I had nothing to do with Ned Morecombe's murder! He was definitely still alive when I saw him through the library window on the way back."

"Wait—you saw Ned through the window?" I gasped. "That could have been the last time anyone saw him alive. Did you tell this to the police?"

He glanced at Julian again, then shook his head. "I couldn't, could I? I wasn't supposed to let anyone know that I'd come over to the house that night. I was supposed to pretend I stayed over at the garage the whole time."

"Did Ned look all right the last time you saw him?" asked Mabel.

He nodded. "Yeah, he was with his sister. Mrs Floyd."

"With Annabel?" I looked at him in surprise. "This is when you were on your way back, you said? What time was that?"

He thought for a moment. "Just before midnight... I remember the clock beside Julian's bed said a quarter to twelve as I was climbing out the window."

"But it couldn't have been Annabel," I protested. "She said she was in bed by eleven thirty. Are you *sure*?"

"Yeah, she was in there earlier with Ned; I saw them when I passed the library window the first time, on my way to the house—"

"What time was that?" I asked quickly.

"Around eleven fifteen or eleven twenty, I think?"

Yes, that fits with Annabel's account, I thought. She'd said that she was in the library with Ned until around eleven fifteen, then she'd left him, popped into the kitchen to speak briefly to Mrs Holmes, and then gone upstairs to bed. *Unless...* An uneasy thought struck me. *Could Annabel have been lying?* I knew she had gone to see Mrs Holmes because the housekeeper had verified that, but afterwards, had she really gone upstairs to bed like she'd said...?

"What were they doing?" asked Mabel.

Cole looked at her blankly. "What do you mean?"

"Ned and Annabel—were they talking?" asked Mabel impatiently.

"Or eating something?" added Florence.

"Or reading books?" suggested Ethel.

"Or having a row?" said Glenda.

Cole gave them a funny look. "Uh... yeah, Ned had a plate of plum pudding, but he wasn't eating it. He was drinking port though, and Annabel—Mrs Floyd had a glass in her hand too." He glanced at Glenda. "And yeah, they looked like they were having a flaming row. I mean, I couldn't hear what they were actually saying through the glass, of course, but I could tell by their expressions. Ned had this jeering sort of look on his face and Mrs Floyd looked like she was going to cry. And I reckon they were still at it when I came back past the window on my way back—you know what family arguments are like," he said with a wry look. "Mrs Floyd had gone over to the other side of the room, so I couldn't see her from the window, but I saw Ned talking to her."

"And he looked fine?"

Cole grinned. "Actually, he looked pretty pis—er, I mean drunk," he hurriedly amended, glancing at the Old Biddies. "He was leaning on the mantelpiece and had this stupid smile on his face."

"I think you've interrogated Cole enough, considering that you're not the police and have no official standing," Julian spoke up for the first time. He was standing stiffly by the bed, trying to maintain a dignified stance as he clutched the edges of his black academic gown together. He gestured to the door. "I'd appreciate it if you could leave now."

Reluctantly, the Old Biddies began shuffling out of the room. I followed them, my mind churning. *It just can't be Annabel... it can't!* I thought. For one thing, Ned *had* to have been overpowered by a man—or at least a strong, athletic woman. And Annabel was neither. She wouldn't have been strong enough to hold him down and suffocate him.

Unless he had been incapacitated.

I stopped in my tracks. In my mind's eye, I saw Ned's body once more, on the night I'd found him: slumped sideways in that armchair in front of the fireplace, his arms flung out limply, his head lolling back on his shoulders... When I'd first seen him—before I'd seen the stocking on his head—I *had* thought that Ned had had too much to drink and fallen into a drunken stupor. That was what his slumped pose had looked like at first. And that's what Cole was suggesting. Well, *could* Ned have been drunk? Was that the explanation for why he hadn't been able to defend himself?

But no... I couldn't buy it. I was sure that a man like Ned Morecombe would've been more than capable of holding his drink. In fact, he probably had a very high alcohol tolerance. I'd seen him myself less than two hours earlier at the end of dinner, and he had been completely lucid. Could he have got so roaring drunk in the intervening time that he had been too weak to resist when someone tried to suffocate him? No, it seemed too far-fetched.

Then I caught my breath as a new idea struck me. I don't know why I hadn't thought of it before. Ned might not have been drunk... but he might have been *drugged*.

Yes, that would explain everything! Something had been put into his drink, perhaps, which had weakened him or maybe even rendered him semiconscious, so that he hadn't been able to put up a fight. I wondered if the forensic pathologist had done the autopsy yet and whether they had found evidence of drugs in his system.

Not that Inspector Pratt would share the information with me even if they had, I thought sourly.

Suddenly, I missed Devlin and realised how spoiled I was when he was around, with confidential police information and forensic findings often shared with me and continual updates on the progress of the investigation. I was planning to speak to Devlin tonight, though. *Maybe I can ask him to check with the forensic department for me*, I thought. *It had to have been a poison that couldn't be tasted easily in the drink; something that—*

I whirled back around to face the bed. "Cole, listen... yesterday, when you were driving us back into town, you took a long time to bring the car around. You said you'd been delayed because you needed to top up the antifreeze?"

"Yeah, that's right. It's usually kept on a shelf in the garage but it wasn't there, so I had to go searching for it. Finally found it in the utility room at the back of the house. I think I remember Mrs Floyd saying she wanted to spray some antifreeze on the garden path next to the vegetable patch, to clear the ice. She didn't want to use salt because that was bad for the soil. I suppose she must have forgot to put it back in the garage after that."

I stared at him. Antifreeze was a well-known poison, which—from what I'd heard—could cause symptoms that often looked very similar to alcohol intoxication: loss of coordination, dizziness and fatigue, nausea and vomiting, even seizures and coma...

I didn't want to ask but I had to know: "Cole, you said you saw Ned and Annabel each holding a drink the first time you looked through the window."

"Yeah, that's right."

I hesitated. "Did you happen to see if Annabel handed a glass to Ned?"

Julian burst out laughing suddenly. "Are you suggesting that my saintly cousin might have murdered her own brother?" He shook his head. "I'm sorry, but even I find that hard to believe!"

CHAPTER TWENTY-THREE

That evening was not how I'd expected to spend Christmas Eve. Oh, I went through the motions of helping my mother with the final touches to the decorations for the house and preparing the next day's big meal, but all the time, I was troubled by my thoughts. Especially by the thought that *Annabel* could have been the murderer.

A cheeky "*Meorrw?*" interrupted my musings. I looked up from where I was rolling napkins into napkin rings, as per my mother's instructions, to see Muesli on the other side of the room, trying to climb up the Christmas tree.

"Noooo... Muesli!" I growled, getting up and going over.

My little cat had been particularly naughty all evening—scampering under everyone's feet, climbing onto the mantelpiece and batting the cards on display off one by one, and attacking any Christmas decorations she could reach with gusto. Her favourite game, though, had been climbing up the Christmas tree and knocking ornaments off the upper branches. I hadn't put up a tree in my own cottage, so Muesli had been delighted when we arrived at my parents' place last night to find a six-foot Christmas tree waiting in the sitting room. She had instantly thought it was her personal jungle gym and spent every waking moment wriggling up through the branches.

"Muesli... you've got to stop doing this!" I huffed as I dragged her out from the middle of the tree once more, scattering pine needles everywhere.

The little tabby gave a defiant "*Meorrw!*" and wriggled out of my arms, flinging herself at the tree again. The branches swayed alarmingly as the tree teetered to one side and, for a moment, I thought the entire tree was going to topple over.

"MUESLI!" I cried, lunging for the tree and steadying it.

"*Meorrw?*" she said, clinging upside down to one of the branches and tilting her head to give me an impudent look.

I bit my lip to stop myself smiling. It was hard to stay mad at my little cat when she looked so adorable and it was obvious that she was enjoying herself immensely. Still, my good humour vanished when I looked down and saw the mess of pine needles on my parents' cream carpet. Guiltily, I glanced across the room to check my mother's reaction—normally she couldn't even bear to see a piece of fluff on her carpets and now, with the prospect of important guests tomorrow, her standards were higher than ever.

But to my surprise, my mother didn't seem to have noticed my little tussle with Muesli. In fact, her polishing cloth, and the silver soup ladle she had been working on, lay forgotten in her lap as she leaned over the coffee table, engrossed in an article in the evening paper. Curious, I went over to see what she was reading. It was a small piece in the corner of the front page, with the headline: "*Country House Murder Causes Rift in Thirty-Year Business Alliance*". My eyes widened as I read the short paragraph underneath:

"*Businessman Neville Smythe has caused controversy with his public comments regarding Ned Morecombe, the man who was found dead at a country house in Oxfordshire earlier this week. The police are treating the death as suspicious and a murder investigation is currently underway. Mr Smythe's daughter, Jessica, was once engaged to Ned Morecombe, until the latter abandoned his fiancée and absconded with his trust fund. The resulting scandal caused great distress for Mr Smythe's only child and it is believed that the businessman has nursed a grudge ever since. When questioned regarding the murder, Mr Smythe is alleged to have said: 'Ned had it coming to him.' He has also voiced several criticisms regarding the dead man's morals and character. The remarks have infuriated Mr Smythe's long-time business associate, Sir Hugh Morecombe—who is Ned Morecombe's father—and there are concerns that this could threaten the alliance between their respective companies. Share prices have plummeted in response, with investors worried about Sir Hugh's actions in retaliation."*

"Oh dear..." said my mother. "Poor Annabel. I'm sure more scandal is the last thing the family needs. And how dreadful of Neville Smythe to make such a heartless remark—surely there was no need to rub salt in the wound, now that Ned is dead?"

Unless it was a sense of glee in justice being served at last? A wild thought occurred to me and I wondered if Neville Smythe could have possibly been involved in Ned's murder. The papers had said that he still held a grudge and his comments about Ned certainly seemed to support that... but surely it was too far-fetched to think that he would orchestrate the murder of the man just because the latter jilted his daughter? Besides, on a practical note, how could he have done it? Neville Smythe hadn't been snowed in at Thurlby Hall with us, so the only way he could have been involved was if he had hired someone to kill Ned.

Is it coincidence that Kelly used to be Neville Smythe's secretary? I wondered, then instantly chided myself. *No, no, this really is getting into the realm of the ridiculous! Surely Kelly isn't some femme fatale sent by Neville Smythe into the enemy's camp to spy on and kill the target? Aside from anything else, no one knew Ned would return out of the blue. And Kelly's connection to Neville Smythe isn't a strange coincidence—it's the very reason she and Sir Hugh met.*

I sighed. Much as I wanted to pin the murder on someone else, I knew in my heart that rather than trying to develop these outlandish theories, I needed to consider Annabel as a serious suspect. Everything in me rebelled against that possibility. I liked Annabel; I felt very sorry for her, and saw her as a victim herself. But I couldn't help remembering the cruel way her father had rejected her and made it obvious that Ned was his favourite...

Seth's words about abused women came back to me: *"...when those women finally snap, they really lose it. Maybe Ned's return was the straw that broke the camel's back..."*

My dark thoughts had me brooding all through the dinner with my parents and I excused myself as soon as I could afterwards. Remembering my plan to call Devlin, I dialled his number with a smile of anticipation. It took a while for him to answer and when the line connected, I could barely hear his voice above the din of loud thumping music, wild whooping, and raucous laughter in the background.

"Bloody hell, it sounds like celebrations are

already in full swing at your mum's place," I commented with a laugh.

Devlin gave a weary sigh. "Yes, people have been arriving since lunchtime and everyone is already completely plastered."

I heard a loud cheer and squeals of excitement, followed by the distinct sound of shattering glass. Devlin cursed under his breath, then his muffled voice shouted: "*Be careful, Mum! You could have hurt yourself! No, don't... no, just leave it... I'll sort it out later...* Sorry," he said, coming back to the call.

"It's okay. At least everyone seems to be having a 'smashing' time," I ventured with a weak laugh.

Devlin didn't sound amused. "It's like chaperoning a party of senseless, underage drinkers... except that everyone here is over thirty and should really know better," he said through gritted teeth.

I felt a stab of pity for him. It didn't sound like he was enjoying Christmas with his mother at all. "Maybe if they have a big party now, things will be calmer tomorrow," I suggested, trying to cheer him up. "Does your mum have anything special planned for Christmas Day?"

"Er... actually..." Devlin trailed off.

"Yes?"

"She's... yes, she's made plans..." He trailed off again.

I frowned. "Devlin, is everything okay?"

"Uh... yes, fine... So, what have you been up to?"

he asked, abruptly changing the subject. "I assume you got back from Thurlby Hall okay? I was worried until I got the text from you yesterday saying that they'd cleared the road to the estate and you were being given a lift back to Oxford."

"Oh yes, I was back in Oxford by late afternoon. I'm at my parents' now."

"And I suppose Dylan Pratt is heading that murder investigation? I hope he wasn't too much of a plonker when he arrived to question everyone," said Devlin.

"Well, actually..." It was my turn to hesitate and trail off, wondering what to say. Devlin was bound to hear about my involvement in the case sooner or later, and better that it came from me than from that "plonker".

I took a deep breath and said: "I was... er... sort of involved in the questioning of all the suspects."

"What do you mean?"

I told him about Sir Hugh's insistence that I get preliminary statements from everyone while we were waiting for the police to arrive, and also about the Old Biddies' discovery of footprints outside the library window.

"What? Gemma..." Devlin groaned. "You promised me that you wouldn't start snooping and meddling again!"

"I'm not snooping and meddling. Sir Hugh *asked* me to get involved, and besides, it made sense to do something proactive instead of just sitting helplessly around, waiting for the police to arrive. We didn't know how long we were going to be snowed in and we could have been waiting for ages…"

"I'm sure Pratt didn't see it that way."

"No, he acted like a complete tosser," I said irritably. "What's more, he actually thinks that *I* might be a suspect! Can you believe that?"

"What do you mean?"

I recounted my maddening interview with Pratt at the police station yesterday afternoon, adding angrily, "That man always jumps to conclusions and then tries to force all the facts to fit his preconceived ideas. It's just arrogance and laziness! Because he doesn't want to do the real legwork required for investigating, and he thinks he has all the answers anyway. I'll bet he hasn't even bothered to read Ned's autopsy report properly—oh, speaking of which: do you think you can you ring up your Forensics department and ask if they've analysed the port that Ned was drinking and the plum pudding he was eating on the night he was murdered?"

"Gemma…!" said Devlin in an exasperated voice.

"Oh please, Devlin. It's just a quick phone call. You know Pratt will never give me that information."

"You shouldn't need that information," said Devlin sternly. "You should leave the murder investigation to the police."

"Yes, but this could *help* the investigation and

Pratt is probably overlooking it! Please, Devlin... it's really important. If there was antifreeze in the food or drink, or if Ned was found to have it in his system, then it means that he could have been killed by anyone, even a weaker woman. That changes everything! Please, Devlin," I begged.

Devlin sighed. "Gemma, I can try... but I'm not the senior investigating officer on this case, plus I'm officially on leave so I have no authority to ask for that information. My request might seem odd and flag up an alert which could get back to Pratt... In any case, you do realise that tomorrow is Christmas Day? The Forensics department is probably already shut and won't reopen until after Boxing Day at least. In fact, I doubt they'll even have got to your case yet... they were still working their way through a huge backlog when I left last week. You're not going to get any reports until well after Christmas."

I bit my lip. I couldn't imagine another week of uncertainty, brooding over the possibility of whether Annabel Floyd could be the murderer.

"Isn't there another way—" I started to say but was cut off by the sound of a shrill scream in the background, followed by angry shouting.

"Gemma... I'm really sorry, sweetheart, but I'm going to have to go," Devlin said hurriedly.

I was taken aback. I'd been looking forward to a long chat, with a bit of romantic banter thrown in perhaps—not this hasty exchange.

"I miss you," I said, trying not to sound too

forlorn.

"I miss you too," Devlin replied in a distracted voice. "Look, I'll speak to you tomorrow, okay?"

I put the phone down and stared at it with a frown. Something had been bothering Devlin, beyond the party guests' shenanigans. And what were his mother's "plans" for Christmas Day that he had been so reluctant to talk about? He had sounded so distracted and completely unlike himself...

I sighed. This Christmas was turning out to have more mysteries than I could handle.

CHAPTER TWENTY-FOUR

"Ah, perfect timing, darling! You can give me a hand with the mince pies," said my mother as I stepped into the kitchen the next morning.

I started to answer, then stopped and stared around. There were pans simmering on the stove and roasting trays in the oven. The kitchen island was covered by mountains of potatoes, baby carrots, parsnips, green beans, and Brussels sprouts, all peeled or sliced. The blender was bulging with a stuffing mixture of sage, onion, sausage, and breadcrumbs. And a row of little jugs, each filled respectively with bread sauce, gravy stock, cranberry sauce, apple chutney, and Hollandaise sauce, stood to attention like soldiers ready to be called into battle.

On one counter, spreads of cheese and crackers

were artfully arranged on platters, alongside pâtés, dips and breadsticks, tiny smoked salmon blini, caramelised fig tartlets, and mini sausage rolls. On the opposite counter, there were gingerbread biscuits, cinnamon buns, traditional shortbread, a sliced Madeira cake, as well as homemade chocolate fudge. I could also see unopened packets of salt 'n' vinegar crisps and Pringle tubes, roasted peanuts and honey cashews, hazelnut biscotti and caramel popcorn... all dwarfed by a huge tin of chocolates. And as my mother swung open the fridge door to get a carton of double cream, I saw that the shelves inside were crammed to bursting with more food, including a chocolate Yule log and a big bowl of raspberry trifle.

"Oh my God, Mother... are you trying to feed the British Army?" I said. "How are we going to eat all this food?"

"Nonsense, darling. It's Christmas! People have to eat and I always say: better too much than too little. Some of this is for tea this afternoon anyway."

I sniggered. "Tea? By the time we finish lunch, I don't think anyone will be able to eat again for a week!"

"Remember, Seth and Cassie might not be able to come for lunch but they'll be coming later for tea. And Mabel, Glenda, Florence, and Ethel too... so there will be more people later." My mother gestured to a space at the kitchen island, then lifted a bowl from the counter and set it down next to me. "Here's the mincemeat we prepared yesterday. You just need to roll out the pastry and make up the mince pies."

I lifted the plastic wrap covering the bowl of mincemeat and sniffed the mixture of dried and fresh fruits, grated citrus zest, nutmeg, cinnamon, and spices. "Oooh... I thought this smelled amazing yesterday but today... mmm... it's like someone captured Christmas in a bottle!"

My mother handed me a slab of dough, wrapped in cling film. "I made up the pastry dough earlier— you just need to roll it out now and cut out the rounds for each pie."

I did as she instructed, rolling out the pastry thinly and then using a pastry cutter to cut out round discs to line a shallow muffin tray. I filled each pastry case with a heaped spoonful of the mincemeat, then covered each again with another disc of pastry, slightly smaller this time. Carefully using the tines of a fork, I pressed the edges of the circles together to seal them, then brushed them all with beaten egg.

"There!" I said.

My mother leaned over to check my handiwork and nodded approvingly. "Good. Now in the oven for twenty minutes."

The smell that filled the kitchen as the mince pies began to bake was mouth-watering. I found it hard to concentrate on the other tasks my mother set me as I waited. The clock had barely counted twenty minutes when I pulled the muffin tray out of the oven. The mince pies looked golden brown and smelled absolutely divine. I fidgeted as I waited for them to cool down enough to be popped out of the tray. Spreading them out, I dusted them all lightly with icing sugar, then stood back and surveyed them with pride.

"Can I taste one now?" I asked eagerly.

My mother looked up from where she was arranging prawn cocktails in individual serving cups and said absently, "Just one, darling."

I grabbed the pie nearest to me and bit into it with relish, feeling my teeth sink through the light, buttery pastry. The filling was hot, nearly burning my tongue as it bubbled out, and a burst of flavours filled my mouth: the fragrant mincemeat, with its subtle mix of tangy and sweet, the plump juiciness of raisins and sultanas combined with the chewy bitter-sweetness of the citrus zest, all overlaid with the warm spices of cinnamon, nutmeg, ginger, and cloves.

I had to admit, I hadn't felt particularly festive when I'd woken up that morning and hadn't been looking forward to the prospect of spending Christmas Day with a bunch of distant relatives I'd never even met... but the delicious, nostalgic flavours of the mince pie instantly put me in the mood.

"Ohhhhh...." I closed my eyes as I chewed reverently. "Mmm... I think that's the best mince pie

I have ever tasted!"

My mother laughed. "It always tastes better when you've put in the hard work of baking it yourself. Now, darling, I need you to arrange them on a platter and take them out to the sitting room, together with some of the other nibbles. And check with your father—he's supposed to be preparing the drinks. Oh, and can you set the table for me?" My mother tucked a strand of hair behind her ear, looking uncharacteristically flustered as she glanced at the clock on the kitchen wall. "The guests will be arriving soon and I want everything to be absolutely perfect!"

As it turned out, however, the guests didn't arrive soon. In fact, even well past lunchtime, there was still no sign of them. My mother's fluster morphed into nervous impatience as she obsessively checked the turkey and other dishes. Everything had been carefully timed to be brought to the table in perfect succession, starting from twelve o'clock, and with every passing minute, things were at the risk of becoming dried out, overcooked, or congealed...

"Oh fudge buckets! Where *are* they?" cried my mother irritably as she checked on the turkey again for the fifteenth time.

I glanced at her. *Wow*. For my mother to use the F-word, things must have been *really* bad.

"Maybe they're stuck in traffic?" I suggested. "Or their train is late?"

"There is no traffic. They came up to Oxford by train yesterday and are staying at The Randolph. They simply had to get a taxi from the hot—*ah!* Is that them?"

My mother went eagerly out to the entrance hall but when she opened the front door, it was not a large, boisterous American family standing on the doorstep. Instead, there was an elderly man in a three-piece suit, brandishing a gentleman's walking cane—the Victorian kind with a carved silver knob on the end—and sporting the most ridiculous toupee I had ever seen. It looked like a furry creature had died on his head.

"Ronnie!" cried my mother. "How lovely to see you. I'm so pleased that you could make it after all."

"Merry—*hic!*—Chrishmush, Evelyn... marvelloush to shee you..." He tottered into the house and caught sight of me, hovering behind my mother. His face lit up and he said with a roguish smile, "Aha! Who's thish lovely young lady?"

"Don't you recognise Gemma?" My mother put a hand on my shoulder. "She was overseas for several years but she's back in England now."

I went forwards and gave him a tentative peck on the cheek, trying to ignore the alcoholic fumes wafting from him. Someone had obviously started on the festive drinks early. "Hello, Uncle Ronnie."

He caught my hands in a claw-like grip and teetered forwards. For a moment, I thought he was going to fall into me, but he caught himself at the last moment and swayed backwards again. "Little Gemma, eh? Come back, eh? Sho what are you doing back in Blighty?"

"I'm running a tearoom, Uncle Ronnie."

"Eh?" He leaned towards me and cupped an ear. "Shpeak clearly! Can't shtand it when young people mumble."

I said again, louder: "I'm running a tearoom."

"Eh?"

"I'M RUNNING A TEAROOM!"

"All right, all right—no need to shout," he said peevishly, regarding me from under bushy eyebrows. "Nothing wrong with my hearing."

"Do come in, Ronnie..." My mother led us back into the sitting room. "Would you like a sherry?"

"Had a couple—*hic!*—already, actually," he chuckled, swaying slightly. "But don't mind if I have another... Hullo, Philip! Shaw the England vershush India tesh match last night... sheven for sheventy-two at shtumps... absholutely shocking!"

My father came forwards to shake hands, smiling in his gentle way. "I'll reserve judgement until both teams have had an innings. Besides, we've got a couple of useful spinners and the wicket's going to take more turn."

"I hope you two are not going to talk cricket all through lunch, Philip," said my mother severely. "Our American cousins won't understand a thing and they'll be dreadfully bored."

Ronnie perked up. "What's thish, then?

American coushins?"

"My cousin Hank, who was born in the States, has just moved to England and he is bringing his family to lunch today," my father explained.

"They've never been to the UK before or experienced a traditional British Christmas," my mother added anxiously. "I really want to make a good first impression and for them to feel comfortable and welcome—"

"Oh, not to worry, not to worry, Evelyn—I've had lots of experiunsh with Americansh," said Uncle Ronnie, waving his glass and sloshing sherry everywhere. "Leave it to me—I know jush how to make them feel at home." He nodded knowledgeably. "Hug them—*hic!*— that's what you need to do. They like that. Make sure you talk really loudly and shmile a lot. Show your teeth."

Oh God. I stared at the elderly man in horror. Uncle Ronnie was even worse than I remembered.

"Er... those are stereotypes, Uncle Ronnie," I said hastily. "Not all Americans—"

The doorbell rang and we heard the babble of voices outside the front door.

"Oh, that will be them now!" said my mother brightly, hurrying out of the sitting room.

A few minutes later, she came back leading a group of people and beaming like a proud tour guide showing off her first clutch of tourists. She was followed by a couple in their sixties: the husband with a good-humoured smile, large beer belly, and more than a passing resemblance to my father, and his wife as scrawny as he was portly, with a thin, anxious face and a figure that looked as if it had been whipped into submission by daily yoga sessions.

My father started forwards but, before he could say anything, Uncle Ronnie lurched in front of him, holding out his arms wide.

"Merry Chrishmush! Merry Chrishmush! You must be Hank, eh?" He lunged and engulfed the man in a bear hug. "Welcome—*hic*—to England!"

Hank reeled back and stared in alarm at the old man who was baring his teeth at him in a chimpanzee grin.

"Uh... thanks. It's real nice to have family on this side of the pond and to celebrate Christmas with them." Carefully, Hank set Uncle Ronnie upright, then turned to my father with a warm smile and held out his hand. "Man, it's been ages, Philip! I think the last time we saw you and Evelyn, the kids weren't even born yet... huh, Madison?"

He glanced at his wife, who was air-kissing my mother with quick, nervous movements. She stepped back as soon as she could, as if afraid she might catch an infection, and said:

"I think I might have been pregnant with Tanya, honey... I remember feeling really sick and they didn't have the brand of anti-emetic I wanted in the local drugstores and I was so worried I might be developing gestational diabetes—"

231

Hank snapped his fingers. "Yeah, that's right. Madison and Evelyn were both in the family way... which means Tanya's the same age as your Gemma, right?" He looked at me with interest, then gestured to the group behind him. "Hey kids... say hello to your English cousins."

A young woman my age stepped forwards. She looked as if she had strayed from some executive board meeting, with her slicked-back ponytail, sharp navy dress, and stiletto heels. She gave a quick, impatient glance around the room, and I half-expected her to raise a laser pointer and ask where the projector was. Behind her were a girl in her mid-twenties busily texting on her smartphone, who barely raised her head long enough to greet everyone, and a boy in his late teens who mumbled in a sullen manner.

Hank gestured to the first young woman and said enthusiastically, "That's awesome about Gemma and Tanya! You guys should sit next to each other at lunch—you'll have loads to talk about, being the same age and all."

"Gemma went to Oxford," said Uncle Ronnie loudly as I cringed with embarrassment. "Best university in the world!"

Hank grinned. "Well, Tanya went to a fancy-pants school too: she graduated *magna cum laude* from Yale... didn't you, honey?" He looked proudly at his daughter. "And then she got a graduate position at one of New York's top investment banks, and now she's a hotshot Senior Analyst for a Fortune 500 company—handles millions of dollars a year! We think she might even make vice president next year."

Tanya smiled complacently, then turned to me and said: "And what do you do, Gemma?"

"I... er... well, I decided to have a career change last year. I was working in Sydney but I decided that the corporate rat race wasn't really for me. So I resigned and came back to the UK." I raised my chin slightly. "I always had a dream of opening a traditional English tearoom, so that's what I did."

Tanya burst out laughing. "No way! You're kidding, right? Seriously, what do you do?"

"I run a tearoom," I said, trying to keep the smile on my face.

She stared at me, her lip curling. "What? You're telling me that your *career* is serving tea and cakes?"

I flushed as I felt everyone's eyes on me. It reminded me of the awful time when I'd first come home and everyone had been horrified at or contemptuous of my decision. It had taken me nearly a year to earn people's respect and not feel ashamed for shunning the conventional path. Now, suddenly, I was back in that toxic mix of angry frustration and defensive embarrassment.

Then my mother spoke up: "Oh, but Gemma serves wonderful tea and cakes at her tearoom. Her scones are known as the best in Oxfordshire. And I think it's marvellous what she's managed to achieve in one year. We're very proud of her."

I smiled at my mother as I felt a rush of love and gratitude. She might have been one of my loudest critics when I'd first come home, but she had since embraced my career change and become The Little Stables's most loyal supporter.

"Thash right, thash right... gotta be happy in your job—thash what I always shay," Uncle Ronnie barked. "Spend mosh of your life at work, don't you? Nothing worsh than being trapped in a job you don't enjoy, eh? Even if it comes with a bloody load of dosh."

Tanya didn't look convinced, sniffing disdainfully and giving me another once-over, as if I were an odd specimen in a zoo. There was an awkward silence, then Hank gave a forced laugh and said:

"Ah, kids! It's always something with them, isn't it? Speaking of which—here are my other two. This is Britney... Britney, honey, can you stop texting for a moment? And this is Cody, my youngest. Oh, and this is my brother-in-law, Shaun... Madison's brother," he added, indicating the last person to enter the room. Shaun was a man in his forties who had a shaggy mullet haircut and wore a black T-shirt emblazoned with the logo of a heavy metal band.

"Whatsuuuuup...!" said Shaun, holding up one hand and making the sign of the horns with his fingers.

"Er... how do you do?" said my father, looking nonplussed.

"Shaun sorta joined us for Christmas at the last minute—that's why we were late—he turned up at the hotel just as we were leaving. He lives in London and he hitched a ride up; can you believe it?" Hank shook his head with admiration. "I hope you don't mind, Evelyn, that I brought him along. After all, Christmas is for family, right?" He guffawed and clapped my mother on the shoulder.

She staggered, attempting to maintain her composure. "Oh! Er... naturally... we're delighted to have him... Um..." She gestured to the sofa. "Won't you all sit down?"

Everyone moved to take seats in the sitting room and I began passing around the nibbles whilst my father organised drinks and my mother fussed around the guests:

"Oh, would you like me to take your coat, Madison? Here, Cody, this is probably more comfortable for you... Let me move this side table closer to you, Hank... Tanya, darling, here's a napkin—you don't want to get any stains on that lovely dress... Ah, Shaun, would you like—"

She broke off suddenly and jerked back with a scream, staring wide-eyed at Shaun's mullet. Or rather, at what was crawling out from beneath his mullet: a large, scaly green lizard with spines down its back, a long, stripy tail, and baggy folds of skin under its neck.

It wriggled out from where it had been snuggled under Shaun's hair, at the nape of his neck, and crawled onto his shoulder, where it clung with talon-like claws and tilted its head, regarding everyone with a beady orange eye.

"Oh yeah... I forgot," said Shaun, grinning and waving to the lizard. "Meet Godzilla. I hope you don't mind me bringing him along. He doesn't like being left alone—he gets lonely—and I was worried the staff at the hotel might freak out if they found an iguana in one of the rooms. Besides, Godzilla is family too..." He turned his head and puckered his lips, giving the scaly lizard a noisy kiss. "Aren't cha, buddy?"

CHAPTER TWENTY-FIVE

There was a frozen silence as my parents stared in shock at the iguana in their sitting room. I glanced at my mother, who had gone white, and, for the first time in her life, seemed to be at a loss in a social situation.

Shaun saw her expression and put a hand up, saying: "Hey... chill, man! Godzilla won't bite or anything. He's really laidback—he likes to spend most of his time just hanging out somewhere warm. And he's real smart, you know—people don't realise how intelligent iguanas are. He's even potty-trained. Yeah, that's right; it was super easy 'cos iguanas naturally poop in water so you just need a place where they can soak, like your bathtub or something, and you gotta be consistent, just like with training puppies, and then once they've associated pooping with water, you can put a dish with water in their tank... and ta-da!"

My mother made a strangled noise in her throat, but before she could answer we heard an inquisitive "*Meorrw?*" and, a moment later, Muesli strolled into the sitting room. Her whiskered face lit up as she saw the visitors and she trotted forwards to demand some attention.

Then she skidded to a stop as she spotted Godzilla.

Her fur puffed up, her back arched, and a deep growl began emanating from her chest as she whipped her tail back and forth. The iguana turned slowly to eyeball her, then began bobbing its head up and down, making the dewlap at its throat flap around.

"Wow... cool, man!" said Shaun, grinning widely. "Godzilla's never seen a kitty before!" He stroked the big lizard on the head. "Whatcha think, buddy? You wanna taste some kitty, huh?" He chuckled, then threw a look at us. "Oh, don't worry—iguanas are totally vegetarian. They only eat flowers and fruit and leaves."

Muesli approached the big lizard cautiously, her fur bristling, and hissed a challenge. The iguana bobbed its head even more vigorously and made a grunting noise, then lashed its tail sideways. My mother flinched as the long, whip-like tail narrowly missed a Lladró sculpture on the nearby side table.

"Whoa, buddy... take it easy," said Shaun,

gathering up the iguana and holding it close to his chest. He frowned. "Can somebody get rid of that cat? It's upsetting Godzilla."

I gaped at him, unable to believe his nerve. *He's the one who brought his bloody great lizard unannounced and he's complaining about* our *cat?* But I could see that my mother was already struggling and I didn't want to make the atmosphere even more strained than it already was. Reluctantly, I scooped Muesli up and carried her out of the room, taking her upstairs and depositing her in my bedroom.

"Sorry, Muesli," I told her, giving her a pat. "It will just be for a few hours, okay?"

"*MEORRRW!*" growled Muesli, lashing her tail and giving me a disgruntled look. Then she jumped onto my windowsill and presented her bum to me.

I sighed and went back downstairs. When I re-entered the sitting room, an uneasy calm had settled over the group. My mother's desire to be a good hostess and her ingrained British compulsion to remain polite in the face of all adversity had obviously overridden her revulsion for the iguana. So she was handing out canapés and pretending that there wasn't a big, scaly green lizard perched atop her sofa. I went over to join her, picking up the platter of mince pies and offering it around to the guests.

"Would you like a mince pie?" I asked Madison.

She recoiled in horror. "Oh no! I don't like meat

pies."

"Actually, these don't have any meat in them. The name is misleading. It's just fruit and spices—it should really be called a 'fruit tart'," I explained patiently.

Madison still looked dubious but Hank leaned over and picked up one of the small golden pies dusted with icing sugar. He turned it over, looking at it curiously.

"Don't you people have minsh pies at Chrishmush?" asked Uncle Ronnie.

Hank shook his head. "Nah. We have pumpkin pie, apple pie, pecan pie—"

"Don't forget sweet potato pie," put in his wife.

"Blimey! Chrishmush without minsh pies! It beggars belief," muttered Uncle Ronnie. "How can it feel right if you don't have traditional nosh like minsh pies... or Chrishmush pudding?"

"Well, you guys don't have eggnog, right? And we don't think it's Christmas without eggnog," said Hank, grinning. He eyed the mince pie in his hand then took a bite and chewed with surprised pleasure. "Hey! These are pretty good!"

"I'm glad you like them. But don't spoil your appetite for lunch," said my mother, giving Hank's hand a mock slap as he reached for a second pie. "In fact, shall we go to the table now?"

Everyone rose and began heading into the dining room. Shaun got up and lifted the iguana from the sofa, placing it back on his shoulder.

"Er... you're not going to bring *that* to lunch, are you?" asked my mother with a look of horror.

"Oh, he'll be no problem," said Shaun, waving a hand. "He'll just sit on my shoulder and chill. Don't worry, it's not like having a dog, always begging for scraps. Godzilla won't be interested in anything on the table... Actually, have you got any salad or raw vegetables we can give him? It seems really mean that he has to miss out on Christmas lunch. He likes leafy vegetables, like kale or Swiss chard, or stuff like carrot tops—you got any of those? Or squash or green beans... or broccoli? At home, I give him worms and crickets sometimes, but I'm guessing you won't have any of that."

My mother was breathing noisily through her nose and looked like she was going to say a *lot* more than "Fudge buckets!" but, after a minute, she managed to regain control of herself and said in a cordial voice:

"I'm afraid I hadn't expected a reptile guest and therefore I'm not adequately prepared. Perhaps after lunch, I can have a look to see if there is any leftover salad for... er... your pet."

"Okey-dokey," said Shaun, sauntering to the dining room with Godzilla riding on his shoulder.

We took our places at the table and the American guests eyed the festive crackers placed on each plate with interest.

"What are these?" asked Hank, lifting a cracker and turning it over quizzically.

"Eh?" said Uncle Ronnie next to him. He cupped his ear. "Shpeak up!"

"What are these?" Hank waved the cracker in the old man's face. "They look like giant candy wrappers, but... they feel like there's nothing in them."

Uncle Ronnie did a double take. "Don't you have them in the Shtates either? Bloody hell, you're misshing out! Thosh are Chrishmush crackers."

"It's traditional to pull the crackers before we start the meal," my mother explained. She glanced at me. "Darling, why don't you show them?"

I picked up my cracker and started to turn to the person next to me, who happened to be Tanya, but her disdainful expression made me change my mind. Instead, I turned to Hank across the table and offered him the other end. He grasped it gingerly and gave a gentle tug.

"No, no, you have to pull harder, Hank," said my father, chuckling. "Don't be polite."

"O-kay..." said Hank, gripping the cracker tighter and giving it a strong tug just as I grasped my end with both hands and yanked hard as well. There was a loud snapping sound, like a miniature gun going off, and the cracker split into two.

The Americans all jumped and Shaun cried, "Holy sh—what was that?"

Uncle Ronnie slapped his knee and cackled with glee whilst I gave Hank an apologetic smile.

"Sorry, I should have warned you. There's a strip

of cardboard inside with a bit of gunpowder on it. It goes off when we pull the cracker." I pulled out the blackened strip from the remnants of the cracker to show him. Then I pointed to his hands. "You got the bigger half so you get the prize."

"Oh yeah? What do I get?" asked Hank eagerly.

The guests watched, fascinated, as I unrolled the festive red and green wrapping to reveal the cardboard roll inside. Wedged in the roll was a green paper hat in the shape of a crown, a little plastic toy, and a tiny slip of paper with text printed on it.

Hank's face fell. "That's it?"

My father laughed. "It's customary for a cracker to contain a paper crown, a useless toy, and a silly joke."

"You have to wear the crown while you eat the Christmas meal. That's part of the tradition," I said, grinning as I unrolled the paper crown and held it out to Hank.

He placed it on his head with good-natured humour, then picked up the tiny piece of paper and held it at arm's length, squinting at the text. "These words are so small... I need my glasses to read them."

"Here, I'll read it for you," I said, taking the paper and reading the words out loud: "'*What did the clock say when it saw itself in the mirror? It's time to reflect.*'"

Everyone groaned and Hank said: "That's a

terrible joke!"

"I want to try one!" cried Madison, grabbing her cracker and turning to my mother. There was a loud *bang* as both ladies lurched backwards, then Madison held up the larger portion of the cracker triumphantly. She shook out the paper hat and plastic keyring, then eagerly unfolded her piece of paper and read out loud:

"*'Why are Christmas trees so bad at knitting? Because they always drop their needles.'*"

Everyone groaned again and Hank said: "That one's even worse!"

Soon the whole room was filled with the sounds of miniature explosions, tearing paper, and laughter as everyone began pulling their crackers and reading the jokes—everyone, that is, except Britney, who still sat with her head down, busily texting on her phone.

"Britney, honey—aren't you going to pull your cracker?" asked Madison. Then she leaned over to her daughter and hissed, "For heaven's sake—can't you get off your phone for one second?"

"Look, Taylor just broke up with Brad, okay?" snapped Britney, raising her head at last. "She's, like, freaking out, and she needs me. I'm the only person who knows how to talk to her. And you *know* she's got depression and anxiety. She could, like, totally spiral down—"

"I'm sure your friend Taylor will manage—the way she's always managed with each of the boys she breaks up with each week," said Madison acidly. "Can't you even put your family first on Christmas Day?" She lowered her voice and added, "Besides, we're at someone's house! It's downright rude of you to be looking at your phone all the time."

"Jesus, don't give me a lecture, okay?" snarled Britney. "I'm not, like, some kid, you know—I'm twenty-seven; I'm an adult woman and I deserve to have time to relax and speak to my friends when I'm on vacation."

Madison turned away, compressing her lips with anger. We had all been listening in an embarrassed silence, and now nobody seemed to know what to say. I eyed Britney, who had slumped back in her seat, busily texting on her phone again. I'd never met such an openly obnoxious and self-centred person.

Then Uncle Ronnie reached across the table and snatched the phone out of Britney's hands. "Young lady, you are a shellfish and arrogant little cow," he said, glowering at Britney.

My mother gasped in horror. "Ronnie!"

Britney gave a wail and looked at her father. "Daddy, he took my phone! And he called me a shellfish!"

"I think he meant 'selfish'," her brother muttered. "And he's right—you *are* selfish!"

"No, I'm not!" snapped Britney.

"Yes, you are!"

"Guys... guys..." said Hank, holding his hands up.

I leaned back as shouts and screams began flying across the table. I couldn't believe that the Christmas meal had degenerated into this. *Maybe it's surprising that* more *murders don't happen at Christmas*, I thought, shaking my head internally. *Still, we've already had the drunken uncle, the uninvited guest, the iguana, and the embarrassing family fight... surely it can't get any worse than this?*

My mother stood up abruptly and, for the first time in my life, I heard her raise her voice: "Er... SHALL I FETCH THE TURKEY?"

People stopped speaking and lapsed into a slightly shamefaced silence. Uncle Ronnie grudgingly handed Britney's phone back and order was restored slightly as we waited for my mother to return from the kitchen. When she walked back into the room a few minutes later, though, carrying the magnificent roast turkey on a large platter, everyone's faces lit up. By the time the golden roast potatoes, honey-glazed baby carrots, sautéed Brussels sprouts, roast parsnips, sage-and-onion stuffing, and crispy "pigs in blankets" had joined the turkey on the table, the good humour and festive atmosphere seemed to have returned. Everyone's mouths were watering as they eyed the spread. Even Godzilla seemed to take an interest in what was on the dining table, climbing down into Shaun's lap so he could poke his scaly head over the edge of the table and eye the dishes in front of him.

My mother made to sit down, then tutted and exclaimed: "Oh, *sugar*! I forgot the gravy and other condiments."

"Here, I'll give you a hand," said Hank, standing up and accompanying her to the kitchen.

They had barely been gone a few minutes, though, when there was a crash followed by the terrible sound of shattering glass and crockery. My mother screamed. We all sprang up and rushed from the dining room into the kitchen, where we found my mother and Hank staring in dismay at the remains of the trifle bowl and the huge mess of broken glass, raspberry compote, sponge cake, whipped cream, and vanilla custard splattered across the kitchen floor.

"I'm... I'm so sorry," stammered Hank. "I don't know what happened—it just sorta slipped from my hands..."

My mother took a deep, steadying breath, then fixed a smile to her face. "It's all right. Accidents happen. Luckily, there's also a Yule log and chocolate mousse for dessert, as well as ice cream and Christmas pudding. I suppose we won't miss the trifle too much."

"We'll help you clean up," offered Madison.

"Oh, no, no, leave it for now," said my mother, dragging her eyes away from the mess on the floor. "The food will get cold otherwise. Let's go and sit down, and eat first, then we'll sort this out." She led the way back to the dining room. "As long as nobody steps in the—"

She broke off and froze on the spot. I crashed into her back, and I felt the others bump into me too as we all piled up in the dining room doorway. My mother made a choked sound in her throat and swayed slightly. I peered over her shoulder, then realised that I had been wrong earlier when I thought things couldn't get any worse...

Sitting at the table was Britney, still with her head down, busily texting on her phone and oblivious to anything else... and on the table in front of her, with its head stuck up the turkey's bum, was Godzilla the iguana, happily munching on some sage-and-onion stuffing.

CHAPTER TWENTY-SIX

I don't know how we did it, but somehow we got through that torturous lunch. Shaun seemed suitably chastened after seeing his pet demolish the dishes spread across the dining table and eat half the Christmas turkey, and he made a visible effort to keep Godzilla out of everyone's way for the rest of the meal. My mother salvaged what she could and we all tucked solemnly into a strange mash of prawn cocktail, soggy roast potatoes, shredded turkey, and slightly iguana-flavoured gravy. Hank attempted to crack a few jokes but my mother's usually unshakable social aplomb failed her and she could barely manage a wan smile in response.

At last, we rose from the table and drifted back to the sitting room where, thankfully, there were still plenty of intact mince pies, cheese and crackers, crisps, nuts, and chocolates. My father hurried to offer everyone drinks again and my mother said in a faint voice:

"Can you get me a gin and tonic, darling? And make it a double, please."

Then the angelic voices of a choir singing "God Save the Queen" drifted from the TV screen and my mother perked up at the sound of the national anthem.

"Ah! The Queen's Shpeech!" cried Uncle Ronnie. He began to sing along in a quavering baritone, waving his arms like a conductor: "*Send her victorioush... Happy and glorioush... Long to reign over us... God shave the Queen!*"

"Ooh! I'd almost forgot!" my mother cried, sitting upright. "Can you put the sound up, darling?"

My parents weren't staunch royalists, but sitting down to watch the Queen address her nation at 3 p.m. was an annual tradition that they never missed on Christmas Day. I obediently pressed the "Volume Up" button and sat next to my mother as we all watched the camera pan across the magnificent exterior of Buckingham Palace. The Americans looked slightly bemused as we sat in reverent silence for the next ten minutes while the Queen reflected on the past year and finally wished everybody a peaceful and happy Christmas.

My mother sighed with contentment and leaned back against the cushions, the colour coming back into her cheeks. "Ohhh... that was wonderful, wasn't it? She has such a lovely, gracious manner, and I do like the dress she's wearing this year. Goes so beautifully with her pearls."

"Marvelloush... marvelloush...!" mumbled Uncle Ronnie into his wine glass.

My mother stood up, her poise restored, and smiled at everybody. "Now, would anyone like a cup of tea?"

As she was pouring out the tea, the front doorbell rang. I went to answer it and was surprised to find the Old Biddies standing on the doorstep.

"Merry Christmas, Gemma! We're a bit early for tea but we knew your mother wouldn't mind."

They trooped into the house, all talking at once.

"...fabulous speech Her Majesty made this year— one of her best yet," declared Mabel. "I always say there's nothing like listening to the monarch after lunch to aid the digestion."

"...the Santa at the grotto in the Westgate Centre was definitely the best one," gushed Glenda. "That lovely bushy beard—his own, you know—and those twinkling blue eyes... and only sixty-six, he told me! Mavis says her toy boy is sixty-two, and he looks *much* older..."

"...still think brandy sauce is the best thing to have on Christmas puddings," said Florence with a thoughtful frown. "Although my neighbour Cora swears by her cranberry toffee sauce and Dot Wilkins from bingo says they always serve theirs with vanilla custard..."

"...couldn't believe it when they said they'd never read *A Christmas Carol*! How can anyone not have read Dickens's classic?" cried Ethel. "That's why I'm giving everybody a copy of the book for their Christmas present this year—oh, except for you, Gemma," she added, reaching into her handbag and pulling out a wrapped parcel. "This is your present."

"Oh! Thank you," I said, smiling and taking the gift.

"It's from all of us, dear," said Florence.

"Yes, but *I* knitted it," said Ethel, puffing her chest out.

I tore the festive wrapping paper open and held up a hideous Christmas jumper with a lopsided reindeer face on the front.

"It's supposed to be Rudolph; it's got a red pompom on its nose, see? That wasn't in the pattern—that was my own idea," Ethel said proudly.

"Er... it looks great," I said, eyeing the sweater with horror.

"Well, put it on, put it on!" they urged me.

There was nothing I wanted to do less. But I also didn't want to hurt their feelings, so I took a deep breath and pulled the jumper over my head. As I grappled with the scratchy, woollen fabric, I heard Glenda's voice, muffled, next to me:

"...and I still think we should have made one for Cole too. The dear boy told me that he'd never owned a hand-knitted sweater—can you imagine? Of course, his mother wouldn't have known how—

she was only a young girl herself when she had him—and how horrible that his father should have abandoned them like that. I always think, if you get a girl pregnant, you should do the honourable thing and marry her! But I suppose it's a class thing: Cole did say his father came from a very posh family and his mother was only a farmer's daughter—"

"Wait... what did you say?" I gasped, struggling to push my head through the folds of the sweater. I turned to Glenda, the jumper still bunched around my neck, and said urgently, "Did you say that Cole's father abandoned his mother when he got her pregnant?"

"Yes, dear. Weren't you listening that day when he was driving us back from Thurlby Hall? He was telling me all about his background—"

"Oh my God!" I cried. "Cole could be the murderer!"

"Cole?" The four of them looked at me blankly.

I recounted what Julian Morecombe had told me about Ned's womanising ways and the two girls from the local village that he had dallied with in his youth. "Julian told me that he had got one of them pregnant and Sir Hugh had to pay the family off. What if... what if Cole was the child of that pregnancy? He would be about the right age. And he could be bitter and resentful that Ned had abandoned his mother and treated her so shabbily... maybe he killed his father in revenge!"

Glenda gasped. "No! That lovely young man? He

would never murder anyone, much less his own father!"

"You don't really know him," I insisted. "How do you know what he's capable of? If Cole was the killer, it would explain a lot of things—like the strange footprints which led to the library window but not away... and that whole thing about Annabel taking the missing antifreeze—that could have all just been a story Cole made up to cover up his own tracks..." I dug in my pocket for my phone. "I'm sure Cole is the murderer! I've got to call the police and tell Inspector Pratt—"

"He's gone up to Thurlby Hall," said Florence.

I stopped. "What do you mean?"

"We called him ourselves a short while ago. We had a new idea for how the police could use our maple syrup cast, you see, but really, he was very rude!" said Mabel, pursing her lips angrily. "He told us that he didn't have time to speak because he was on his way to see Sir Hugh."

"Now?" I said, puzzled. "It's Christmas Day."

"Well, apparently everything was quiet at the station anyway and Sir Hugh is really angry about the lack of progress so far—and you know, he's a great friend of the Detective Superintendent, so Inspector Pratt said he was going to give a personal update on the investigation," explained Glenda.

"I do feel a bit sorry for Inspector Pratt, though, having to be on duty on Christmas Day," said Ethel.

I was barely listening as I dialled the police

station and asked to be redirected to Pratt's mobile phone.

"I'm sorry but I'm not authorised to do that," said the duty sergeant. "You can leave a message for the inspector and I'll see that he gets it when he returns—"

"No, you don't understand... this is really important," I said. "It's about an ongoing murder investigation. I... I have information which could reveal the identity of the killer! I need to speak to Inspector Pratt about it right away—"

"As I said, you can leave a message and I'll make sure that the inspector gets it when he returns to the station."

Aaarrgghhh! I wanted to scream with frustration. Taking a deep breath, I thanked the sergeant and ended the call. The Old Biddies looked at me expectantly.

"I've got to speak to Pratt! He's already at Thurlby Hall; he could arrest Cole and question him—" I broke off as I glanced at the hall clock, then made a sudden decision. "I'm going to the Hall myself. It's only fifteen minutes or so by car. I just need to speak to Pratt for a few minutes—I can be back within an hour." I grabbed my mother's car keys from the hook by the door. "Can you tell my mother that I'll be back soon?"

I'd barely started the engine, though, when the passenger door was flung open and Mabel climbed into the seat next to me. I gaped at her as the rear doors opened and Glenda, Ethel, and Florence piled into the car as well.

"What are you doing?" I demanded.

"We're coming with you too," said Mabel. "If you're going to unmask the killer, then, as partners in this investigation, we should be there."

I exhaled in exasperation. "We're not partners! We're—"

"Besides, the police might still need our maple syrup cast," added Glenda, holding up the orange blob that was looking more and more shapeless every time I saw it.

I started to argue, then decided not to waste time. They could tag along if they wanted to. Swinging the car out into the street, I stamped on the accelerator, saying: "Buckle up. We're going to nab a murderer."

CHAPTER TWENTY-SEVEN

There were still remnants of the snowstorm around Thurlby Hall and I had to drive carefully to avoid the drifts of dirty snow which had thawed into slippery slush at the sides of the driveway. I parked the car in front of the house, noting the discreet vehicle nearby which probably belonged to Inspector Pratt, then hurried up to the front door. Mrs Holmes opened the door and raised her eyebrows in surprise when she saw me with the Old Biddies.

"Oh! I didn't realise Mrs Floyd was expecting company—"

"She isn't. I... I came to speak to Inspector Pratt, actually. Is he here?" I asked.

"Yes, he's up in Sir Hugh's rooms at the moment." The housekeeper looked doubtful. "They said they weren't to be disturbed under any circumstances."

"Have they been together long?"

Mrs Holmes glanced at the clock on the wall by the front door. "The inspector arrived about twenty minutes ago."

I hesitated. I could wait, but the two men might remain closeted together for a long time. *No*, I decided. *This is important enough to interrupt their meeting.*

"I have to speak to Inspector Pratt. It's about the murder investigation and I'm sure Sir Hugh would want to hear it too, so they won't mind me interrupting," I said, hurrying past her and starting up the staircase.

"We're coming too, Gemma!" cried Glenda as the Old Biddies all started to follow me.

"No, no... it'll be too many of us," I protested, imagining Pratt's face if we all piled into the room. He would instantly be annoyed and probably refuse to listen to me. "Why don't you go and sit with Annabel until I finish?"

To my relief, they didn't argue for once and tottered off towards the drawing room as I continued up the staircase. I made my way down the warren of corridors until I found the door to Sir Hugh's suite of rooms. Knocking softly on the door, I opened it and stepped in. The two men looked up and Pratt scowled as he saw me.

"What do you want?" he demanded. "I told Mrs

Holmes that we were not to be disturbed."

"I know—I'm sorry, I wouldn't have interrupted except that I have important information which could help to solve the case!"

Pratt didn't seem impressed by my announcement. Instead, he gave me a patronising look and said, "I'm sure you can tell the duty sergeant at the station about whatever little clue you think you've found—"

"It's *not* a little clue," I said, irritated by his manner. "I think I know who the murderer is."

Pratt scowled again. "Now, look here, Miss Rose—who do you think you are? I'm not wasting—"

"No, wait," said Sir Hugh, holding up a hand. "If Miss Rose has information which may help us find Ned's killer, I want to hear it."

Pratt started to retort, then caught himself and clamped his mouth shut, scowling even more ferociously. I took a deep breath and quickly told them my theory about Cole.

"...so I think you need to question Cole again and look into his background—find out if his mother was a girl in the local village —" I broke off as my gaze fell on the framed photographs of Ned on the side table, which Sir Hugh had been looking at the other day.

I picked up the one of Ned standing with a pretty girl next to a tree. I could see now that the tree trunk had the shape of a heart etched into the bark, with the letters "*N & N*" faintly visible inside the heart, but my attention was focused on the girl's face. I frowned, staring at it intently. Was there a resemblance to Cole? Or was it just my imagination?

"Julian told me that Ned had got a local girl from the village pregnant when he was in his teens..." I said, still looking at the photograph.

"Ah, yes, I remember that summer," said Sir Hugh, shaking his head and smiling. "My poor wife got her knickers in such a twist about that, but really, I told her, boys will be boys. We paid the family a great deal of money and arranged for her to have an abortion."

"Do you remember... was it this girl?" I asked, holding up the photograph.

Sir Hugh shrugged. "I can't remember what she looked like exactly... I do know that the girl who got pregnant was called Helen. Yes, Helen Croft, that was her name. Her father was Les Croft; one of the local farmers—"

"And Nell is a nickname for Helen, which makes it very likely that she was the same girl as the one in the photo," Pratt cut in impatiently, glancing at the "*N & N*" in the photo. He gave me a supercilious look. "Yes, I know what you're thinking and we're already ahead of you, Miss Rose. When I questioned Julian Morecombe, I asked him about the two girls he mentioned in your notes and we've checked up on them. Helen Croft—the girl that Ned got pregnant—did abort the baby. She went on to marry a Cypriot and is now living in Cyprus with her husband and two grown children. The other girl, Sandra Davis, has moved up to Leeds; she's divorced and now living with a boyfriend. Both of them have alibis and were confirmed to be hundreds of miles away on the night of Ned's murder."

"But are you *sure* Helen Croft had the abortion?" I asked. "What if she kept the baby? You still need to check up on Cole's mother and make sure her name isn't Helen or Nell or anything similar—"

"I don't need to," Pratt said smugly. "We've already run a background check on him. Cole Barlow was born in Surrey, to a farmer's daughter who'd had an affair with a wealthy local landowner. He was brought up by his mother and his grandparents, and his father still lives down the road from them, although he hasn't officially acknowledged Cole. Oh, and his mother's name, by the way, is Liz—short for Elizabeth. There is no nickname or variation of Elizabeth that starts with an 'N'..." Pratt thrust his face into mine. "So you can forget your stupid little theory that Cole was Ned's illegitimate son and killed him for revenge or something."

My cheeks felt hot. Could I have got it so wrong? But if it wasn't Cole, then where did that leave us? The other suspects passed through my mind: Kelly... Julian... Richard... Annabel—at the last, I jerked mentally away from the thought. No, I just couldn't believe that Annabel could be the killer! *It has to be one of the others*, I thought. Then I recalled something—something that I'd forgotten to mention in my statement.

"Wait, there's something else," I said. "I didn't put it down in my statement because I was so focused on Thurlby Hall that I wasn't thinking of what had happened before but... I'd met Ned a few days earlier."

"Yes, at the Oxford train station—you mentioned that in your statement," Pratt said impatiently. "You had tea with him at The Randolph in Oxford."

"Yes, but what I didn't mention was that Ned had to rush off after he got a phone call—a call from London."

"We know who called Ned down to London. Yes, Miss Rose, contrary to what you think, I do know how to do my job," said Pratt sarcastically, seeing my look of surprise. "We've been checking all calls that Ned made and received in the time since he arrived back in the UK, as well as retracing his movements. We know he arrived in the country a few days ago and came straight to Oxford at first. In fact, he checked into The Randolph Hotel. However, he cancelled the room within an hour of checking in and left again, this time for London. And this was straight after he received a call from London... which we traced to a well-known member of an underground gambling ring."

"Gambling?"

"Yes, Ned owed a lot of money and they were hounding him for payment. That is why he rushed down to London—to placate them. He told them that he would be getting his hands on a lot of money soon and asked for an extension into the new year, which they granted him. Then he came back to Oxford and headed to Thurlby Hall..." Pratt gave me a sneering look. "Now, do you have any other little theories you'd like to run by us?"

I flushed.

"I suggest that you leave detective work to the *professionals* from now on," Pratt added in a condescending tone.

I stepped back, chagrined and humiliated. Turning, I started for the door—then I stopped short. I stared at the wall opposite where the large oil painting of the nude woman was hanging. Whirling back, I ignored Pratt and addressed the older man:

"Sir Hugh—sorry, can I just ask you one more question? Normally, when you put the painting back after you open your safe, do you always make sure that it's straight?"

"Of course," said the old man. "I can't stand it when paintings are askew."

"Then I think someone was in here, trying to open your safe on the night of Ned's murder."

His brows drew together. "What do you mean?"

I pointed at the oil painting. "When you called me up here on the morning after the murder, we were talking about your safe and you pointed out where it was to show us that it was hidden behind the painting. I just remembered now that you straightened the painting because it was askew... which suggests that someone other than yourself must have moved it since you last accessed the safe."

Sir Hugh stared at me for a moment, then he hobbled across the room and took the painting down. We watched silently as he turned the combination and opened the safe.

"Is anything missing?" I asked as he peered at the two levels of compartments inside, which were filled with various documents and boxes.

"No... but you're right, someone has been in here. I remember placing the latest new will on the top shelf." He indicated a brown document envelope. "And now you see it's on the bottom shelf, as if someone just threw it in there."

"Whoever opened the safe must have been in a hurry to leave," I mused. "They threw the will back in, shut the safe door, and put the painting back, but didn't have time to adjust it so that it was hanging straight."

Sir Hugh raised his head and narrowed his eyes thoughtfully. "You know, now that you mention it... I think I did hear someone in here, although I didn't realise what the sounds were at the time. I'd actually been woken by the grandfather clock downstairs striking midnight; it doesn't normally wake me—I've been living with it long enough now to tune it out. But that night... well, I suppose the excitement of Ned's return meant that I wasn't sleeping as deeply as I normally would have. I lay in bed for a bit, trying to get back to sleep, and that's when I heard the sounds from in here. My bedroom adjoins this private sitting room, of course, but at night I normally close the double doors between them, so the sound was quite muffled. I didn't think much of it at the time, but now... it all fits! It was a sort of shuffling, like someone moving around softly, and there was also a very faint creak—which I'm sure now was that painting being moved."

I frowned. "Are you sure you heard the sounds in here *after* midnight?"

"Yes, I was lying in bed counting the chimes before I heard the sounds in here."

"And you didn't see anyone in here when you got up? You must have rushed out when you heard the scream."

"Well, I tried to," said Sir Hugh. "But I got such a shock when I heard the scream that I tried to get out of bed too quickly and I fell. Bloody old age! There was a time I could have sprung out of bed and been down those stairs faster than you could blink, I tell you! Now I lose my balance if I try to do anything quickly," he said gruffly. "Anyway, I was a bit stunned and by the time I'd managed to get myself back on my feet, find my walking stick, and make my way out of the bedroom, the sitting room here was empty."

"Miss Rose, I really don't know what you're trying to achieve with all these questions," said Pratt impatiently.

"Don't you think it's relevant that someone broke into Sir Hugh's safe?" I demanded.

"Well, nothing was stolen, was it?" said Pratt dismissively. "I think it's time you stopped playing amateur sleuth and left the investigations to *real* detectives. And let me remind you that you're still a suspect yourself. Don't think you can distract me from investigating *you* by trying to confuse things."

"I'm not—"

"Now, if you'll excuse us, we have important police business to discuss."

He bundled me out and, before I knew it, I found myself in the corridor, staring at a closed door. Seething with anger and frustration, I turned and stomped back downstairs. In the main hall, I bumped into Mrs Holmes carrying a tray with teapot, cups, and shortbread biscuits. She was heading towards the drawing room and smiled as she saw me.

"Ah... that's good timing. I'm just taking this in for Mrs Floyd and your friends. They're in the library." She looked at me curiously. "Did you... er... manage to speak to the inspector?"

"Yes... a fat lot of good it did," I muttered, staring down at my feet. The memory of my humiliation at Pratt's hands filled me again and I felt myself cringe. How could I have got it so wrong? I had been so sure that I had the answers! But I couldn't deny that Pratt had done his homework and he had effectively disproved all my theories. *Except that thing with Sir Hugh's safe*, I thought. *There was something there...*

Looking up again, I asked: "Mrs Holmes, when you saw Richard—Mr Floyd come back into the house on the night of the murder, are you *sure* you saw him go upstairs? He didn't go into the library?"

"Oh yes, he came in and went upstairs."

"But are you sure? Maybe at the angle that you were looking at, from the kitchen doorway down the hall, you could have made a mistake?"

She shook her head slowly. "I suppose I could have... but I don't think so. I'm pretty certain he headed for the staircase."

I sighed. Nothing about this case made sense. It would have helped if Pratt had been willing to share more information with me—maybe even brainstorm hunches together—but all he seemed to want to do was humiliate me at every chance possible.

The housekeeper looked at me in concern. "Are you all right, miss? You look a bit down."

I smiled wanly. "I'm all right. Just a bit frustrated with the police."

Mrs Holmes hesitated, giving me a slightly shamefaced look, and said: "I hope I didn't make things awkward for you by speaking to the inspector."

I looked at her in surprise. "What do you mean?"

"When Inspector Pratt was questioning me... well, I felt like I had to be honest... and he said I had to tell him if anyone had said anything—well, negative, like, about the younger Mr Morecombe..." She broke off and looked at me apologetically. "I had to tell him that you were really angry after Mr Morecombe tried to kiss you and that you'd said..."

"I said I'd kill him if he touched me again," I said dryly. "It's true, I did say that—I'm not denying it."

"I knew you didn't mean it! And I tried to tell the inspector that," said Mrs Holmes quickly. "But... well... I'm not sure if he believed me. I hope it didn't make trouble for you."

I smiled at her. "It did a bit, but it's okay. Don't feel like you need to apologise! You did more than enough by coming to my rescue that afternoon. So many things have been happening one after the other that I haven't had the chance to thank you properly."

"It was disgraceful, what he did. The younger Mr Morecombe, I mean. I know you're not supposed to speak ill of the dead but really...!"

"Yeah, he was a bit of a creep. You know, he'd already tried it on with me a couple of times before and I'd made it clear that I wasn't interested."

"Some men just don't know how to take no for an answer," said Mrs Holmes, compressing her lips. "Especially when you'd told him already that you had a boyfriend. He should have respected that."

"Don't worry—my boyfriend is actually with the CID too, so as soon as he returns after the Christmas break, I'm sure he'll sort things out. He won't let the police harass me."

"Oh, good. Well, tomorrow's Boxing Day so it won't be long now..." She shook her head. "I can't believe that Christmas is nearly over. The whole thing has been like a dream this year..."

A nightmare would be more accurate, I thought as I followed her to the library. Just inside the doorway, I paused and looked around the room whilst Mrs Holmes bustled over to Annabel and the Old Biddies. I hadn't been in here since the night I'd found Ned's body. It was strange seeing it again in the cold light of day.

Most of the Christmas decorations from the tea party were still hanging around the room, although they looked slightly sad and pathetic now. I noticed that the row of red velvet stockings, each embroidered with one of the family members' names, had been removed from the mantelpiece. And in the mirror above where they had been hanging, I caught a glimpse of my own reflection. I'd forgotten that I was still wearing the Christmas jumper that the Old Biddies had given me (no wonder Inspector Pratt hadn't taken me seriously!) and the lopsided reindeer face looked even more hideous in the reflection, especially given my elegant surroundings: the library shelves filled with leather-bound books and, through the open doorway behind me, the stately décor of the foyer, with the lavish wood panelling and ornate wainscoting and that simple Henning Koppel clock on the wall by the front door...

I caught my breath. Whirling around, I stared at the clock through the doorway, then I turned back again to look at it through the reflection in the mirror. That silly joke from my Christmas cracker at lunch echoed suddenly in my head.

"Oh my God!" I whispered.

I dashed back upstairs and ran through the corridors, bursting into Sir Hugh's sitting room once more. Pratt looked up and scowled ferociously.

"Miss Rose, I told you—"

"I know who the killer is!" I cried.

Pratt gave an exaggerated sigh. "Oh, for God's sake, not this again..."

"No, I'm serious!" I insisted, advancing into the room and looking Sir Hugh straight in the eye.

"If you want to know who murdered your son, come down to the library and I'll tell you."

CHAPTER TWENTY-EIGHT

I took a deep breath and looked around. Everyone had assembled in the library and there were wildly differing expressions looking up at me: from the open contempt of Inspector Pratt to the hopeful eagerness of Sir Hugh, from the scowling impatience of Richard Floyd to the bored indifference of Kelly. Annabel's face, as usual, was a smooth, blank mask, and Julian's held a wary anticipation. The Old Biddies were whispering excitedly amongst themselves, and behind them, Cole and Mrs Holmes stood at the back of the room, trying to conceal their vulgar curiosity behind polite staff detachment.

I cleared my throat and began speaking: "Three nights ago, I came into this room searching for my cat, Muesli, and I found Ned in an armchair there."

I pointed at an empty space in front of the fireplace. "He had been murdered."

"The police have taken the armchair for analysis," Pratt said importantly. "And we'll be conducting a detailed forensic examination to find some *genuine* leads to the killer, not a bunch of silly ideas cooked up by amateurs."

I ignored him and continued: "Ned had been suffocated by a Christmas stocking over his head and there were also remnants of a glass of port and a plate of plum pudding found on the floor next to his chair. Because of the snowstorm, which had cut off all access to Thurlby Hall, I knew that Ned's killer had to be one of the people who had been trapped here in the house..." I paused and looked around again at the assembled group. "Which means that it had to be one of us."

A few people shifted uncomfortably and there were several sideways glances around the group.

"The next morning, Sir Hugh asked me to question everybody about their movements the night before... and I began to get an idea of who the murderer might be." I turned to face Richard Floyd. "It seemed to me that the most likely suspect was you."

The businessman made an angry movement and started to say something, but I held up a hand, forestalling him.

"You had a convoluted alibi which was full of holes and inconsistencies, and which seemed to leave a long gap of time unaccounted for—more than enough time to have committed the crime. You are also a hard-headed businessman, used to ruthless manoeuvres to get what you want, and most of all, you had plenty of motive. It was obvious that there was no love lost between you and Ned, and—having spent your whole life working towards the top position in the company that you had helped to build—you were faced suddenly with the prospect of Ned swooping in to take all the reward. And Ned was even taunting you about it!"

"That doesn't mean that I killed him!" snapped Richard. "I told you, I never went to the library that night!"

"And I didn't believe you—until I realised *why* you were lying: because you were covering up for where you *really* were." I paused, then said softly: "You were in Sir Hugh's sitting room, breaking into his safe."

There was a murmur around the room and several people turned to stare at Richard Floyd. The businessman flushed and hesitated, then said sullenly:

"All right! I admit it—I lied. I wasn't in my bedroom when I heard the screams. I was actually in Sir Hugh's private sitting room." He cast the old man a bitter look. "I overheard you talking about your new will earlier in the evening. It drove me crazy, brooding on it all through dinner, and when I was out smoking, I decided that I *had* to know exactly what was in the new will. I knew you'd keep it in the safe in your sitting room and that the safe is behind that painting of the nude. It would have been easy to nip in while you were sleeping—"

"But the safe is locked," protested Sir Hugh.

Richard gave a harsh laugh. "Come on! That safe is the easiest thing to crack! Anyone could have guessed the combination: it's Ned's birthday. He was your favourite. All I had to do was try the numbers forwards or backwards—"

"So you opened the safe," I cut in.

He made a disgusted sound. "Yes, but I didn't get time to look at the will. I'd barely got it open when the screaming started. I had to abandon the whole thing. I chucked the will back in, shut the safe, shoved the painting back, and got out of the room as fast as I could. By the time I got back to the landing, Annabel had come running out of our bedroom. So yes, I was never in our room that night," he admitted grudgingly. "But I couldn't let anyone know that, so when you questioned me, I pretended that I had been preparing for bed and that I'd heard the screams and run out onto the landing first, before Annabel was fully awake."

"So although Richard had lied about his whereabouts that night, his alibi still held good," I said, swinging around to face the others again. "He couldn't have been murdering Ned because he was upstairs trying to open Sir Hugh's safe. Which means that the killer had to be one of the others.

But who? Julian?"

I turned to look at the Oxford don who bristled indignantly. "After all, Julian had lied as well. He'd said that he had gone up to bed early and was alone in his room... when in fact, he'd had a late-night visitor: Cole Barlow the chauffeur. The two were having an affair and Julian had invited Cole to come to his room after dinner. In fact, I heard Cole arriving and mistakenly thought that it was Kelly going to Julian's room."

"Julian... and Cole?" said Annabel, her mouth dropping open as she turned around to stare at her cousin.

Kelly sniggered. "Didn't you know, Annabel? Bloody hell, I thought everyone knew that your cousin was a flaming old queen!"

"I take offence at that!" cried Julian, standing up, his face red.

"Julian? What's this they're saying about you?" demanded Sir Hugh.

Julian Morecombe hesitated, then drew himself upright and looked his uncle in the eye. "I'm gay."

The old man's eyebrows drew together. "You're WHAT?"

"I like men," said Julian baldly. "I always have. Ever since I was a boy... I was never interested in girls."

"But... but you flirt with every woman you see," spluttered Sir Hugh. "You're an outrageous womaniser, an eternal playboy—"

Julian gave a weary smile. "It's an act. I pretend to be chasing women all the time so that nobody will think anything else or wonder why I'm not married..."

"And that's why Ned was taunting you, wasn't it?" I asked. "He threatened to reveal the truth to your uncle—"

"And you think I might have murdered him to prevent him from exposing my secret?" said Julian with a contemptuous laugh. "Well, you know what? Ned might have done me a favour. I hadn't wanted to come out of the closet but now that I've been forced to... I realise how tired I am of pretending, of living a lie..." He took a deep breath and turned back to his uncle, meeting the older man's eyes defiantly. "I'm not going to be ashamed of the truth anymore. Even if it means that I'll be disinherited from the title and the estate."

"I thought we were here to find out who murdered Ned, not take part in some sexual identity support group," Pratt said sarcastically. He gave me a scornful look. "I hope you're not going to trot out Cole Barlow next as Ned's illegitimate child and possible murderer because we already know that I've debunked *that* theory."

"But you haven't explained the mystery of Cole's footprints outside the library window," I said, glancing over at the chauffeur, who looked uncomfortable at having the attention suddenly on him.

"What footprints?" scowled Pratt. "That was just a load of bunk dreamt up by those crazy old coo—*er*—" He glanced over at the Old Biddies, who were glaring at him, and hurriedly amended his words: "—I mean, your old friends. The SOCO team never found any footprints."

"That's because the wind changed direction and fresh snow blew under the eaves of the house, covering the prints," I shot back. "And in fact, that helps to explain the mystery of the footprints as well. You see, the trail of footprints led to the library window, then stopped abruptly. The logical thing to assume was that the person making those prints climbed in the library window—"

"I didn't!" cried Cole. "I never went into the library—I swear! Okay, I admit that I climbed down the ivy from Julian's bedroom window and I walked along the side of the house. I was heading back to my rooms over the garage, all right? But then I saw Richard—Mr Floyd—come around the corner of the house, so I had to duck down really quickly and hide. As soon as Mr Floyd went back into the house, I ran across the lawn and back to the garage." He looked around the group with a pleading expression. "I swear—I never climbed into the library. Ned was alive and well when I saw him through the library window, just before I ran back to the garage."

"Hang on, hang on—if you did that, then how come your tracks ended at the library window? Why didn't Miss Rose and her friends find your footprints going across the lawn?" demanded Pratt.

"For the same reason that your SOCO team didn't find the footprints by the house," I answered for the chauffeur. "It was snowing when Cole climbed out of Julian's window and so he kept under the eaves when he was walking along the side of the house... and his footprints in the snow there would have been preserved because they were sheltered by the overhang. But after he left his hiding place by the library window, Cole decided to run straight across the lawn to the garage... which means that he was out in the open. So when the fresh snow fell, it covered up his tracks across the lawn. In the morning, when my friends and I went out to search for footprints, we only found the tracks that were under the eaves. Of course, even those tracks eventually disappeared later that day because the wind changed direction and began blowing snow under the eaves, so that everything was covered up by the time the police arrived."

I swung around to Cole and added with a reassuring smile: "In any case, I believe you, Cole—I don't think you murdered Ned. For one thing, you had no motive... unlike someone else." I turned to the blonde woman sitting closer to me. "Such as you, Kelly."

"Me?" Kelly jerked upright from the lazy position she had been lounging in. "*I* didn't kill Ned! I barely knew him!"

"But he represented a serious obstacle to your ambitions. Not just for yourself but for your future children. Yes, Sir Hugh might be elderly, but men *have* fathered children in their seventies, and any son you have with him will be the next male heir— eligible for not only his personal fortune but also the estate and the title."

Kelly gave an incredulous laugh. "You think I would murder a man to protect children I might not even have?"

"No," I admitted. "I did play with the idea but I realised that it was too far-fetched. Besides, I was stumped over how you could have done it. Ned was a tall man still very much in his prime. He would have fought and struggled if someone tried to suffocate him, so whoever his murderer was, he or she had to have been strong enough to hold him down." I eyed her assessingly. "And you're a fairly petite woman, so you couldn't have managed to overpower him. That is... unless he had been drugged."

"Drugged?" said Sir Hugh in shocked tones.

I nodded. "I think Ned's port or the plum pudding he was eating was spiked with antifreeze. A lot of it would have been needed for him to show the symptoms so quickly... but that's not a problem: antifreeze is sweet, so even a large amount would have been easily masked by the natural flavour of the port or the plum pudding, since they're both sweet as well." I glanced at Pratt. "I don't suppose you could confirm that from the autopsy report?"

"The... the full report with the toxicology analysis isn't ready yet," blustered Pratt. "It's Christmas... everything is shut—"

"It doesn't matter. I'm sure Ned was drugged and antifreeze would have been a logical choice. There was a bottle handy in the garage. And if Ned was weakened by the poison, then he could have been overpowered by anyone—even a slim, fragile woman... like his sister," I said, turning at last to Annabel.

She looked up with startled eyes. "Me?"

I nodded grimly. "I didn't want to believe it. I kept resisting the suggestion that you could have anything to do with your brother's death. But... things started cropping up that I couldn't ignore: first of all, you're the one who removed the bottle of antifreeze from the garage—"

"But that was for the garden path! And that was before Ned even arrived!"

"—and then Cole mentioned that he saw you through the library window having an argument with Ned and looking very upset—"

"It... it wasn't an argument," said Annabel, putting her hands up to her flushed face. "We were... Ned was taunting me, jeering in that horrible voice he used to use when he was a boy... saying that no matter what I did... no matter what I sacrificed... Daddy still wouldn't love me..." She stopped and took a shuddering breath. "I stormed out and went to see Mrs Holmes in the kitchen, then I went up to bed. I wasn't in the library with Ned when Cole saw him," she insisted.

"I also remembered something else last night," I continued as if she hadn't spoken. "On the night I discovered Ned's body, when we were all standing in the library, you got very worried when Muesli tried to investigate the spilled port and plum pudding on the floor next to Ned's armchair. I remember you quickly asking Mrs Holmes to clean the mess up 'in case anything is poisonous to cats'—those were your exact words. It's true that pets often tragically poison themselves by eating human food like chocolate... But could it have been because you *knew* that the pudding or port had been laced with toxic antifreeze?"

Annabel gasped. "How could you... You think that *I murdered Ned?*"

"It would have been easy enough for you to do. I'm sure, as Ned's sister, you knew about his old habit of drinking his favourite port at Christmas. Cole says he saw the two of you through the library window, holding glasses together. You could have laced Ned's glass with antifreeze before giving it to him, and then pretended to storm out. You then used the pretext of seeing Mrs Holmes to kill some time while you waited for the poison to take effect. It also helped to establish your alibi, because you could make sure that, afterwards, your housekeeper would say that you went up to bed before eleven thirty."

"No..." said Annabel in a faint voice.

"Instead of going upstairs, though, you could have returned to the library where you found your brother now weak and confused, and it would have been easy to pull his stocking over his head and suffocate him. It would have been over in minutes—"

"No!" cried Annabel. She had clasped a hand over her mouth and was staring at me with horrified eyes. "No, no, no... I would never... how could you think that I could murder Ned?"

"It would have been understandable," I said gently. "You'd spent your whole life trying to make your father happy—you'd even married a man you didn't love to please him. And now, after all the sacrifices you'd made, you had to stand back and watch as the brother, who had never done anything worthwhile, swanned back into your lives and got all your father's affection again. Could anyone bear that kind of disappointment and rejection? Surely even a saint would snap in those circumstances?"

Annabel shook her head vehemently. "I... I didn't..." She gulped. "Gemma, I... I thought you were my friend. How could you... how could you suggest that I did those things?"

I was silent for a moment. Everyone was staring in bewilderment, their eyes going from me to Annabel then back again.

At last, I spoke up: "I said you *could have* done

those things, Annabel... but in fact, you didn't. Because you're not the person who murdered Ned Morecombe." I turned suddenly and pointed to the back of the room. "*You're* the one who killed him."

Heads spun around, eyes widened, and mouths dropped open as everyone saw who I was pointing to.

"Mrs Holmes," I said to the stolid, grey-haired woman in the apron. "Or rather, *Miss* Ellen Holmes... or perhaps I should really call you by the name you always used as a girl... Nell?"

CHAPTER TWENTY-NINE

There was a shocked silence in the library. Then the housekeeper stepped forwards, her head held high.

"Yes," she said, her eyes blazing. "I killed him. I murdered Ned... and I'm not sorry!"

"*You* killed him?" said Sir Hugh hoarsely, staring at her. "But... but why?"

"He deserved it! For what he did to me... to my hopes and dreams..." Her voice broke and she gulped back sudden tears. "I was only a girl—barely seventeen—it was my first job, working here at Thurlby Hall, and Ned... he... he dazzled me... he would bring me flowers... tell me how beautiful I looked... it was thrilling—the handsome young master of the house paying attention to *me*, the junior maid... Ned told me his engagement was a sham, that he was only doing it for the family business... he said he didn't love that rich girl in London—he loved *me*, only me..." She swallowed a sob. "So I let him touch me... and kiss me... and then... and then when I got pregnant, I thought... I thought he would look after me, like he'd promised..."

She clenched her hands, her voice suddenly shrill. "But it was all a lie! Ned just laughed in my face... he said he was leaving and the baby was my problem... and then he was gone... gone... and I had nobody to turn to. I didn't dare approach Sir Hugh for help ... the police were here, asking about missing jewels... everyone was screaming and shouting... it was a disaster, they said—the scandal, the humiliation... everything was falling apart, they said... Hah!" She spat. "I'll tell you what was falling apart—my life was falling apart. My parents—they disowned me... I had no friends, no money and there was the baby—I knew I couldn't keep it... I was so scared the day I went to the hospital—oh God, it hurt so much—and the pain didn't go away... days and days and days... an infection, they said... there was only one way to save my life..." She looked around the room, dry-eyed now. "The nurses were very kind... they explained—there was too much damage, too much scarring... but I knew what they were really telling me: that I would never have a baby again."

Ellen Holmes took another step forwards and

looked Sir Hugh in the eye. "That was why I killed your son—because he not only robbed me of my girlhood but of my womanhood too. Oh, I tried to forget... tried to find happiness with another man... but the scars were too deep, not just in my body but also in my mind—and besides, what man would want a barren woman like me?" she asked in a choked voice.

"Mrs Holmes—" cried Annabel, jumping up and running over to the woman. She reached out to put a compassionate hand on the housekeeper's arm but Ellen Holmes jerked away.

"I don't need you to pity me," she said thickly. "I said I'm not sorry for what I did and I meant it— even though I will have to go to prison... I... I think it was meant to be." She turned towards Inspector Pratt and held out her fists, crossed, towards him, in the classic gesture of someone about to be handcuffed. "I expect you'll want to arrest me now."

Pratt looked stunned. "Er..." Then he bristled and said, "Hang on... hang on... I'm not going to accept everything just like that! I need proof that she's the killer."

"Proof? She's confessed—what more proof do you need?" growled Sir Hugh.

"Well, for starters... how Miss Rose here decided that Ellen Holmes was the murderer," said Pratt, shooting me a challenging look.

Everyone in the room turned back to me, their faces expectant.

"It was a few things which sort of came together," I said slowly. "Small things which had niggled me but which I brushed aside at first... like how Mrs Holmes seemed vaguely familiar when I first saw her here at Thurlby Hall—I told myself that it was because she resembled the illustration of Mrs Claus I'd often seen on Christmas cards. When she walked in on Ned trying to kiss me against my will, I found it a bit odd that she said: 'It's not as if he's a young man *anymore*'—almost as if she'd known him as a young man... and then there was a strange remark she made when we were talking about Ned sexually harassing me and how he wouldn't take no for an answer—she said: 'Especially when you'd told him already that you had a boyfriend'... That puzzled me because I couldn't understand how she could have known that I'd told Ned that. I'd never mentioned my boyfriend to Ned here at the Hall..."

"Oh..." cried Ellen Holmes, putting a hand to her mouth.

"But it was the discrepancy with the time in the statements which really bothered me," I continued. "Richard insisted that he'd come back into the house at ten *past* twelve whereas Mrs Holmes maintained that he had come in at ten *to* twelve, according to the clock on the wall beside the front door... and then a Christmas cracker made me see the truth."

"A Christmas cracker?" said several people, looking puzzled.

287

I nodded. "Or rather, the silly joke inside a Christmas cracker. It said: *'What did the clock say when it saw itself in the mirror? It's time to reflect.'* And I realised that ten minutes *past* midnight could look like ten minutes *to* midnight if a clock is viewed through a mirror—especially if the clock has no numbers, like the minimalist Henning Koppel clock by the front door." I paused a moment to let that sink in. "When I asked Sir Hugh earlier upstairs, he confirmed that he heard Richard entering his sitting room and breaking into his safe *after* midnight... which meant that Richard's account of the time he came back into the house was correct. He *did* come back in at ten *past* twelve... and I realised that the only way Mrs Holmes could have got the time wrong was if she had been looking at the *reflection* of the clock. And the only place she could have done that was if she had been standing in the library at that moment and looking at *that* mirror..."

I pointed at the mirror above the mantelpiece, which showed the open library doorway on the opposite side of the room, with the front door and foyer beyond. The stainless-steel Henning Koppel clock hanging on the wall beside the front door was clearly visible in the reflection.

"Mrs Holmes must have been standing here in the library when Richard came back into the house. She had probably just finished killing Ned and was hiding in here, until the coast was clear for her to go back to the kitchen. And when I questioned her, she must have thought that she could strengthen her alibi by mentioning that she saw Richard come into the house while she was looking out of the kitchen—in other words, that she wasn't anywhere near the library. It was clever and it might have worked, except that she forgot her reading of the clock was through the reflection in the library mirror. If she had been looking at the clock from the kitchen doorway, she would have read the time correctly.

"Once I realised that, everything else fell into place," I continued. "I realised why Mrs Holmes had seemed familiar and why she had known that I'd already told Ned about my boyfriend... because she had been there when we were having tea at The Randolph last week and had overheard our conversation. *She had been one of the waitresses serving us.*"

I turned to the housekeeper. "In fact, you were the waitress who spilled tea on Ned, weren't you? I remember now... you must have been walking around his chair with the teapot as he was talking about being the prodigal son and it must have been a shock as you rounded the chair and saw his face properly for the first time. You recognised Ned and you heard what he said—that he was coming back home for Christmas—and the shock made you spill the tea. I remember that you kept your face averted as you cleaned up and then you hurried away, and a different waitress served us afterwards—"

"Yes, that was me," said Ellen Holmes. "I knew Ned instantly, although he didn't recognise me at all. In fact, he didn't even recognise me when he arrived here at the Hall! When I confronted him that night, before I killed him, he didn't even believe me at first. He kept insisting that I was too old and haggard to be the pretty young girl he'd known. Hah!" She laughed without humour. "People are always shocked when they learn that I'm only in my early forties—because I look ten or fifteen years older. Well, let me tell you something: pain and stress, grief and suffering... they all leave their mark... and the years have been a lot kinder to Ned Morecombe than to me," she added bitterly. "Anyway, even if I hadn't looked so different, I wasn't too worried. People never pay much attention to waitresses and other serving staff—especially rich people who are used to being waited upon. We're just faceless servants in the background; the only time they notice us is if we make a mistake..." She rounded on Annabel. "Even you're guilty of that."

"Me?" said Annabel, blinking.

"Yes, you didn't notice me hovering around your table, did you, when you were having tea with Gemma and her mother? But I heard everything you said—about how your old housekeeper was leaving and how you were desperately looking for someone to replace her." Ellen Holmes smiled grimly. "As soon as you left, I looked up the agency with your advertisement and put in an application right away. I knew that if Ned was returning to Thurlby Hall at last, then I had to be there... to finish what he had started twenty-five years ago." She gave another hollow laugh. "It was almost ridiculous, how easy it was to come back into this house... to get close to Ned again... to have the chance to kill him—"

"That's why you said you thought it was meant to be," I said suddenly.

Ellen Holmes nodded. "It *was* meant to be. How else could you explain the perfect coincidence of everything? That I should have been working my shift at The Randolph on the day you and Ned came in... that Mrs Simms should decide to give her notice this Christmas... and that Annabel should happen to have brought the antifreeze in from the garage and leave the bottle in the utility room..." She stopped and gave me a sad smile. "And maybe you taking over the catering for the Christmas tea party... and being snowed in here at the Hall—you, the girl with the reputation for being a clever detective—"

"Now, just a minute!" Pratt protested, whilst the Old Biddies piped up: "We helped as well!"

"—that was all meant to be too," said Ellen Holmes softly. She saw my face and said quickly, "Oh, don't feel bad. I don't hold anything against you. In fact..." She turned to gaze out of the library window, at the barren winter landscape, and gave another smile. "In fact, for the first time in twenty-five years... I will be at peace this Christmas."

CHAPTER THIRTY

"Come along, Gemma, dear! Your mother will be wondering where we are," ordered Mabel.

I glanced over my shoulder to see her leaning out of the front passenger window of my car and the other Old Biddies in the back, all beckoning impatiently.

"I'm coming—just a minute!" I called, then I turned back to face the elegant woman standing on the front steps of Thurlby Hall. "Annabel... I just wanted to say I'm sorry for what I said about you, back in the library. I hope I didn't offend or hurt your feelings—"

"No, no... in actual fact, I'm grateful to you," said Annabel.

"Grateful?" I said, wondering if I'd heard right.

"Yes, it was a bit of a shock at first but then...

your words really made me think. I might not have *done* the things you said, but a lot of what you said I *felt* was true... I *did* resent my brother; I *was* hurt and furious that no matter what I did to try and please him, my father never seemed to appreciate me..." She stood up straighter. "But then I realised that it was my own fault that I was feeling those things."

"Oh no, it's not your fault—" I protested.

Annabel held her hand out. "No, hear me out, Gemma... I realised that I'd got it all wrong. I'll never be able to change the way others think or behave—but I can change the way *I* react to them." She smiled suddenly. "I've spent my whole life trying to make my father love me, but if he won't do it naturally, then it's a lost cause and I shouldn't be wasting myself on him. Or on anyone else who doesn't value me..."

She took a deep breath. "So I've decided that after the New Year, I'm going to ask Richard for a divorce... and I'm going to get myself a flat and move out of Thurlby Hall. Maybe... maybe even get a job—something *I* want to do—not something to please others." She grimaced. "I know it won't be easy, especially as I'm older and have no qualifications to speak of... but perhaps I could do some volunteer work first."

I stared at her, a smile spreading slowly across my face. "Annabel... I think that sounds wonderful! Good for you!"

"Oh, and there's something else..." She reached into her pocket and pulled out her phone, tapped the screen a few times, then turned it around to face me. "What do you think? They say it's hard finding someone again when you're middle-aged and single... but he sounds like he might give me a chance."

I gazed down at the screen which showed the website of a local cat rescue, with a series of photos of felines looking for homes. Annabel was pointing to a picture of a grizzled old tabby with the caption:

"I'm a handsome 15-year-old boy who is feeling sad today as all weekend I watched the younger cats head off to their new homes. I sat patiently and waited as people walked past my cage but no one stopped to look at me. Maybe it's because I'm a bit shy and I might growl a bit when you first meet me... but I promise I don't mean it! I just need a quiet home where I can feel safe and someone who will be patient with me... Will you take a chance on a golden oldie like me and give me someone to love?"

I felt a sudden lump in my throat and had to blink several times before I could look back up at Annabel.

I smiled. "I think it sounds like a match made in heaven."

***

I climbed up the front steps of my parents'

house, with the Old Biddies at my heels, and quietly unlocked the door. Stepping into the hall, I was just wondering which of the two—loudly announcing our return or slipping furtively back in to join the others—was more likely to earn my mother's forgiveness, when the air was rent by a bloodcurdling yowl.

"Muesli!" I gasped and ran into the sitting room, where I found my parents and the guests all staring transfixed at the centre of the room.

My little tabby cat was in a face-to-face standoff with Godzilla. While I was gone, Muesli must have somehow got out of my bedroom and come back downstairs. Now she was making ugly faces at the iguana and lashing her tail, her green eyes narrowed to slits as she hissed and spat. The big lizard was bobbing its head up and down, and lashing its own tail, its legs splayed out defensively and its spines erect on its back.

I looked in exasperation at Shaun, who was making no effort to separate them. Instead, he was watching them avidly and saying: "Woah, man... this is more awesome than the WWE SmackDown!"

"Oh, for heaven's sake...!" I cried, marching into the room and scooping my cat up in my arms.

"Marvelloush show... *Hic!* Marvelloush..." mumbled Uncle Ronnie, teetering sideways and sagging onto Hank, who tried desperately to prop him up.

"Darling! Where have you been?" cried my

mother, looking frazzled. "Mabel said something about you popping out for a minute... and then you all disappeared!"

"I'm sorry, Mother. It was urgent—I had to go to Thurlby Hall," I said, struggling to hold on to a squirming Muesli, who was still trying to shoot death glares at the iguana.

"Thurlby Hall?" said my mother in puzzlement.

"Gemma worked out who committed the murder!" squeaked Ethel proudly.

"With help from us," Mabel reminded everyone.

"And our maple syrup cast," said Glenda, holding up the orange blob.

"Hey—you mean the case that's been in the papers?" said Hank, looking impressed. "So who did it?"

They all gathered around me as I told them briefly about Ellen Holmes's confession. I noticed for the first time that Seth and Cassie were at the back of the group; I was delighted to see my two best friends and I couldn't wait to have a proper catch-up with them and tell them the details of everything that had happened. By the time I had finished answering everyone's questions, though, Seth had been dragged into a discussion with Hank and my father, whilst Cassie had been cornered by Shaun, who seemed to have been smitten by her sultry looks and was trying his best to impress her.

I glanced between them, then decided that Cassie probably needed rescuing more. It looked like Shaun had his iguana tucked safely under his mullet once more, so I set Muesli down, gave her a pat, then headed towards Cassie.

"...and did you know I was the best wing spiker on my college team? Yeah, they called me Shaun the Slammer. I could jump up super high and—*wham!*—slam a ball across the net so fast, you wouldn't even see it coming." Shaun glanced around, then mimicked a sideways sweep with his arm. "Man, I haven't got the space here or I'd show you... There was this one time when the setter dumped the ball over the net 'cos he thought he could catch the defence off guard but he didn't realise that I was—"

"Hi," I said, sidling up to join them.

Cassie turned to me with relief. "Gemma! Er... Shaun was just telling me all about playing on his college volleyball team... Um... Have you got a drink? Do you want me to get you one?" she asked, already making a move to get away.

"I've got a better idea," I said, giving her a conspiratorial smile. I turned to the man next to us. "Um... Shaun... I've heard so much about this drink that you Americans call 'eggnog'. Hank says in the States, you never celebrate Christmas without it. I'd love to try it and I'm sure Cassie would too. Can you make some up for us?"

"Me?" Shaun looked taken aback. "Well... um... sure, I guess... I mean, I haven't actually made it myself but I suppose I could Google a recipe... But I think you gotta make it, like, ahead of time and let it chill in the fridge—"

"Aww, can't you just try? Please?" Cassie and I chorused, giving him our best cajoling smiles.

Shaun blinked, no match for a double dose of feminine charm. "Uh... yeah, okay... you guys wait here... I'll go and ask your mother if she has any eggs..."

He lumbered off and Cassie blew a loud sigh of relief. "Bloody hell, Gemma, if I had to spend one more minute in that man's company, I think I would've been the next murderer on your CV! He's in his forties, for heaven's sake, and he still acts like a teenage headbanger."

I laughed. "You should try having a whole lunch with him... and his iguana!"

"Yeah, I heard about the iguana eating the Christmas turkey," said Cassie, chuckling. "I almost wish I'd been here. It sounded hilarious!"

I gave her a dark look. "It wasn't funny at the time, I promise you. And Godzilla wasn't eating the turkey—he was eating the stuffing in the turkey's bum. Apparently iguanas are vegetarians... haven't you heard?" I asked mischievously.

Cassie groaned and rolled her eyes. "Oh my God, yes! Shaun has already told me more than I ever want to know about iguanas." She cast a glance around the sitting room and grinned. "Still, you have to admit, this is probably the most exciting Christmas Day you've ever had."

"You mean the worst Christmas I've ever had," I muttered. "Seriously, the lunch was torture, and even before that, things were so strained and awkward... and now I've got the whole evening to get through." I eyed the guests. "Actually, Hank is very nice—I like him—and his wife, Madison, seems sweet, just a bit neurotic. It's the other members of his family... But I suppose I can't really complain because the other worst guest is a member of my own family!"

Cassie followed my gaze to the old man standing by the bar. He was flushed bright red, his toupee was askew, and he was struggling to stand upright. Before he could help himself to another drink, however, he was confronted by the Old Biddies, who gathered around him, arms on their hips and accusing expressions on their faces.

"Hullo, hullo... can I get you lovely ladiesh a drink?" asked Uncle Ronnie gaily.

Mabel gave him a disgusted look. "You, my man, are completely off your trolley!"

"Rubbish!" said Uncle Ronnie, looking aggrieved. "I might—*hic!*—be slightly pished but I'm not drunk."

Mabel snatched the gin bottle out of his hands. "No more drinks for you—unless it's plain water."

Uncle Ronnie bristled and started to retort, then he took one look at Mabel's face and thought better of it. Turning his back on them, he beat a hasty retreat, muttering, "Bloody crazy old bat!"—then his face brightened as he spotted Cassie and me, and he tottered over to join us.

"Gemma! You never told me that you have shuch a pretty friend," he said, beaming. Then he caught sight of something above our heads and added, "Ah! Thish looks like my lucky day!"

I looked up and groaned inwardly. We were standing right under the mistletoe. *Nooo!* I thought in dismay. I had put the traditional "kissing bough" up in the hopes of giving Seth a bit of a chance with Cassie—not for my drunken old cousin to smooch my best friend!

"Come now... give ush a kish!" said Uncle Ronnie, approaching Cassie with his sunken lips puckered.

"Er..." Cassie flinched and leaned backwards, trying not to recoil too visibly.

"Ah—Uncle Ronnie, we haven't had the Christmas pudding yet! And I don't think anyone could light it better than you," I gabbled, grabbing his arm and steering him away from Cassie. "It's such an important British tradition. We've got to make sure the Americans see it done properly, don't we?"

The old man drew himself up to his full height. "Of coursh! Of coursh! Got to show 'em how it's done..."

He tottered obediently after me as I went over to where my mother was standing with Shaun, listening politely as he read out the list of ingredients needed for making eggnog from his phone and trying to ignore the iguana eyeballing her from underneath his mullet. She looked up as we approached, her expression slightly desperate.

"Mother, I think we should have the Christmas pudding now," I said brightly. "Uncle Ronnie wants to do the honours and light it."

"Oh, of course, darling," said my mother, stepping away from Shaun with relief. "I'll just fetch it."

She disappeared into the kitchen, where the Christmas pudding had been steaming gently above a pan of simmering water, and returned a few minutes later bearing a large mound on a platter. Rich, dark, and moist, filled with sweet dried fruits and fragrant spices, doused in brandy, and maybe even containing a surprise in the form of a silver coin, a thimble, or a ring... the Christmas pudding, also known as plum pudding, was the ultimate finale to the festive celebrations.

And setting it alight was the most exciting part of serving it. Uncle Ronnie cleared his throat importantly and lifted a bottle of brandy, which he started pouring liberally over the pudding.

"Er... maybe not too much," I protested, remembering that the pudding had originally come from Mabel and had already been billowing with alcoholic fumes when she'd given it to my mother.

"Nonshensh!" Uncle Ronnie cried. "It's not a deshent Chrishmush pud if it doesn't have a good dollop of the shtrong shtuff."

"Yes, but—"

He poured the last of the brandy into a soup ladle, then held the latter above a candle flame to warm the spirit. Fumes swirled upwards from the ladle, then suddenly, the brandy caught fire, burning with a fiery blue flame.

"Aha! Shtand back and watch the magic!" cried Uncle Ronnie, brandishing the ladle as he approached the pudding. He tipped the ladle sideways, pouring the flaming brandy onto the dark brown mound.

There was a *WHOOSH!* sound and a gust of heat hit my face as the pudding erupted into a mountain of flames.

My mother screamed, people gasped and cried out, and Uncle Ronnie staggered backwards.

"My hair! My hair!" he cried, trying to smack his head where his toupee had caught fire.

"Get that toupee off his head!" shouted Mabel, trying to reach him.

Shaun shoved everyone else aside. "I've got this! They don't call me Shaun the Slammer for nothing!"

He raised his beefy hand and whacked the old man across the head. The flaming toupee flew to the other side of the room and Uncle Ronnie reeled backwards, then toppled over. My mother screamed again as the old man crumpled to the floor.

"Shaun! What have you done?" cried Hank, aghast. "You've knocked him out!"

I rushed to join my mother by Uncle Ronnie's side, whilst everyone else hovered around us, watching anxiously as we tried to revive the old man. Thankfully, he came around pretty quickly, blinking in confusion and saying: "Blimey! That brandy packed a wallop!"

Everyone started talking at once, exclaiming in relief, offering suggestions, and above the din, I could also hear Muesli's demanding yowls.

"Not now, Muesli," I called as I helped my mother raise Uncle Ronnie up.

"*Meorrw! Meeeeorrw!*"

"Not now, Muesli!"

"*MEEEEEEEORRW!*"

I turned around irritably to scold my cat, then gasped as I saw what she was trying to tell me.

The toupee, which had been knocked off Uncle Ronnie's head, was now lying underneath the Christmas tree, amongst all the gaily wrapped presents. With all our attention on the old man, no one had noticed that his toupee was still burning and the flames were licking dangerously close to the tree's lowest branches. In fact, some of the needles were already starting to smoulder.

"The Christmas tree! It's going to catch fire!" I gasped, springing to my feet.

Seth whirled and dashed across the room. He stamped repeatedly on the burning toupee, putting it out just in time. Meanwhile, Hank rushed over to the tree and yanked the plug for the fairy lights out of the wall, whilst Cody doused the smouldering branches with a glass of water.

"Man, it would have been really serious if the tree caught fire," said Hank, shaking his head. "I saw this video from the NFPA back home, and this burning Christmas tree destroyed a whole room in less than a minute!"

My mother scooped Muesli up and cuddled the grey tabby close to her chest.

"Oh Muesli, darling—you saved the day!"

EPILOGUE

Bing Crosby's rich baritone, crooning about chestnuts roasting on an open fire, brought a familiar wave of warmth and nostalgia, and I smiled as I looked around. After all the excitement with the Christmas pudding and Uncle Ronnie's flaming toupee, it was a relief to see the calm and order around the room. Tanya, Cody—and even Britney, to my surprise—were happily playing charades with their father and mine. Uncle Ronnie was sitting in an armchair, enjoying being fussed over by my mother and Madison. Shaun was showing Godzilla off to the Old Biddies. And over in the far corner— my smile widened—Cassie and Seth were standing together under the mistletoe.

"... that was pretty heroic of you, Seth, to just jump on the burning toupee like that," Cassie was saying. "You might have burned your foot, you know!"

Seth blushed and gave an embarrassed cough. "Oh... well..." Then he glanced up and saw the mistletoe. Slowly, he leaned forwards. "Um... Cassie..."

I smiled to myself and turned away to give them some privacy. Glancing out the window, I saw that dusk had fallen and snow was beginning to fall again—white flakes swirling against the windowpane, catching the light from the house and glittering against the darkened sky beyond. *It looks like we're having a "white Christmas" after all*, I thought with another smile. I turned back to scan the room once more and felt a sudden rush of affection for everyone there—yes, even drunken Uncle Ronnie and Shaun and his iguana. For all the stresses and squabbles, it was nice to celebrate Christmas with family. I felt a sudden pang. *If only Devlin could be here too....*

The front doorbell rang and I straightened in surprise.

"Who on earth can that be?" my mother said. She caught my eye. "Darling, can you see who that is, please?"

I made my way out to the hall, wondering who the caller was. I knew we weren't expecting any other guests, so who could be calling so late on Christmas Day?

The door swung open and Devlin O'Connor

stepped in from the cold.

"Devlin!" I gasped in delight as he swept me into a hug. "What... what are you doing here?"

He laughed and set me back on my feet. "Spending Christmas where I really want to be."

"But... your mother!" I cried. "You can't have left her on Christmas Day?"

"Well, actually, she was the one who left me first," said Devlin dryly. "Yes, I arrived home to find that my mother had decided to book a last-minute holiday with her new boyfriend. They found a cheap deal for a week in Tenerife and they flew out this morning."

"What? This morning? But... didn't she realise she'd be leaving you alone on Christmas Day? Especially after you'd made the special trip to spend Christmas with her?"

Devlin shrugged. "You know what my mother's like. She probably booked the tickets on an impulse and never thought about me until afterwards."

"Oh Devlin..." I put my hand on his.

He covered my hand with his and smiled. "It's okay, Gemma. I'm not upset. Maybe I should be but... you know, I've come to accept my mother for what she is. I know she still loves me, in her own way. She's just... well, she's like someone who never grew up, a thoughtless teenager who just thinks of themselves but doesn't really mean any harm."

"Yeah, I know what you mean—I've met a couple of those myself recently," I said wryly.

Devlin shook his head in amazement. "In fact, Mum even told me that she'd invited loads of her friends around so that I'd have plenty of people to get hammered with on Christmas Day... as if getting drunk with a bunch of strangers was my idea of the perfect Christmas! So last night, I decided that I wasn't hanging around to be the dutiful son anymore." He gave me a slightly guilty look. "I almost told you when you rang, actually—you sounded so down—but I wanted it to be a surprise."

"It's a wonderful surprise!" I said, squeezing his hand, then adding in admiration: "I don't know how you managed to get here. It's Christmas Day—none of the trains are running."

"I've got a mate in the Force up there—I knew he was driving down south today to spend Christmas with his family, so I got a lift with him. I'd actually hoped to arrive earlier but the weather was terrible and the roads were chock-a-block." Devlin's arms tightened around me and he smiled down at me, his blue eyes twinkling. "Anyway, I'm here now."

"You're the best Christmas present I could have asked for," I said, throwing my arms around his neck.

Devlin lowered his head, but before he could kiss me, we heard a familiar plaintive voice in the hallway behind us.

"*Meorrw? Meeeorrw?*"

We turned to see Muesli trot out of the sitting room. She stopped short as she saw Devlin.

"*Meorrw!*" she cried, bounding over to her favourite person and purring like an engine as Devlin picked her up.

I was wrong, I thought as we walked back to join the others, with Muesli nestled against Devlin's chest and his other arm around me. *In spite of the madness, mayhem—and murder!—this has turned out to be a wonderful Christmas after all.*

FINIS

THE OXFORD TEAROOM MYSTERIES

A Scone To Die For (Book 1)

Tea with Milk and Murder (Book 2)

Two Down, Bun To Go (Book 3)

Till Death Do Us Tart (Book 4)

Muffins and Mourning Tea (Book 5)

Four Puddings and a Funeral (Book 6)

Another One Bites the Crust (Book 7)

Apple Strudel Alibi (Book 8)

The Dough Must Go On (Book 9)

The Mousse Wonderful Time of Year (Book 10)

All-Butter ShortDead (Prequel)

For other books by H.Y. Hanna,
please visit her website:
www.hyhanna.com

GLOSSARY OF BRITISH TERMS

** NOTE: we say "drink driving" in the UK, unlike "drunk driving" in the US.

Biscuits – small, hard, baked product, either savoury or sweet (American: cookies. What is called a "biscuit" in the U.S. is more similar to the English scone)

Blighty - an informal (and usually affectionate) term for Britain or England; it was originally used by British soldiers in World War I and World War II.

Blimey – an expression of astonishment

Bloody – very common adjective used as an intensifier for both positive and negative qualities (e.g. "bloody awful" and "bloody wonderful"), often used to express shock or disbelief ("Bloody Hell!")

Blusher – a cosmetic cream or powder which is applied to the cheeks to give it a rosy colour (American: blush)

Bollocks! – rubbish, nonsense, an exclamation expressing contempt

Bugger! – an exclamation of annoyance or dismay

Bum – the behind (American: butt)

Chock-a-block – very crowded; crammed full of people or things

Chuck – throw, but can also mean "throw away" depending on context

Clotted cream - a thick cream made by heating full-cream milk using steam or a water bath and then leaving it in shallow pans to cool slowly. Typically eaten with scones and jam for "afternoon tea"

Cuppa – slang term for "cup of tea"

Dodgy – shifty, dishonest

(a) Domestic – short for "domestic dispute"; an argument, usually between a husband and wife

Dosh – slang term for "money"

(to) Get your knickers in a twist – to get very agitated or angry about something

Hammered – very drunk

Jumper – a warm, often woolly garment, which is worn by being pulled over the head, similar to a sweater. Contrast this with a cardigan, which has buttons down the front. (NOTE: this word has a different meaning in the United States, where it refers to a type of girl's dress, a bit similar to a pinafore)

Knickers – (women's) panties

Lift – a compartment in a shaft which is used to raise and lower people to different levels (American: elevator)

Nappies – a piece of disposable absorbent material wrapped round a baby's bottom and between its legs to absorb waste. (American: diapers)

Nosh – slang term for "food"

Off your trolley – very drunk

Peaky – tired, pale,

Pissed – drunk (not to be confused with the American meaning of this word, which means "angry" – in the UK, that meaning would be conveyed by "pissed off")

Plastered – very drunk

Plonker – an idiot

Porter – usually a person hired to help carry luggage, however at Oxford, they have a special meaning (see Special terms used in Oxford University below)

Posh – high class, fancy

Pudding / Pud – in the U.K., this refers to both "dessert" in general or a specific type of soft, jelly-like dessert, depending on the context.

Queue – an orderly line of people waiting for something (American: line)

(to) Ring – to call (someone on the phone)

Row – an argument (pronounced to rhyme with "cow")

Santa's Grotto – usually found in a department store or shopping centre at Christmas time, this is a temporary area (often in the shape of a cavern) that is brightly decorated with Christmas ornaments and where children can meet an actor dressed up as Santa Claus, take photos with him and possibly receive gifts from him.

Shag – (v) to have sexual intercourse with or (n) the act.

Sloshed – very drunk

Tosser – a despicable person

Up the spout – slang term for "pregnant"

Whinge – to moan and complain (usually in an annoying way)

Willy – penis

SPECIAL TERMS USED IN OXFORD UNIVERSITY:

College - one of thirty or so institutions that make up the University; all students and academic staff have to be affiliated with a college and most of your life revolves around your own college: studying, dining, socialising. You are, in effect, a member of a College much more than a member of the University. College loyalties can be fierce and there is often friendly rivalry between nearby colleges. The colleges also compete with each other in various University sporting events.

Don / Fellow – a member of the academic staff / governing body of a college *(equivalent to "faculty member" in the U.S.)* – basically refers to a college's tutors. "Don" comes from the Latin, *dominus*— meaning lord, master.

Fresher – a new student who has just started his first term of study; usually referring to First Year undergraduates but can also be used for graduate students.

Michaelmas Term – the first term in the

academic year (autumn), followed by Hilary Term (spring) and Trinity Term (summer).

Porter(s) – a team of college staff who provide a variety of services, including controlling entry to the college, providing security to students and other members of college, sorting mail, and maintenance and repairs to college property.

Porter's Lodge – a room next to the college gates which holds the porters' offices and also the "pigeon holes"—cubby holes where the daily mail for students is placed.

Quad – short for quadrangle: a square or rectangular courtyard inside a college; walking on the grass is usually not allowed.

CHRISTMAS MINCE PIE RECIPE

MINCEMEAT

This is the key ingredient to mince pies! You can buy ready-made mincemeat but it is easy to make your own and you can add/adjust the different fruit portions and sweetness to suit your taste. Below is a traditional recipe but modern variations can also include dried cranberries, dried apricots, even dried tropical fruits like pineapple. You can also substitute rum or sherry instead of the traditional brandy. Contrary to popular belief, mincemeat does not need to be made months in advance—even a few days of marinating will produce wonderful flavours.

** Note: the traditional mincemeat recipe calls for "suet" which is a form of animal fat. This can be hard to source or you may not wish to use it. Alternatives can be used, although the end result might taste slightly different. Vegetable shortening is recommended as the best alternative, although butter can also be used (I personally tested the mincemeat recipe with butter and thought it tasted great!)

MINCEMEAT INGREDIENTS:

- 1 large Bramley (or Granny Smith) apple, finely chopped *(the skin can be left on if you wish)*
- 120 g (4¼ oz/⅔ cup) raisins
- 75 g (2¾ oz/½ cup) currants
- 85 g (3 oz/½ cup) sultanas (a.k.a. golden raisins)
- 55 g (2 oz/⅓ cup) mixed peel (mixed candied citrus peel)
- Finely grated zest of 1 lemon
- Finely grated zest of 1 small orange
- 2½ tablespoons lemon juice
- 2½ tablespoons orange juice
- 100 g (3½ oz/½ cup, lightly packed) dark brown (muscovado) sugar
- 40 g (1½ oz/¼ cup) chopped blanched almonds or almond flakes
- 65 g (2¼ oz/½ cup) suet *(or vegetable shortening or butter) – this should be finely grated or chopped into small pieces. Putting the butter in the freezer briefly makes it firm enough to chop or grate easily.*
- 1 teaspoon ground cinnamon
- 1/4 teaspoon ground nutmeg
- Large pinch of ground cloves
- 80 ml (2½ fl oz/⅓ cup) brandy

MINCEMEAT INSTRUCTIONS

1) Mix all the ingredients in a large, heatproof bowl and combine well – in particular, make sure that the pieces of suet/butter are well distributed and thoroughly mixed in with the other ingredients. Cover and set aside in a cool place overnight (or 12 hours) to marinate, so that the flavours have time to mingle and develop.

2) Preheat the oven to 120°C (235°F/Gas ½). Cover the bowl loosely with foil and cook for 2 hours, stirring occasionally.

3) Remove the bowl from the oven and set aside to cool, stirring it from time to time. The fat/butter should have melted and coated everything.

4) Once it has cooled, it can be transferred to sterilised jars and stored in the fridge (or even a cool, dark cupboard) for up to 6 months. Alternatively, it can be used immediately to fill mince pies in the recipe below.

SHORTCRUST PASTRY (aka. "PIE DOUGH" in the U.S.)

Ready-made (frozen) sweet shortcrust pastry, (known as "pie dough" in the U.S.), works very well. *(A U.S. reader has recommended Pillsbury as making a "wonderful refrigerated ready-to-use pie dough").*

However, if you would like to make it from scratch, here are two recipes: the first is a traditional British recipe for shortcrust pasty and the second is a tried and tested "easy pie dough" recipe from Kim McMahan Davis of the *Cinnamon and Sugar... and a Little Bit of Murder Blog* who has kindly offered to let me share it with my readers.

(A) Traditional Shortcrust Pastry:

SHORTCRUST PASTRY INGREDIENTS:

- 375g (3 cups) plain flour
- 260g (approx. 1 ¼ cup) unsalted butter, softened
- 125g (1 cup) icing sugar, plus extra for sprinkling
- 1 egg
- A little cold water

SHORTCRUST PASTRY INSTRUCTIONS:

1) Mix the flour, icing sugar and butter in a large bowl, using your fingertips to gently rub the butter into the flour, until they are thoroughly mixed and the mixture resembles coarse breadcrumbs.
   * *You can also do this in a food processor (on pulse mode), which will be quicker and might be better as you want to handle the flour as little as possible.*

2) Add in a bit of water at a time and mix gently (or pulse in the food processor) until the mixture comes together

3) Tip the mixture out onto a floured surface and gently fold until you get a smooth dough—but be careful not to overmix or knead too vigorously, otherwise the dough will become tough.

4) Divide the dough into two halves, wrap in cling film (plastic wrap) and chill in the refrigerator for 30 minutes.

5) Preheat oven to 220C/200C fan/gas 7.

6) On a lightly floured surface, roll out one of the dough halves thinly (to about 3mm).

7) Use a round cutter that's slightly larger than the holes in a shallow tart pan (eg. 7cm) to cut out rounds of pastry to line each hole.

8) Fill each pastry case with a generous dollop of the mincemeat.

9) Roll out the second portion of dough and cut slightly smaller rounds (eg. 6.5cm) to place as lids over each pie.

10) Brush the edges of each pie with a bit of egg wash (egg beaten with a little water), then press gently down along the edges to seal. You can use the tines of a fork to press the two sections of dough together around the edges of the pie, as well as giving it a pretty ridged edge.

11) Place in the oven and bake for about 20 minutes or until the crusts are golden.

12) Remove from the oven and allow the pies to cool slightly, before gently taking them out of the tart pan. Place on a rack to cool. Sift icing sugar over the top of the pies and serve warm.

(B) Easy-Peasy Pie Crust

(from Kim McMahan Davis of the *Cinnamon and Sugar... and a Little Bit of Murder Blog*)

PIE DOUGH INGREDIENTS:

- 2-1/2 cups (12-1/2 ounces) all-purpose flour
- 2 tablespoons (1 ounce) granulated sugar
- 1 teaspoon salt
- 1-1/4 cup vegetable shortening *(dairy-free and vegan version)*
- OR
- 3/4 cup vegetable shortening and 1/2 cup (1 stick) unsalted butter, all thoroughly chilled.
- 1/4 cup vodka (any brand), chilled
- 2-3 tablespoons ice cold water

PIE DOUGH INSTRUCTIONS:

1) Place flour, sugar and salt in a food process and pulse 5 times until combined. *(Alternately, you can mix in a large bowl with a fork.)*

2) Add shortening (cut into medium/small pieces) and butter if using (cut into small cubes) and pulse about 15 times. (*Or use a pastry cutter*

and work shortening and butter in until it becomes small pea-sized.)

3) Scrape down bowl and pulse 3 or 4 more times.

4) Mix 2 tablespoons of ice cold water with the chilled vodka and sprinkle over the flour mixture. If you live in a very dry place or have central air or heat going, you may need to add the additional tablespoon of water. This dough can handle being more moist than traditional pie crust recipes.

5) Pulse just until the dough begins to stick together. It took me about 6 pulses. You don't want it to come together in a ball. Overworking the dough is what makes it tough. *(Or use a fork to work the liquid into the dry ingredients.)*

6) Transfer the dough onto a non-stick surface and divide dough in half. Compress each half into a ball and flatten, then wrap well with plastic wrap.

7) Refrigerate for at least an hour and up to 3 days.

8) Remove one disk from the refrigerator and place on well-floured work surface. Flour the top of the dough along with your rolling pin.

Continue from Step 9 in the Shortcrust Pastry recipe above.

Enjoy!

ABOUT THE AUTHOR

USA Today bestselling author H.Y. Hanna writes funny and intriguing British cozy mysteries, set in Oxford and the beautiful English Cotswolds. Her books include the Oxford Tearoom Mysteries, the 'Bewitched by Chocolate' Mysteries and the English Cottage Garden Mysteries—as well as romantic suspense and children's mystery novels. After graduating from Oxford University, Hsin-Yi tried her hand at a variety of jobs, before returning to her first love: writing. She worked as a freelance writer for several years and has won awards for her novels, poetry, short stories and journalism.

A globe-trotter all her life, Hsin-Yi has lived in a variety of cultures, from Dubai to Auckland, London to New Jersey, but is now happily settled in Perth, Western Australia, with her husband and a rescue kitty named Muesli. You can learn more about her (and the real-life Muesli who inspired the cat character in the story) and her other books at: **www.hyhanna.com**.

Sign up to her newsletter to be notified of new releases, exclusive giveaways and other book news! Go to: **www.hyhanna.com/newsletter**

ACKNOWLEDGMENTS

I am so grateful for my wonderful members of my beta reading team, who always find time to fit me into their busy schedules—even reading multiple versions of the manuscript with constant plot changes and character revisions! So a big thank you to Connie Leap, Kathleen Costa, Basma Alwesh and Charles Winthrop for helping me make the story the best it can be. My thanks also to my editor, Chandler Groover and proofreader, Heather Belleguelle—I feel very lucky to have the support of such a fantastic team.

To Kim McMahan Davis of *Cinnamon and Sugar... and a Little Bit of Murder* blog—a huge thank you for letting me share her pie dough recipe and also for coming to my rescue (and teaching me some essential tips about baking!) when I completely messed up the shortcrust pastry for my test mince pies!

And, of course, I can never thank my amazing husband enough for always being there for me. Without his unwavering support, encouragement and enthusiasm, I could never have achieved everything that I have. He is one man in a million.

Finally, to my readers—thank you for your passion and enthusiasm for my books, for all your encouragement and your lovely messages on email and social media which always make my day... and for being the loveliest fans an author could ask for.

Made in the USA
Coppell, TX
24 February 2021